FRACTURED BY DECEIT

A PSY-IV Team Novel

JAMI GRAY

Cover Art: Robin Ludwig Design, Inc.
Publisher: Celtic Moon Press, First edition, 2019
ISBN: 978-1-948884-31-0 (ebook) ISBN: 978-1-948884-30-3 (print)

Sign up for free reads from Jami!

Join Jami's newsletter to be the first to hear about new releases, free books, special prices and other nifty events.

Sign up at: https://www.subscribepage.com/jami-gray-books

What Readers Say...

About Arcane Transporter:
"Taking a refreshing approach to fantasy magic, this fast-paced, economical thriller is told from a highly likable perspective." —Red Adept Editing

About PSY-IV Teams:
"This story is an emotional roller coaster, from betrayal, anger, fear, love..." —InD'tale Magazine

About the Kyn Kronicles:
"...a fantastic paranormal action novel is quite possibly the best book I've read this year. I could not put it down, and had to exercise serious self-control to keep from staying up all night to finish it." —The Romance Reviews

About Fate's Vultures:
"...if you like your characters with a bit more bite, with secrets, with hidden agendas, and all those sorts of things, and your worlds are a far more deadlier place, then this is for you." —Archaeolibrarian

FATE'S VULTURES

Lying in Ruins

Beg for Mercy

Caught in the Aftermath

Fear the Reaper

PSY-IV TEAMS

Hunted by the Past

Touched by Fate

Marked by Obsession

Fractured by Deceit

Linked by Deception

BOX SETS

PSY-IV Teams Box Set I (Books 1-3)

The Collapse: Fate's Vultures (Books 1-4)

The Kyn Kronicles Box Set (Books 1-6)

Arcane Transporter Box Set I (Books 1-3)

Arcane Transporter Box Set II (Books 4-6)

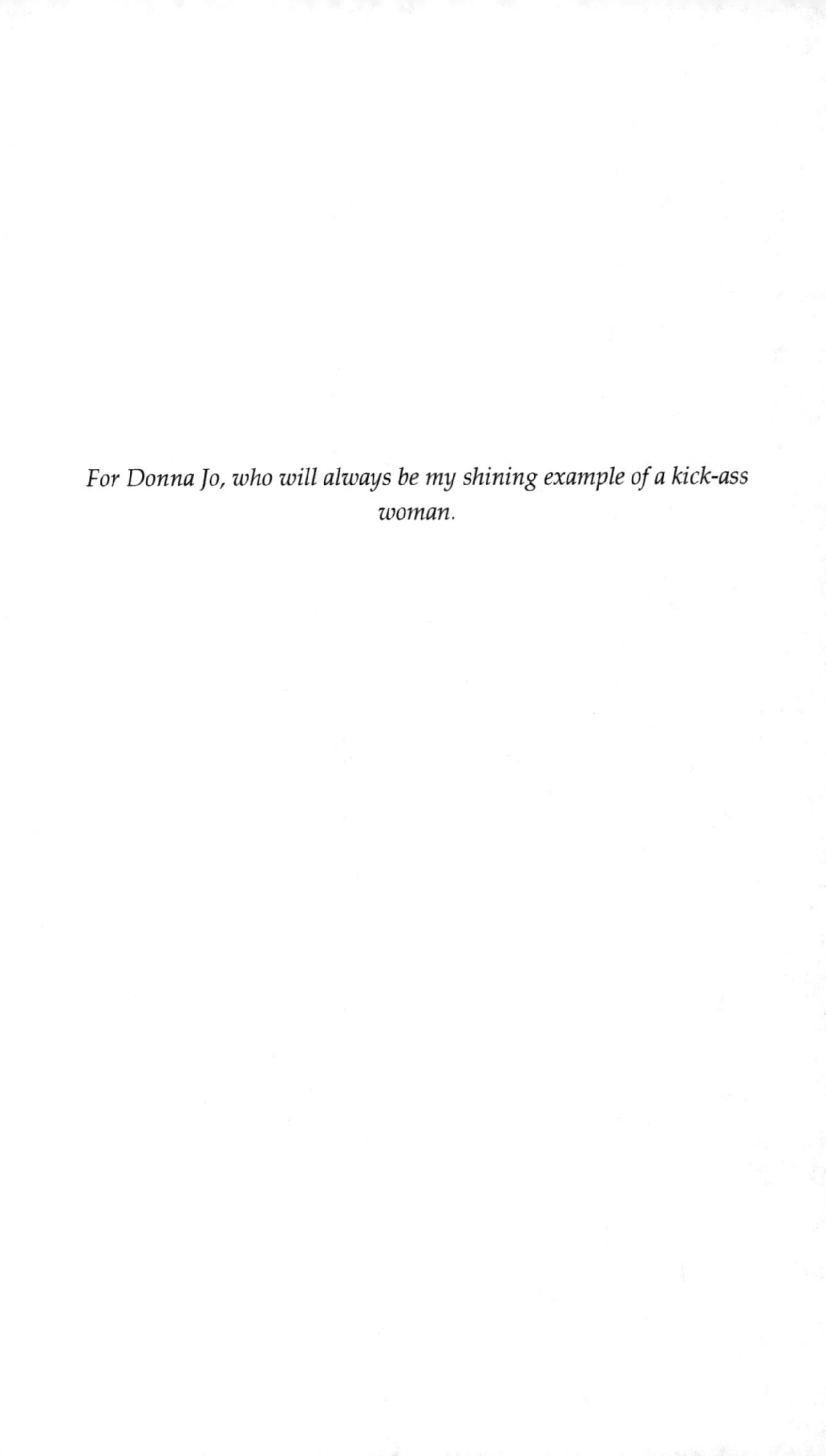

For Donna Jo, who will always be my shining example of a kick-ass woman.

Acknowledgments

As always, my undying thanks go out to my Knight in Slightly Muddy Armor and my enduring Prankster Duo. How you all put up with me while in writer mode, I'll never figure out, but will love you to the moon and back forever.

To my writing partners in crime - DeAnna, Dave and Camille - without whom I'd never get into so much creative trouble.

To my beta readers - JoAnn, Monica, and Nana - you guys keep me in line when everyone else is still trying to figure out where that line is.

To my readers - you are the reason I keep doing this. Thank you!

Love you all!

Contents

Prologue

How long does it take for a mind to break?

Since time had long since lost meaning, I wasn't sure, but I had a feeling I might be close to discovering the answer. Too bad I wouldn't be in any shape to appreciate it.

"My name is Megan Rouser. I have a brother, Dev, and a sister, Keelie, and my parents…" I faltered under the smothering weight of despair. *Do they even know I'm still alive? Is anyone even looking for me anymore?*

Ice stroked a bitter finger along my spine, and I pressed my forehead against my drawn-up knees, squeezing my eyes tight as I rocked. My heart beat a frantic fist in my chest, making it hard to breathe. The cold finger became a claw piercing my neck. Its nails slowly sank into my mind. Agony seared me as if every nerve ending had been dipped in fire.

I threw my head back and opened my eyes to a gray fog, blind to everything but pain as my muscles seized in protest. The vicious claw tore through my brain in unrelenting demand. The pain rose to a new excruciating level. A scream tore from my raw throat and bounced off the walls until the sound encompassed my entire world. A hellish agony-infested inferno turned the blinding gray to ash.

"Give me what I want." That sibilant voice weaved its way through the pain.

"No." My answer never changed, because under my agony lived a deepening rage that refused to die. I no longer had any idea what the interrogator wanted or who it was. Once upon a time, before the days had blurred into one horrific endurance test after another, I had a clue, but not anymore. Now it was nothing more than a brutal entity asking the same damn question on an endless loop.

Something warm dripped over my lip as the cracks in my mind widened and stretched. The pressure on my head increased until blackness edged my mind. I reached for it, knowing the oblivion would be temporary. Still, it was better than this, anything was better than this. The never-ending nightmare didn't leave me many options. It was getting harder to resist slipping into the dark and the final exit it offered. What would it matter if I never woke again? It wasn't like I was going to be missed.

Hold on, Megan. The whispered demand chained me in place as a flickering outline cut through the encroaching darkness. Recognition came, but the belief that normally followed my personal talisman of hope didn't because I no longer had faith in it. I'd been here too long, and this thing—hallucination? Apparition?—could not sustain my faith that help was coming. Not anymore.

"I'm sorry." Why I apologized even as my heart ached, I didn't know. Some small still-sane part of me knew my illusionary guardian wasn't real, no matter how many times it had saved me in the past. It was nothing more than my desperate hope given form, but even that wasn't enough anymore.

The pressure on my mind snapped away so fast that the back of my head knocked against the hard wall behind me.

Freezing at the unexpected reprieve, I blinked my vision clear. My prison remained unchanged, which was no surprise since it was self-made, an attempt to stay safe—well, as safe as I could get, anyway.

Gray stone walls, like those found in a castle, surrounded me. Ragged pages filled with my rough, manic jumble of sketches of demonic eyes and faces covered the stone. Some were marred with heavy black lines as if a child had tried to scratch them out of existence. Some shifted, following my movement, much like the fantastical drawings from one of my favorite stories of a boy wizard. An unseen wind riffled through the paper layers, revealing older images—a flash of the indistinct figure serving as my imaginary savior—but before it came into focus, the nightmarish images fluttered back into place, hiding it.

No door broke the stone-and-paper-covered walls. Other than an occasional visit from the figment of my damaged mind and fractured hope, I was the sole occupant. It took five steps to cross the room. I knew because I'd counted. Hazy light filtered through a narrow window high above me and forever out of reach.

Warm wetness touched my sore, swollen lips. Unlocking my arms, I raised a shaking hand to brush it away. Bright-red smears stained my dirt-encrusted fingertips. Another nose-bleed. I wiped my fingers against my dusty, dirty pants, adding another crimson mark to the fabric.

Concentrating on sucking air in and letting it out, I tried to make my mind blank, waiting to see if the monster who'd been playing with me for what seemed like forever would come back for another round. I was met with silence. Instead of easing my tension, this sent dread crawling under my skin, leaving me chilled. Imagination was a dangerous thing when fueled by fear, and I had no shortage of that.

A harsh, bitter laugh sliced through the unsettling quiet,

leaving me on edge. It took a second for me to realize that the horrible sound was coming from me. I stuffed my scraped fist against my mouth, choking back my rising screams. My body shook as the last piece of me shattered into unrecognizable pieces—such an ironic end, considering how often I'd been accused of living in my mind. Now that I really was living in my mind, all I wanted was to get off the damn stage.

A muted roll of thunder drifted from the window above. Dust rained down, and my prison shook for the first time in… ever. Scrambling to my feet, I tried to figure out what was happening. Considering that this was a mental construct built deep in my own subconscious, this disruption was unexpected and unusual. Maybe it was a reflection of my mental collapse.

Another rumble sent me stumbling to the center of the room, and I craned my neck back, focusing on that narrow strip of light and watching it darken. The thunder gained strength until it reverberated in my bones. Wind slipped through the window slit, riffling the sketches with ghostly fingers, the soft rustling filling my ears until they were stuffed full of white noise. Under my dread, a numbing fatal acceptance rose.

The end was coming.

Stuck in my self-made prison, I had two choices—I could either wait it out or dare to step outside my crumbling protections and brave the storm. I stared at the walls, the sketches rising and falling in a strange dance. *Hmm, die now or later?*

A door wavered into existence, proof that my choice had already been made. Like a woman walking to her execution, I shuffled across the floor and lifted my hand until it hovered above the newly exposed doorknob. Swallowing against a dry throat, I let my hand drop until the solid fixture was cool against my palm. Closing my eyes, I turned the handle.

Something hot and solid cupped my face, chasing back the cold that seemed to be my new normal. "Megan, can you hear me?"

Deep and resonating, it was nothing like the monster's voice. My pulse kicked in because there was a hint of familiarity to it. Unfortunately, I wasn't all that trusting of my own perceptions.

"Megan, come on. Open your eyes. Show me you're still here."

It's not real. It's not real. My mental mantra didn't do jack to stop the sickening mix of hope and fear crawling through me. I didn't want to open my eyes to another cruel game because I was pretty sure I wouldn't survive it. I'd been tricked too many times before when the monster wore the mask of someone I loved. But this voice tugged at something buried deep. It belonged to… I tried to place it but failed.

"Megan, open your eyes."

With no way to escape the command, I opened my eyes— which felt as if they weighed a ton—and stared into a rich, velvety darkness with hints of gold.

"That's it. Good girl."

Not liking the term, I frowned and licked dry lips. "Not a girl." The denial came out rough and didn't sound like me.

"No, you're definitely not." Humor lightened those eyes, and the one eyebrow marred by a scar lifted. "Sorry."

A faint muffled explosion of pops made me jerk my head out of his hands, and I scrambled back until my spine hit something hard. A yank on my leg and the harsh sound of metal scraping concrete followed. My attention snapped to my feet, where a chain was locked around my ankle. I stared, blinking, as it hit me. I looked back at the man kneeling in front of me. "This is real?"

His earlier humor disappeared, replaced by a grim wariness. He nodded, his gaze anchoring mine.

Please don't let this be another game. Needing physical proof, I reached out, unsurprised to find my hand shaking.

His nostrils flared, and those eyes darkened into velvet, but he leaned in until my fingers could brush the strong line of his jaw. Heated skin, slightly rough with the beginnings of stubble, rasped against my fingers. His hand covered mine, pressing it close.

Heat, flesh, bone—it was all there under my hand. *Real. He's real.* Hot tears rose, the first in a long time, and slipped down my face. "You're real."

"I'm real, Megan." He tilted his head and frowned. The hand lifted from mine and touched his ear. "Copy, asset retrieved. Rendezvous in three."

Without him holding it in place, I pulled my hand back, curling it into a fist to hold onto the remnants of that touch. It took a moment to realize the asset he was talking about was me.

My sluggish brain ground into gear, and I finally took in the rest of him—the patterned cargo pants and dark shirt, the weapon strapped across his chest, the other ones at his waist, the ear piece and mic partially hidden by his dark hair. *Soldier. Rescue team.* They finally found me.

Before I could appreciate the wonder of that, another volley of muted shots drifted to where we sat. The dull thump of a muted explosion followed on its heels, barely earning a glance from him but making me jump. *Right, okay. So we need to get out of here.* Bracing my hand against the wall, I tried to stand, only to be mocked by the rattling scrape of the chain and the legs that wouldn't support me.

"Hold up." His hand landed on my shoulder, holding me in place. "We need to get that off your ankle first."

"Hurry." I managed to get that one word out from between clenched teeth. As I stared at the metal cuff, anxiety and the need to get it off tore my shaky composure to shreds.

Desperate not to buckle under the circling madness, I focused on the soldier's deft movements as he used a lock pick on the manacle.

The teasing sense of familiarity hit again, but I couldn't pin it down. It was too hard, and my head pounded. Needing a distraction to avoid spiraling into the pit at the edge of my mind, I asked, "What's your name?"

He shot me a quick look, his lips curving slightly. "Bishop." He handed me a canteen. "Small sips."

The name rang a bell. I heeded his advice, taking a small sip. Then I frowned, trying to remember something I'd spent way too long avoiding. The effort almost hurt. "The colonel's Bishop?"

"The one and only."

A tremble—whether of fear or relief, I didn't know or care—moved through me. The next question was harder to get out. "How long?"

He lifted his head and shot me a narrow-eyed glance before going back to work on the lock. Fortunately, he didn't pretend to misunderstand my question. "Six months."

Shock ricocheted through me, leaving another layer of numbness in its wake. *Six months?* The canteen shook, sending a splash of water over my hand. My stomach knotted.

Bishop looked up, took the canteen, and stowed it away before going back to work on the metal cuff. I heard a dull click, and then the pressure on my ankle disappeared, revealing a pale band of skin surrounded by dirt and bruises and old cuts. His warm, firm arm wrapped around my waist, hauling me up. "Time to go."

Reeling at the rapid change of position, I braced one hand against his hard chest. The other went to the arm holding me, my nails digging in as I turned my head to blink at my rescuer.

Whatever he saw in my face left his jaw tight and his eyes hard. "Time to move, Megan."

Biting my lip, I looked down and tried to take a step, only to find that my legs still refused to work. Choking back a sob of frustration, I admitted, "I don't think I can walk."

"Hang on."

It was my only warning before he shifted his hold and swung me up into his arms. I looped my arm around his broad shoulders as he straightened, somehow managing to avoid the weapon strapped to his back.

As he headed out of the cell, a sense of foreboding wrapped me in a suffocating fog. An evil voice whispered a warning. *If he takes me out of this hell, it will follow and swallow us both whole.* The chilling grip of dread clung tight, leaving me fighting the terrifying urge to demand that he leave me behind. Closing my eyes, I buried my face in his neck, biting my lip to hold the words back. Still, a mortifying whimper escaped.

The arms holding me tightened. "Just hang in there, Megan."

His words were an eerie echo of the ones my imaginary protector used. They managed to finish what six months of captivity had started, and with freedom only steps away, I finally broke, falling into the darkness.

Chapter One

FOUR WEEKS LATER

"Honey, I don't think you being alone is a good thing right now."

"Mom, look, I'm fine." Pinching the bridge of my nose, I stared at the laminated countertop as if it contained advice on how to deal with overprotective parental units. I used to do that with ease, but now it seemed to take every bit of energy I possessed.

"No, you're not." Underneath the love was a depth of worry that four weeks of having me back couldn't erase. "You've only been out of the hospital a couple of weeks, and Keelie says you're not sleeping well."

"Keelie called you." Shifting the phone against my ear, I tried to tone down my frustration at having my every move reported by my baby sister.

Mom's tone softened. "Of course she did. She wouldn't head out of town and not let us know. She's worried about you." Her unspoken, *We all are,* came through loud and clear.

"I know."

Her concern was typical of my close-knit family and something I'd yearned for while I was locked away with the faceless monster I still couldn't seem to escape. But now that I had them back, I didn't find their concern comforting. It was more like a smothering weight. *Doesn't that make me the worst daughter ever?*

"How about this: I will be fine."

Her quiet sigh signaled her surrender. "I know you will be, baby, but…"

I dropped my hand to trace random patterns on the counter. "Mama, I'll be okay. It's just going to take time." Hearing myself repeat my therapist's favorite phrase made me wince as I watched the sunlight spilling through the glass patio door. "Keelie needed to get back to work, and she'll only be gone a week."

"I'd feel better if you had a friend stay with you."

I managed not to snort. For that, I'd need to actually have a friend. Being MIA for six months had done a hack job to my social life. Not to mention I had a new aversion to socializing. "I'm fine." Since that came out sharper than I wanted, I added, "I promise to call or text you every day, okay?"

"Every day, Megan."

With the end of the discussion in sight, I agreed. Again. "Yes, Mom."

"I love you, sweetheart."

The swath of sunlight blurred, and my throat tightened. "I love you too, mom."

We exchanged goodbyes, and I disconnected my phone and set it facedown on the counter. My eyes burned, and I tried to blame it on another sleepless night, but I knew better. After Keelie had left the previous afternoon, I spent most of the day wondering when my mom would finally break down and call. She managed to make it twenty-four hours before calling me, which was better than I'd expected, especially since this was the first time I was truly alone since my rescue four weeks before.

Bracing my hands against the counter's cool surface, I spread my fingers wide, pressing in. The scrapes and cuts that had once marked my skin were healing. Unfortunately, I was now the bearer of thin white scars that encircled my wrists, thanks to the wire restraints used to bind me to the chair during my question-and-answer sessions. A familiar dread crept in, dimming the sunlight until Keelie's apartment wavered into a terrifying grayness. I pushed harder against the counter, concentrating on how it warmed under my palms even as a line of cold sweat broke out along my spine.

This is real. I am real.

"I'm okay." The sound of my own voice eased back the nightmare, just as my therapist had told me it would. I wasn't sure if I was pissed or annoyed by that fact. I was going to stick with annoyed since that seem to be my theme for the day. As this was my first go-around with the whole therapy thing, I had no idea if that was the correct response or not. Honestly, I wasn't sure I gave a damn. Then again, I was finding it hard to give a damn about much of anything lately.

Give it time.

Frustration joined my irritation, and I turned away from the counter to pace. If I ever got back to normal, I was banning those three words from my vocabulary. Logically, I knew that four weeks was not a lot of time in the grand scheme of things, but I still felt trapped by my inability to shake the horror that shadowed every waking moment. I felt trapped by the nightmares that wouldn't leave me alone and a sense of loss I couldn't understand—and by the suspicion that someone was watching me, just waiting to pounce.

According to my all-knowing therapist, all of it was just a by-product of six months of captivity bundled into one diagnosis—post-traumatic stress disorder, or PTSD, a label I never considered would apply to me and my relatively normal life. *I mean, seriously, how much danger could a noncommissioned officer expect to face while serving as the administrative assistant to a retired colonel who now works in the private sector?* The low-danger nature of the job was one of the reasons I chose to remain an NCO when I joined the marines. I wasn't looking to make a name for myself—I just wanted a successful career before I found the mysterious "one" to share my 2.5-kids-and-dog life with. You know, the normal American dream.

Unfortunately, I'd gotten pulled into a nightmare to end all nightmares, and my goals had changed. Now I just wanted to make it through a full night without waking up in a cold sweat, with a raw throat and blood-curdling nausea-inducing images seared into my mind. The lack of sleep and the low level of apprehension I couldn't shake left me feeling as if the nightmare wasn't really over.

Hang in there, Megan. The fading echoes of my imaginary protector drifted through my mind, triggering that elusive sense of loss.

"He's not real." Saying it out loud didn't help this time, which was no surprise. My therapist's explanation hadn't stopped me from mourning someone who didn't exist but was simply a coping mechanism. Logically, I understood it, but somewhere deep inside, it wasn't sinking in.

Welcome to the crazy train. Next stop, mad ramblings and wild hair. That thought had made me give a sharp, humorless laugh. Rubbing a hand over my face, I blew out a hard breath and resumed my pacing, trying to yank my mind off the jumbled path it was determined to tread.

A flash of movement outside the patio door stopped my restless movements as a colorful little bird did a flyby. A pang of jealous longing hit me, and the walls went from comforting to confining. Needing the escape, no matter how minor, I unlocked the slider and stepped onto Keelie's tiny balcony. My baby sister managed to afford a nice but cute—another word for *small*—apartment on the fifth floor of a complex with a sliver of a view of San Diego's coastline. It wasn't the remodeled bungalow I once shared with two other women, but it worked, especially since Keelie's roommate had recently gotten married and was only staying on the lease to give herself an exit strategy.

Instead of a half wall, the balcony was a series of iron rods, which gave me a chance to people watch from my lofty perch. It was a pastime I used to enjoy, but ever since I'd gotten back, it wasn't the same. Curling up in one of the two chairs, I pressed my bare feet against the railing. Eventually, my claustrophobia receded. The sounds of the city drifted up—the hum of traffic, a dog barking somewhere, and off in the distance, the deep toll of one the many cargo ships dotting the harbor.

My gaze drifted to the scramble of life below. For a moment, I considered going back in and unearthing one of my sketch pads. Almost seven months without them should have left me jonesing for the creative outlet and comfort. Instead, the thought of putting a pencil to paper left me in a cold sweat. I was scared the madness in my head would bleed onto the page.

Right, no sketching.

Unable to get lost in the possible stories associated with each passing face, my mind detoured, wandering down darker roads. *How much ugliness lies under all the friendly smiles and pretty faces?* I squeezed my hands into tight fists, forcing my thoughts back to brighter paths before I got lost in the murky alleys. But it was hard not to wonder if the guy in board shorts and a baseball cap, checking his phone as he sat on a bench, was the same one I'd seen hanging around at other times. *Is he watching me? Is he working for the monster?*

Laughter, like shiny bubbles, burst from a group of young women juggling surfboards and tote bags. Baseball-cap man turned to watch them walk by, and even from my perch, I swore I could hear his appreciative whistle.

See? Perfectly normal—unlike me, thanks to my warped psyche.

Yeah, something was seriously wrong with me. With the sun warm against my skin, despite the cool late-January breeze, I rubbed my bare heels against the railing's edge and tried to enjoy the moment. Watching the minor drama play out below, I noted a familiar red-and-white bag from a nearby Mexican restaurant being carried by one of the women. Like Pavlov's dog, my mouth watered. *Hmm, maybe I should brave a public appearance.* My stomach rumbled an agreement, and since it tended to be extremely picky lately, I took that as a cosmic sign.

I got to my feet and was heading back in for some shoes when something made me pause and turn, catching a flash of sunlight hitting something in the distance, blinding me for an instant. Shadows rushed at me. The hated voice filled my ears and echoed through my skull, harsh and unrelenting.

Give me what I want.

I don't have it.

Don't lie. Give it or die. I don't care.

I stumbled, pitching forward, and threw my hand out to stop my fall. The rough stucco wall scraped against my palm, but I barely noticed as my nightmares slithered into the light. I caught a glint of teeth. A faceless blur moved closer as the teeth grew, threatening to swallow me whole.

You think you'll escape, but you won't. It touched my face, making me flinch. *You can't escape me. I won't let you go.*

A horn honked, shattering the hellish tendrils and slamming me back to the present. I sucked in air, trying to breathe around my pounding heart, my vision blurred by a sudden piercing ache slicing through my head. Even worse, the sensation of being watched hit my back like a venomous arrow.

Blinded by panic, I half fell, half tripped inside. I slammed the door closed behind me as I put my back to the wall, getting out of sight. Body shaking, mind breaking, I slid down the wall until I could wrap my arms around my knees. The past rose up in a hellish wave, threatening to suck me under.

You'll be okay. The assurance that had once provided comfort now lashed at me, scoring deep wounds. It didn't matter whether it was a coping mechanism or a figment of my imagination—I was far from okay and very much on my own.

My anger and despair rushed out on a choked sob. "I'm not. I'm not."

They were watching, waiting. Despite being out of that hell-hole, I was still trapped, still caught in whatever evil web had shattered my life. That voice, the one that belonged to the endless questions, was still there, still whispering its evil in my mind.

The nightmarish images, memories—whatever the hell they were—circled, waiting to land, but I couldn't let them. I knew to my marrow that if they settled in, I was well and truly done. The only thing left of my future would be four padded walls.

You could make it all go away.

The insidious thought found a foothold, offering relief from the sounds and images stalking my every waking moment. I was so damn tired. I just wanted a moment of peace and quiet. Was that too much to ask?

Open your eyes, and show me you're still here.

The memory of Bishop, rough and commanding, yanked me back from the crumbling edge. "I'm still here." My voice shook, but the words were true—I was still here. For six months, I'd managed to hold on. There was no way in hell I would let go now. I just needed... help. And I knew exactly who to ask.

Chapter Two

BISHOP

"I don't like it." That was putting it mildly. I was not one to normally question Colonel Charlene Delacourt's orders, but that didn't mean I wouldn't. The idea of buddying up to Megan Rouser to find out if she was a player or a pawn in this shitastic game of lies and deception we had going with Falcon did not sit well with me.

The lines of stress on the colonel's angular face deepened, and her response was clipped. "You don't have to like it."

Uh-huh. "Why me?"

"You've already established a connection with her."

The knowledge that the colonel had picked up on that fact made me itch. Granted, my habit of stopping by the hospital until Megan's release a couple of weeks earlier couldn't be missed, but I could try to ignore it. "I got her out of that hellhole. Not sure how much of a 'connection' that really is." I ignored the bitter taste of a lie.

"You rescued her," the colonel patiently continued, not about to let me wiggle out of this. "Not only that, but you were the one she chose to speak to when she finally talked. Tell me how that's not a connection, Bishop."

She was right—I felt a connection. The problem was, it might be one-sided. I couldn't seem to get Megan out of my thoughts, and I couldn't rationalize that reaction, which made me leery. As for Megan, after I carried her out of that warehouse, she'd shut down, turning mute and unresponsive for almost four days. On day five, following the doctor's advice, I sat at her side and kept up a one-sided conversation. For some reason known only to her, that worked, and she finally started talking.

Still, I wasn't about to give in to the colonel gracefully. "Give me another reason, something a bit more concrete, because I'm not as sold on this as you."

One eyebrow rose, and dry amusement lightened the grim lines of her face. "Risia."

Well, shit. My arguments crumbled into dust. There was no arguing with a woman who could see the future, and Risia Lacoste, the team's seer, had an accuracy that was off the charts. But when another solution came to mind, I threw my best friend under the proverbial bus and said, "What about Wolf?"

A man has to try, right?

Delacourt gave a small grimace. "You know he won't try unless Megan gives him permission."

Frickin' Boy Scout telepath. Okay, that description wasn't exactly fair. Wolf could bend and break a mind as easily as read it, so setting boundaries was crucial to his mental well-being. And working on a mind shrouded by trauma for the sake of expediency definitely crossed one of Wolf's lines.

Unable to sit still, I rose and began to pace. "You really think I can get her to give him permission?" I was shaking my head before she could answer. "There's no way she'll allow him near her after what she's survived. You're asking for a miracle."

"Maybe, but we can't afford to wait any longer." The colonel was starting to sound impatient.

I get it. Damn, do I get it, but... "She's been home from the hospital—what, two and half weeks?—after spending six months having her mind jacked around. I think you might want to cut her some slack."

Sympathy flashed over the colonel's features. "If I had that option, I would."

Her answer settled into my brain, and in a flash of clarity, I understood. "You're worried about your inside man."

Grim resolution came back to her face with a vengeance, confirming what I'd said. I knew Delacourt had someone embedded deep inside Falcon, the evil mercenary group that was playing yin to our quasi-military-psychic-team yang. We might not be an acknowledged part of the US military, but we had enough ties to be problematic, which meant we had to play by the rules. Falcon didn't. They didn't play nice either.

We knew they were behind Megan's kidnapping—not that we had actionable proof. Nope, what we had was some serious-as-shit suspicions with a heavy dose of skepticism, but proof was what we needed to shut Falcon down. To that end, Delacourt had an operative deep inside Falcon, so thoroughly undercover that months passed before he or she could confirm our lead on Megan's whereabouts without raising suspicions. Blowing the cover of an embedded operative never ended well —hence the cautionary handling.

As I stopped in front of her desk, my mouth moved before the ideas swirling in my mind coalesced into something solid. "You need to pull them out, sir." Certainty bloomed with no damn rhyme or reason and changed to dread—the mysterious operator was running out of time. That realization was a psychic punch that left my bones humming. "As soon as you can."

Her gaze didn't falter. "We're working on it."

Work faster. I locked the words behind my teeth because they wouldn't help.

"Our operative is not the only reason," she added in a low voice as she straightened the already neat papers on her desk. "Although it's a damn good one."

I had to ask. "Do I want to know?"

She met my gaze. "Answers are being requested from above, and people are getting impatient."

In other words, someone was pressuring Delacourt about team operations and outcomes. That was not a good thing, considering that our team had been quietly trying to chase down whispers about a high-ranking traitor working with Falcon. Having eyes on us would make our search that much more difficult. So far, we'd managed to stop the illegal sale of a shipment of stolen weapons and block the auction of a hijacked list of undercover operatives, but our luck was bound to run out at some point. Although Delacourt maneuvered better than any bomb tech I knew, the situation was more volatile than TAPT—triacetate triperoxide, the notoriously unstable explosive.

Although the PSY-IV teams weren't officially part of the military—deniability and all that—the colonel still had to answer to the higher-ups, especially since they were the ones who ensured our funding. I wasn't a fan of politics, which was why I was standing on one side of the desk, and she was sitting on the other.

If you don't do this, she won't be on that side for long.

The realization rang with crystal clarity, but I tried not to react. I sensed a shadowy figure standing close to the colonel, shrouded in malice and manipulation—as if my suspicion that the traitor was someone close to Delacourt needed more weight. Proof was worth a hell of a lot more than some unexplainable psychic instinct.

Gritting my teeth, I turned away and moved to the large

window overlooking the bland parking lot of the even blander building housing our off-the-books teams made up of ex-military and Special Forces personnel who all shared one common trait—psychic abilities. Which reminded me… "What about her brother? Isn't he one of ours?"

Behind me, the colonel's chair creaked, and the air shifted, telling me she had moved. "Devon and his team are currently OCONUS. The mission has no set return date at this time."

So Dev is out of the country. I felt a flash of satisfaction and a strange possessiveness that left me uncomfortable. *Why in the hell do I want to be the one responsible for Megan?* I decided to deal with that question later. Rubbing my neck, I blew out a hard breath and surrendered to the inevitable. "How's this supposed to work?"

"She hasn't been cleared to drive yet. Her follow-up appointment is tomorrow at the base hospital."

Which means… I turned back to the colonel. "I'm her ride."

Delacourt nodded. "Her younger sister, Keelie, left town yesterday."

It took me a moment to recall the information we'd gathered on Megan's family when we were planning her rescue. "She's the one who works with service dogs, right?"

"And splits her time working with disaster-recovery efforts." Delacourt bent over her desk and scribbled something on a sticky note before offering it up. "Her address, which is where Megan is staying."

I took the piece of paper, barely glancing at it. "She's staying there alone?" Why that concerned me, I wasn't sure, but it did.

Delacourt settled a hip against her desk and held my gaze. "Yes, at her insistence."

The sticky note crumpled in my fist. "Tell me you have eyes on her."

Faint amusement drifted over the colonel's normally stoic face.

My fist uncurled. *Yeah, there are eyes on her.* "What time's her appointment?"

"Oh nine hundred."

At least it wasn't the butt crack of dawn. "Fine, but don't hold your breath." I turned on my heel and headed to the door. Before I could get to it, a knock sounded. Looking back over my shoulder, I caught Delacourt's nod—the slight movement of her silver-streaked cap of black hair. Then I yanked the door open and stepped to the side.

The colonel's latest administrative assistant and Megan's replacement, a fresh-faced intern, popped her head in, worry lining her face. "Apologies, Colonel, but there's a Ms. Rouser here to see you, and she's insistent."

She barely got the last word out before I brushed past her to the front office. Standing in front of the desk, in loose jeans and a shirt that hung over what had once been generous curves before she'd suffered months of captivity, was the face that had haunted my dreams for the last few weeks. Or longer, if I were to be brutally honest. There was no escaping the low punch of hunger I felt or the sudden protective urge to lock her away from everyone and everything.

Megan's arms were wrapped over her stomach. She was too damn thin. *Hell,* the bruises under eyes were almost as dark as her hair. But it was her disconcertingly blank expression that made me feel a surge of anger. Shoving that reaction aside, I managed to say, "Megan."

Her gaze met mine, and for a moment, her mask slipped, revealing a breath-stealing fear inside the startling blue eyes. She blinked, and it disappeared, replaced by cool distance. The abrupt change sent ice through my veins.

"Bishop." Her tone was as neutral as her expression.

Delacourt and the intern joined the welcoming party and

caught Megan's attention. Something too fast to catch drifted over Megan's face as she swallowed hard and lifted her chin. "I'm glad you're here. I need to speak to both of you."

Delacourt stepped around me. "Megan, what's wrong?"

Megan's gaze darted between the intern, the colonel, and me before she looked away and took a step back.

Don't let her run.

Before I could stop myself, I followed, taking a step forward. "Don't." If I let her leave, things would go very badly. No way in hell would I ignore my instincts. That never ended well.

Her head came up, her eyes widened, but she gave me a jerky nod before straightening her spine. She turned to the colonel. "I know I don't have an appointment, sir, but I just need a minute."

"Of course." Delacourt turned and headed back into her office.

Megan's wary gaze came back to me, and her eyes gave a flash of puzzled recognition. Maybe our strange connection wasn't as one-sided as I thought, but now wasn't the time to find out. I held her gaze, unable to look away. She moved stiffly forward, stepping around me with a studied casualness, ensuring we didn't touch.

I pivoted and followed, staying close enough to catch the small shiver she tried to hide and the light scent of something sweet and spicy. Shaking off the intriguing smell, I followed them into the office, closed the door, and leaned back, blocking the only exit. Not that Megan would make a break for it, but hey, it was better to be prepared.

While Megan settled in my recently vacated seat, Delacourt said, "It was my understanding you weren't cleared to drive."

Those too-thin shoulders rose and fell in an awkward shrug. "I took a Lyft."

The slightly amused curve of the colonel's lips did little to soften her serious expression. "Well, that's something, then."

"Wait." Lines creased Megan's forehead. "How did you know about the driving restriction?"

The colonel held her gaze but didn't answer.

Megan sighed, and I swore she sounded relieved instead of annoyed. "You're watching me."

Before more could be said, the door at my back vibrated under a pounding fist. In unison, Delacourt and Megan turned in my direction. I didn't budge but raised a brow in question.

Megan's gaze flicked to the door and back to me, her stoic mask irritatingly intact. "That's probably whoever you all have watching me."

My lips twitched. *Ditched her eyes, did she?* Catching Delacourt's chin lift, I straightened, turned to block the doorway, and opened it a crack to communicate but not far enough to encourage entry. Imitating the sonorous tones of one of my favorite creepy butlers, I said, "Yes?"

Rabbit, the team's tech genius, narrowed his hazel eyes and dropped his raised fist. "She in there?"

Keeping my smirk hidden, I repeated, "Yes."

"Damn it, Bishop. Girl moves faster than a ghost." The south dripped from his disgruntled voice.

Not willing to let him off the hook, I held my position and expression. "Really?"

A snort sounded from the tawny-haired woman behind him—Rabbit's partner, Jinx. "More like he couldn't tear his eyes from a cluster of surfer chicks."

I worked hard not to smile at Jinx's disgusted tone or the flush riding Rabbit's cheeks as he turned to glare at her. "It wasn't them I was checkin' out, woman."

"Uh-huh."

"Did you see the size of the burritos they were carryin'?" Rabbit continued. "They were magnificent."

"Enough," I said. "I've got her from here. I'll call when I get her back."

"Great." Jinx grabbed Rabbit's arm and tugged him back. "Since you're so hungry, let's go feed you before you molest the next set of food-carrying females."

"I'm more likely to molest a chicken wing about now, *chere*," Rabbit muttered.

Shaking my head, I shut the door and turned back to the room, crossing my arms over my chest. The colonel was pinching the bridge of her nose though she had a small smile, but Megan was white knuckling the chair's armrests, her spine rigid, as she stared out the window, biting her lower lip, lost in whatever was going on in her mind.

Delacourt's smile disappeared as she looked at the young woman. "Megan," she called softly.

Megan turned her head with an unusual stiffness that set my instincts on edge. "Yes."

"Are you okay?"

"No." Those blue eyes shifted between Delacourt and me. "I need your help."

Delacourt straightened and left her desk. Once she was seated beside Megan, she leaned forward, her arms braced on her knees, and covered one of the younger woman's hands. "You know I'll help if I can."

I caught the slight flaring of Megan's nostrils and the lessening in the tension around her eyes at Delacourt's touch. As a tell, it wasn't much, but for someone like me who made a career of such things, it was all too clear. Megan was bonedeep scared.

She took a deep breath and proved my instincts right. "I think I'm losing my mind."

Chapter Three

Hearing no automatic denials from the colonel sitting next to me or the man guarding my only escape route, I wondered if my concern that I was losing my mind should be upgraded from possibility to fact. The colonel had someone watching me, and although Bishop's big body blocked a lot, I caught a glimpse of the familiar baseball cap from earlier. So yeah, Baseball Cap was watching me, which explained my sense of being stalked, but he wasn't working for the bad guys, which eased some of my paranoia but not all of it. I still had no explanation for the voices and the nightmares.

I opened my mouth to add to my little revelation, but their lack of response froze my vocal cords. Finding the words to explain the craziness spinning through my mind was nearly impossible. Doubts rushed in, making me wonder what I thought I was doing. Maybe coming here was a bad idea. Perhaps I should consider checking myself in to a mental-health facility and taking the damn drugs the therapist kept trying to push on me. At least, then, the numbness I couldn't seem to shake would have a legit reason for existing.

"Megan."

Hearing my name in that rough rasp, I felt some of the paralyzing pressure ease. I looked up and met the gaze of the man who'd brought me out of hell and somehow managed to become my talisman. *Bishop.* My therapist would probably have a field day when I told her about the weird sensation of knowing Bishop way more than I actually did—that having him there made me feel safe and steadied my world. I latched onto his calm steadiness and strange familiarity as I realized that although neither the colonel nor Bishop had denied my insanity claim, they weren't reaching to phone the men in white coats either. This could be a good thing.

"I need to understand," I said.

"Understand what?" the colonel asked.

Her question unlocked a flood of thoughts and words. They tumbled out one after another. "Why me?" I couldn't hide my scalding anger. Before they could answer, I said, "I don't know why they chose me. I don't know anything—not really. Not anything important. I push… pushed papers, arranged schedules, made appointments, filed reports. It makes no sense why they took me or why they held me for six months." I rubbed my forehead because that wasn't exactly true—I had an idea of why. I just didn't want to admit it.

Implacable and calm, Delacourt called me out. "You know the truth about what we do."

Yeah, I did. No matter how safe my previous job had seemed, there was no escaping the fact there were still risks involved. Security clearances weren't for giggles. I held her gaze. "So I know the teams are psychic. What good does that do anyone?"

"You're an access point." The hard edge in Bishop's voice sent shivers down my spine. I turned to him as he continued. "You had access to the colonel, her office, and all our records. The chance that you saw or heard something was probably high enough for them to risk taking you. Add in the fact you're basically a civilian with no training in surviving interrogation, and you become the weakest point. Hell, if they couldn't get to our team, they could use you against your brother and his team."

It hurt to hear him refer to me as the weakest point, even if his words were somewhat true. But the pieces of his theory weren't fitting together. "If I was leverage, then why didn't they contact him? Why keep me for six months?" Anxiety crawled through me as my suspicions grew. I met his eyes, and something about this man gave me the strength to voice my insidious fears. "I think they did something to me."

Over the last few weeks, my confidence in my own perceptions had eroded, and despite my best intentions, I couldn't say any more. Suffocating pressure returned with a vengeance, bringing the sickening feeling of standing outside of myself as I fell apart. Everything around me was nothing more than a desperate dream. A frantic warning to wake up reverberated through my mind. The tightness in my chest grew as panic set its claws deep and dragged me toward the hazy blackness edging my vision.

Something heavy and warm pressed against the back of my neck, and I followed its lead, bending forward. The touch, rough and solid against my chilled skin, was so unexpected it almost hurt. It gave me something real to focus on.

"Breathe, Megan." Bishop's deep voice accompanied a soothing stroke along my spine, anchoring me. "You're okay. I've got you."

Sucking in much-needed air, I opened my eyes, only to be caught by the velvet darkness of his gaze. Staring into those eyes, I couldn't have stopped my whispered confession if I'd tried. "There's something wrong with me."

His face darkened. "Then we'll fix it."

"Promise?" The stupid question escaped before I could lock it down.

"Yeah."

I knew better, but it didn't stop me from holding tight to his reassurance. *Why did I have to fall apart in front of him, of all people?* I shoved the humiliation back into its warped cage. That useless panic attack proved I was right—the voices and nightmares weren't going away. In fact, they were getting worse, almost as if someone or something was determined to drive me insane. That sounded paranoid even in the privacy of my own mind, but I couldn't shake my conviction. Whether or not anyone ever believed me, I knew something bad had happened, and the memory of it was buried deep.

My stomach pitched as a new fear rose, one I hadn't considered: what if I was a danger to those around me? I'd be damned if I'd put my friends and family at risk. Maybe I should consider checking myself in to a mental health facility, even if it meant being locked away for the rest of my life. It wasn't the best life goal to have, but it was better than nothing.

Having an option, no matter how drastic, eased the encroaching panic. I took a deep breath, then another until my pulse was no longer a deafening beat in my ears. With the air moving steadily through my chest, I managed a nod, letting Bishop know I was okay. Well, as okay as I could get nowadays.

The hand at my neck lifted, but the one on my back stayed. From his crouched position in front of me, he studied me. Not sure what he was looking for, I waited.

Finally, he asked, "You good?"

"Yes, thank you." My stilted politeness was wince worthy.

The seconds stretched before he moved. Then, instead of getting up and walking away, he caught both of my wrists, his thumbs brushing over my skin until they rested on my pulse. "You think they did something to you?" He turned my earlier statement into a question, getting us back on track.

This time, I managed to nod and not freak out.

"Megan." In all the years I'd worked for the colonel, I'd never heard her speak so carefully. This didn't bode well. "You told the doctors you couldn't remember anything. Has that changed?"

Yes and no, but that answer won't work. "Maybe." My answer came out hesitant. Bishop gently squeezed my wrist, regaining my attention, and I tried to explain it to him. "Flashes here and there that don't make sense, but I *know* something's not right. With me, I mean."

The colonel's hand landed on my shoulder. Before I could stop, I jerked back, pulling against Bishop's hold and recoiling from the colonel. Her hand fell away.

Not cool, Megan. I turned my head with difficulty, because of the stiff muscles in my neck, and managed to face her, bracing for her reaction.

Instead of reproaching me, she spoke with wary compassion. "That's normal—"

"For PTSD patients," I said. "I know. My therapist mentioned it." There was nowhere for my frustration to go. This was the reaction I'd expected, so why was I so damn disappointed? "This isn't me feeling guilty for what happened or blaming myself." *At least, I hope not.*

Before I'd splintered into unrecognizable fragments, I was blessed with a relatively normal life. My childhood, minus the unusual quirks of my siblings, was trauma free. I was happy with my accomplishments, satisfied with my chosen path, and relatively whole. My dreams were pretty straightforward, not the nightmares that plagued me now.

Turning away from the resigned compassion in my former boss's face, I stared at my lap, where Bishop's fingers covered the thin white scars. An image wavered for a moment then reformed. Bright-red blood seeped under his fingers to drip to my knees, and the hellish whisper, with its final solution, was back, taunting and cruel.

Before my emerging nightmare could strengthen, Bishop's voice cut through it. "Those flashes—are they always the same?"

His question snapped me back to the here and now. Swallowing hard to ease my dry mouth, I answered, "Not exactly."

"How *not exactly*?"

"Sometimes, I'm back in that cell, in that chair, and he won't stop asking me." I tried to tug my hands free, but Bishop wouldn't let go.

"Asking you what?"

"To give him what he wants."

Bishop's jaw tightened. "What does he want?"

"I don't know."

"You said 'sometimes.'"

I managed a nod, trying my hardest not to get angry at his persistence. It had been my choice, *my choice*, to walk in here and ask for help. The reminder tempered my irritation but did nothing for the tension locking my muscles in place.

"And the other times?"

Yeah, this is where it's bound to get tricky. Part of my rehabilitation was mandatory therapy appointments. As I'd told the colonel, I was highly aware of the symptoms associated with post-traumatic stress disorder. Hell, no one would let me forget about my diagnosis. I tried sharing my worries with the therapist, but she was a broken record of well-meaning but useless advice and prescriptions. I even tried talking to Keelie about it, figuring my little sister's work with trauma survivors would make her a good sounding board. Unfortunately, every time I tried, I froze, the words trapped by my fear of seeing pity and terror in my sister's face. My continued silence carved a chasm between us that broke my heart, but I couldn't seem to find a way to fix it.

I couldn't seem to fix anything lately. I wanted so badly to reach through the emotional wall between my family and me, but something held me back. I seriously considered making it all stop in the most final of ways so I could finally escape that smothering sense of terror and grief. The decision to come to the colonel, the one person who might be able to help me—or in the worst-case scenario, stop me—was my last option for regaining my sanity. When Bishop had stepped out of her office, I took it as a sign that I was doing the right thing.

Lifting my chin, I met Bishop's eyes, my mind jumping from thought to thought like a hummingbird on crack before landing on something my dad once told me: *Sometimes the only way is through.*

It was time to suck it up and wade through. Setting my jaw, I reigned in my crazy and licked my lips. "In one nightmare, I'm at a desk, in front of a computer, and I'm... happy." *And satisfied because no one will ever guess.* "In another, I'm in a house overlooking mountains, standing at a window with a drink. There's a news channel on behind me, chattering about another massacre in a conflicted area, and I raise the glass like I'm toasting someone, but no one's there. The last one..." My throat closed. Even knowing I needed to share this one, I really didn't want to. Bishop's gaze didn't waver, and I forged ahead. "There's a girl. She's crying, begging." *Her voice hoarse from endless screams, and her pleas emerging like tortured whispers.* "And I... I make her stop."

"How?" Bishop asked softly.

Unable to hold his gaze, I looked to my lap, my fingers curling and uncurling in his hold. "I kill her." The three words reignited the memory of perverse pleasure at the sensation of her slender neck under my hands, my fingers squeezing, choking. Her harsh sobs, the rake of her nails against my hands—all of it causing a twisted hunger that left me covered in filth. My stomach cramped. A tremor ran through me as my newly acquired shell gained another crack. "That's not me." *That can't be me because if it is…* My brain stumbled to a halt, horror rising in a choking wave.

"Megan."

The pressure on my wrists disappeared. Freed from the restraint, I jerked back, lurching to my feet, trying to outrun the monster inside of me. Something caught me, trapped me. A white noise of terror shoved reality aside, leaving behind a desperate need to escape.

"Megan, stop it."

The sharp command pierced my panic, acting like a whip. On its heels was the whispery echo of the taunts I'd endured, and I forced my body to still. I sucked in air as if finishing a marathon and realized Bishop's arms were wrapped around me, one at my waist, the other holding my arms tight against my chest. His hold made me loosen the threads of the sadistic web until the colonel's office reshaped around me.

"You're safe, Megan. Safe."

The rumble of Bishop's voice next to my ear cut through the nightmare, leaving me weak and shaky as my adrenaline levels eased down. Held tight in his arms, I could not collapse into a pitiful pile at his feet. Using his support and verbal reassurances, I concentrated on pulling my shit together.

"That's it. Just breathe with me. You're doing great."

I followed his lead until my pulse leveled out and my legs remembered how to hold me. "I'm okay." It came out rough but clear.

"You are," Bishop agreed, his low voice vibrating against my spine. "You survived. You didn't break."

Startled to hear my own personal mantra aloud, I tilted my head back as much as possible against his chest to find him staring down at me. "Not yet." My denial was automatic but true. "These things I'm seeing… they aren't me."

A dark and dangerous look slipped across his face. "No, they aren't."

The surety of his answer gave me something to hold on to. What I wanted to say next would sound crazy. If I'd grown up with different siblings or had another kind of work life, I might have gratefully embraced the white-jacket diagnosis and taken their damn pills. But I knew that despite the fact I was boringly normal, there were others who had extraordinary, and sometimes frightening, abilities—people who could do amazingly good or evil things.

Unable to look away, I whispered, "It's him."

Chapter Four

BISHOP

I had to let her go because hearing the fear in her whispered admission left me with an urge to slam my fist into something—although I would have preferred hitting whoever was behind this whole mess. I let her go and backed up to the desk until I could grip the edge.

"You don't believe me." Megan turned to Delacourt then back to me, her jaw jutting out. "Look, I know it sounds crazy, but you both know it's a possibility."

There was no way to argue with her even if I'd wanted to. Knowing Falcon and the psychics they employed, I was aware that what she'd described could be the aftermath of having her brain fucked with by a telepath as much as it could be PTSD. Hell, it could be both. I was leaning toward the telepath explanation, thanks to my earlier vision of the shadowy threat directed at the colonel and my knowledge of Falcon's lack of ethics.

The colonel shifted in her seat then shot me a grim look. If Megan was right, it didn't bode well—for us or for her. If Falcon had access to a skilled telepath, the kind of damage they could create was, excuse the pun, mind-boggling.

Megan didn't miss our silent exchange. "Tell me I'm wrong."

"I can't," the colonel answered.

Megan gave a jerky nod then rubbed her palms against her knees. "Can we find out?"

Trying to hide my grimace, I looked down. The need to gain Megan's permission for Wolf to poke around in her mind was no longer an issue. As hard as it was to believe, she was all but putting her head on the chopping block. I couldn't figure out if that made her brave or reckless—or both.

"Maybe," the colonel answered cautiously as she studied Megan's face. "It would mean working with a telepath."

In her lap, Megan twisted her fingers together until they were bloodless. "But the telepath—they could find out?"

"His name is Wolf, and if anyone could, it would be him." Delacourt reached out and gave Megan's hands a gentle squeeze, and the younger woman flinched. "We can't offer any promises. This isn't exactly a science. You need to be sure this is what you want."

"Right now, I just want to know I'm not crazy."

"You're not crazy," I said, but I worried that her determination to figure out what was happening might not outweigh the downside of opening her mind to Wolf.

"I hear a *but* in there," she muttered.

She was right—it was a huge-ass *but*. "But to find out if your suspicions are right, you'll need to face a process that's similar to what you endured."

As my explanation sank in, her mask cracked. Fear and aversion seeped out before anger and resolve sealed it up tight. "I know that." She turned away and studied Delacourt and then seemed to come to a decision. "I want to make sure they didn't do something to me. Something that would put those around me at risk." After a tense moment during which the colonel failed to react, Megan's eyes narrowed. "You already thought of that."

When the colonel stayed silent, I answered, "Yeah, we did." If Megan had the courage to ask, she deserved an answer. It was obvious she had enough shit messing with her mind—no sense in adding more.

She turned from the colonel to me, her head tilting in consideration. "Were you going to tell me?" Before I could answer, she raised a hand, palm up, in the universal sign for *Shut it.* "Never mind. Stupid question. Of course you were."

I blinked. Maybe I was too used to the cynical bent of my fellow teammates, but her quick acceptance was startlingly trusting, especially considering her recent ordeal.

She turned back to the colonel. "I understand that the safety of the teams come first, and right now, I'm an unknown risk." She gave a brittle smile. "I can't share what I can't remember, and I can't remember how much, if anything, they were able to pull from me or do to me. What I can tell you is that I don't want to be the reason someone gets hurt or killed. So if there's a chance to find those answers, I'm willing to take it."

Her desire for answers was blinding her to the bigger picture. Frustrated, I said, "Not at the expense of your sanity." Why the hell was I so determined to handle her with kid gloves?

She turned those baby blues to me and shot back, "It's not your choice to make."

Before I could argue, the colonel waded in. "I'll set up a time to meet with Wolf tomorrow. You take tonight to think it through. If you change your mind—"

"I won't," Megan said.

I wanted to roll my eyes at her adamant tone.

Delacourt continued, "If you do, we'll find another solution."

At that blatant prevarication, I kept my disbelieving snort to myself.

Megan's chin lifted. "If you had another solution, this wouldn't be a conversation."

It was obvious that Megan's time as the colonel's assistant had left her with no fear of calling Delacourt out on her shit.

"Take the night, Megan," the colonel ordered.

Megan nodded and got to her feet.

The colonel rose as well. "I'll call you once I talk to Wolf."

"Thank you," Megan murmured.

I pushed up from the desk. "Come on. I'll take you home." Her stomach rumbled, and much-needed color streaked her cheekbones. "Dinner first," I amended as I moved to the door and held it open for her, surprised to realize I was happy to have a reason to spend more time with her.

She tried to wiggle out of it. "I've got food at home."

"Not enough for me."

"Who said you were invited?" she said, showing me a peek of who she must have been before this mess occurred.

Putting a hand on the small of her back, I nudged her through the door. "Consider it payment for playing taxi."

She turned her head and, from under thick lashes, shot me a playful look that stirred things best left alone right now. "So, does that mean dinner's coming from a drive-through?"

"I'm sure I can dig out enough change for somewhere with table and chairs." I held the door open as she passed through, and she gave a muffled snort.

⚫◆⚫

I grabbed the tray holding three orders of steak tacos and followed Megan to a nearby table. A local San Diego favorite, Nina's Cocina was humming with diners, but luckily, we were able to nab a spot in the back corner. Megan took a seat with her back to the door, and I set the tray down and took the other side. As I settled in, Megan distributed the food and placed the required pile of napkins in the center then nabbed one of the three unmarked bottles of salsa.

"You've been here before?" I asked.

She finished lining her two tacos with salsa. "Yep. Keelie and I make it a point to hit it at least once when I visit."

Strange that we haven't run into each other. While I enjoyed food, I wasn't the biggest fan of cooking, and this was one of my preferred stops. "Guessing you didn't use to live on this side of town."

Setting the salsa down, she shook her head. She lifted her taco. "Rent out here is through the roof. I shared a place with two roommates over in Ocean Beach. What about you?"

"Just moved into a house with Rabbit. It's close by and makes for a short commute." I nabbed the salsa and doctored my tacos, the scent of grilled meat making my mouth water.

Mouth full, she made a humming noise. When she finished her bite, she asked, "Rabbit's on your team, right? Like Wolf?"

Since I was busy chewing, I nodded. When my mouth was empty, I added, "Rabbit was the one following you."

"Huh." She put her elbow to the table, leaned against her hand, and watched me. Considering her unfocused gaze, I figured she wasn't watching me eat but was thinking about something else.

"'Huh,' what?"

She blinked, and her lips curved the tiniest bit. "He wasn't what I pictured for someone nicknamed Rabbit." She picked at her food and popped a piece of steak into her mouth, her eyes skating around to the other tables.

Curious, I asked, "What did you picture?"

She shrugged. "I don't know. Less southern charmer, more geeky federal agent."

Southern charmer? I almost choked on my taco. Then I raised a brow in question.

Color rose up in her cheeks, and she dropped her attention to her food. "When I worked with Delacourt, I heard some of your nicknames, but you guys didn't exactly hang around the office, so I kind of made up my own faces to go with them."

Now I was really curious. I sucked down some soda and tried to keep it casual. "You know I have to ask…" I waited until she looked at me then asked, "Did I match what you imagined?"

Judging by how deep the color in her cheeks went, she'd missed the mark with me by a mile or five, but she proved she was game by holding my gaze and answering, "Maybe."

I understood that was all she would give me. Male satisfaction perked up, and I grinned, unable to resist teasing her just a bit. "Exceeded your expectations, didn't I?"

I was rewarded with a laugh, and it sounded good. Hell, it looked even better because as the shadows drifted away from her for a moment, the woman who'd haunted my imagination to an unhealthy degree revealed herself.

Amusement lingered in her tone. "That has to get tiring."

"What?"

A wicked glint sparked in her eyes. "Carrying around an ego that size."

"Hey, haven't you heard? Confidence is sexy."

She gave a delicate snort and went back to her taco.

We spent the next few minutes eating in companionable silence. I was glad to note that her earlier stress seemed to ease. She wasn't as jumpy as before, and the stiffness she'd carried was no longer evident. Unfortunately, there was no missing the exhaustion in her face. It made me wonder when she'd last slept. No doubt, her sleep was far from easy, especially considering those nightmares she'd mentioned. The reminder left me frowning at my empty plate.

"Something wrong?"

I lifted my head, forcing my expression to smooth out. "Nothing important." I gathered the used napkins and dumped them onto my plate. Eyeing her barely touched second taco, I asked, "Do you want me to get a box for that?"

She wiped her mouth and shook her head. "It never tastes as good reheated. Guess my eyes were bigger than my stomach." She crumbled her napkin, dropped it on top, then added her basket to mine. "I'm just going to use the restroom before we leave." She pushed her chair back and got to her feet.

I did the same. "Sounds good. I'll meet you at the car."

She gave me a nod and headed down the short hall to the bathrooms. I kept an eye on her until she disappeared behind the closed door, then I got up to dump our plates. Putting on my sunglasses, I stepped out the door into the early evening. With the nice weather, people were out and about. Laughter and music from a nearby bar mingled with the sounds of passing cars. The street was narrow, and traffic moved along at a crawl. Not wanting to hoof it all the way down to the corner to cross at the light, I waited for a break then jogged across the street to where I'd left my Jeep and beeped the locks. An itch at my neck had me doing a quick scan of my surroundings. Tourists and more tourists, interspersed with locals. I clocked a guy sitting on a bench a few car lengths down, his attention directed at his phone. Nothing seemed out of place or a cause for alarm.

Rubbing the back of my neck, I got in the Jeep and started the engine, still trying to figure out what was setting me off. It wasn't unusual to have such flashes—just part and parcel of the job—but as I waited for Megan, I eyed the passing faces just in case. The man on the bench raised his phone, and I couldn't help but sneer as he took a selfie. I never did understand the fascination people had with social media. *Who the hell wants that many people up in their business?* Shaking my head, I caught sight of Megan darting across the street, checking right and left for traffic.

She rounded the hood, and a movement behind her caught my eye. Selfie Boy was getting to his feet, his phone lifted in Megan's direction. *Could be getting a new angle for his photo.* Unable to shake my unease, I had my door open and my feet on asphalt when Megan reached the other side.

She stopped and looked at me over the hood. "Bishop?"

"Get in," I ordered, not taking my attention from Selfie Boy, who had done an about-face and was disappearing into the crowd.

I stopped at the front bumper, torn. I could attempt to chase the unknown guy down, but that would leave Megan alone, which I didn't think was wise. And what would I do when I caught him? Demand to see his phone? Yeah, that would go over well, considering he hadn't really done anything that could be construed as a threat. *Better to get out of here and get Megan home.* I turned and saw Megan's pale face through my window. Her mask was back in place.

Well, shit. So much for a relaxing dinner. Running a hand through my hair, I turned on my heel and got back in the Jeep.

Megan waited until I'd snapped the seatbelt in place before asking, "What was that?"

I pulled out into the street. "Hopefully nothing."

"That's not exactly comforting."

Yeah, well, it wasn't meant to be. "I thought I saw something, but…" I shrugged as I kept my eyes on the road. "I can't be sure, so hopefully it was nothing other than me being paranoid." When she didn't say anything, I snuck a quick glance to see her biting her bottom lip. I took one hand off the steering wheel and squeezed her knee. "I was probably overreacting. Hazard of the job."

Cold fingers encircled my wrist and held on. "I don't think I'd like your job."

"It has its moments," I murmured as I kept an eye out for any tails. I could feel the tiny tremors in her fingers. "You're staying at your sister's, right?"

"Yes."

"Alone?"

"Yes." Her fingers tightened then let my arm go. "Why?"

Even though I didn't want to, I took my hand from her knee. "I'm not comfortable with you being by yourself tonight."

"I'll be fine." There was a bite to her words.

Recognizing ruffled feminine pride, I changed tactics. "I'm sure you will, but I'd rather be sure, so humor me, okay?"

"Bishop, we barely know each other."

I slid her a glance and asked a question I was fairly certain I knew the answer to. "Do you think I'd hurt you?"

She answered quickly, "No."

"You got someone else you can call?" When she stayed silent, I pressed my point. "I'll have Rabbit bring my bag over. If it makes you uncomfortable to have me around, I can stay in my Jeep." It would make for a very uncomfortable night, but there was no way I could leave her alone tonight, even if I was stuck keeping watch from a distance.

I could feel her staring at me, and when I stopped at a red light, I checked. *Yep.* She was staring at me with an expression I couldn't read. "What?"

She bit her lip, shook her head, and turned away. "You can stay, but I don't think you'll fit on Keelie's couch."

Something told me that her answer had absolutely nothing to do with whatever was running through her mind, but with nothing to go on, I went with the direction she'd offered. "I've slept in worse. Don't worry."

She gave a soft sigh. "Fine, but you can't say I didn't warn you."

The light turned green, and I hit the gas.

Chapter Five

It was after midnight when I finally closed my bedroom door, leaving Bishop on the too-small couch in the living room with a blanket and pillow. Uncertain about the feelings spinning through me, I leaned against the door and stared at my feet as I dug my toes into the carpet. Despite my earlier comments in the Jeep, it wasn't the size of the couch that left me struggling—it was Bishop. Or to be more precise, it was my reaction to the man. He made me feel safe. Until my rescue, I'd been nowhere on his radar. Maybe I'd spent too much time with my therapist, but I couldn't help but wonder if the reason I felt safe with him was because his was the first face I saw when I was rescued.

Maybe, or maybe it's because you spent way too long daydreaming about him.

An uncomfortable heat simmered in my cheeks. Although I'd never been introduced to the men and women on Delacourt's teams, I'd managed to match some of the faces to names as they came through the office. The first time Bishop swept through with his dangerous, sexy, predatory grace, he left an impression—to the point where he showed up in some of my artwork. That same impression might explain why, during the weeks of having my mind twisted, my shadowy protector shared an uncomfortable number of characteristics with Bishop.

When it came to Bishop, I couldn't shake the feeling that if I dared to reach out and touch the impossible, I might be in for the ride of my life. Despite the temptation to find out, I wasn't sure my courage was up to the challenge—not when my mind was a hot mess and when no one, including me, knew if I was a threat or not. Bishop deserved someone he could trust.

Ignoring the painful pinch of that truth, I shivered and pushed away from the door to shuffle into the bathroom. I went through my nightly routine, my thoughts whirling as I tried to grapple with the fact I was in no shape, mentally or emotionally, to follow through on the temptation to play with the built six-foot-two hottie in my living room—not that Bishop had done anything to encourage me other than being the perfect gentleman all night. His solid presence kept me company as I indulged in a Monty Python binge. Between enjoying in the dry English humor and fighting the urge to lay my head on Bishop's broad shoulder and sink into the security he wore like a coat, I managed to combat the darker thoughts lurking just outside the light. Unfortunately, spending time with him left me wanting more. Even if I was mixing my imagination with reality, I couldn't ignore that having him with me was both a blessing and a curse.

I shook my head as I brushed my teeth. *What the hell was I thinking? Wrong time, wrong place.* Hell, with my luck, whatever draw I'd felt was probably one-sided. Especially considering his blunt assessment that I was the *weakest link*. Harsh though it was, the label wasn't wrong. So I was not what a focused, determined man of action would find attractive.

I spat out a mouthful of toothpaste, rinsed, and wiped my face. I worked a desk job for a reason, and as much as I enjoyed escaping into a good story and imagining myself in some intrepid heroine's shoes, the reality was terrifyingly different. Burying my face in the towel, I took slow, deep breaths as the nightmares surged forward, turning the sullen embers of desire to ash. As my fears slithered back in, I lifted my head and opened my eyes, the reflection of the bright fluorescent lights forcing my demons to scramble back into the dark. I carefully folded the hand towel, set it on the counter, and turned away from the face that no longer felt like my own.

Back in the bedroom, I stripped and threw my clothes into the hamper next to the dresser. After tugging on the oversized T-shirt that doubled as my pajamas, I hit the switch on the overhead light, leaving the lamp on my nightstand as the single guard against the darkness. I crawled into bed and under the covers, turned to my side until I was facing the lamp, and waited while my body temperature slowly heated the cold sheets.

You become the weakest point. The words had not only hurt, but they'd also pissed me off—not that Bishop had said them to be mean. He was simply stating a fact. I just didn't want him to think of me as weak, even if that was exactly how I felt. While the majority of the last six months was a blur, there was one point during that bleak time when I'd finally stopped fighting and given up. I couldn't say exactly when, and I couldn't even explain why. All I knew was that I'd spent the first few days, maybe longer, fighting back, determined to outlast my tormentors. Eventually, it became obvious that escape wouldn't be an option, and I shut down and hid. There was nowhere to hide, but I tried. When that failed, I started praying for someone to save me because I obviously sucked at saving myself. That was when my imaginary protector had stepped in like some hallucinatory crutch.

I snorted in disgust. Some heroine I'd turned out to be. Self-disgust and self-pity rose, and I fought them back, my choked whisper barely penetrating the quiet of my room. "I'm here. I'm alive. I didn't break." *Not yet, at least.* But that thought tumbled into that aching void I couldn't seem to heal.

My eyes burned as I stared at the lamp I couldn't turn off if I wanted any chance of sleep. Okay, so being kidnapped and tortured hadn't managed to unleash my inner kick-ass warrior, but I had survived. That counted for something. So what happened next would be my choice. Either I would continue to let the monster win and push me over the crumbling edge into a selfish, suicidal decision I couldn't take back, or I would fight back. Granted, fighting back meant relying on the strength and skills of others, but if that was what it took, then so be it. *No shame in using the expertise of those around you.*

Tomorrow, I would take the first step and let Wolf poke around in my head. The decision didn't leave me with the warm fuzzies, but at least it meant I was doing something. *That counts, right? Then again, depending on what he finds, maybe not.*

Unwilling to slip into the rabbit hole of possibilities that would hold sleep back indefinitely, I got up on an elbow and nabbed my phone from my nightstand. Thumbing through my playlists, I found one with nothing but instrumentals, hit Play, and set the phone on the speaker dock. Then I closed my eyes and sought sleep.

⋅•◆◆•⋅

I woke with my heart pounding and my mouth stretched wide around an airless scream. Terror locked my muscles in a painful grip, making my struggles useless. Remembered restraints morphed from cruel metal into a tangle of sheets. Half-formed images danced across my mind. Clinging to the light from the lamp, I fought to bring my heart rate down as the wisps of paralyzing fear faded, leaving behind a dull ache. Bit by bit, the familiar surroundings of my bedroom reformed, but the unsettling sensation of something lurking just beyond the light persisted, leaving me shaky.

"It's just a dream." A whisper was the best I could manage, but the sound of my own voice helped, pushing the unease back another step.

I dragged air into my lungs until I was sure my body would work. Shifting to my side, I drew my legs up, huddling under the covers like a little kid. My thoughts spun without catching, and no matter how hard I tried, I couldn't remember what had chased me awake. I wasn't sure if that made it better or worse than my normal nightmares.

When my body finally calmed, I checked the time. *Just after three. Great.* Experience told me there was no way sleep would return, nor was I keen about being alone in my mind, which didn't seem like the safest place at the moment. Normally, I'd shuffle out to the front room and zone out in front of the TV, but with Bishop camped out on the couch, that option was out.

Blowing out a breath, I uncurled from my protective ball and forced my body upright. Sitting on the edge of my bed, I scrubbed my hands over my face as exhaustion gnawed at me. A sketch pad taunted me from the bookcase, but I turned away. There was no way I would breathe life into the images stalking me. If I'd liked alcohol, I might have seriously considered seeking oblivion at the risk of my liver.

I left the bed, dragging the throw with me as I did the next best thing—I sought refuge in my chair and my Kindle. Books were to me what comfort foods were to others. I pulled up one of my favorite authors and revisited my favorite storyline. It took concentrated effort to get lost in the story. By the time I heard Bishop moving around, it was closing in on five thirty. When the door to the hall bathroom closed, I figured it was safe to get up. I pulled on a pair of PJ pants and snuck down the hall to the kitchen. My eyes burned, and the only cure was a shot or three of caffeine.

I hit the empty front room to see Bishop's blanket neatly folded over the back of the couch. Piled on the coffee table were his phone, wallet, keys, change, and sunglasses. His bag was open on the easy chair, but that was the extent of his presence. Since it seemed he was really awake, I made sure to brew a full pot of coffee instead of the two cups I normally needed to function. I had my breakfast options narrowed down to eggs and toast when his rumbled "Morning" jerked my attention from the fridge. The man who stepped into the kitchen and leaned against the counter short-circuited my brain while hot-wiring my hormones.

Holy mother of pearl. I knew he was built, but man, oh man, he is... wow. I was just as susceptible as the next woman to a good-looking guy, but Bishop, bare chested and fresh from the shower, took good looks to another level. The man hid a ton under his T-shirts and jeans. I wasn't sure if I was relieved or disappointed to see the line of dark hair arrow from that broad chest and down those well-defined abs and disappear into his jeans. Who could get muscles like that? I'd thought such things existed only in books. Before my mind could delve into things best left alone, I managed to bring my gaze back to his face, taking note of the stubble shadowing his jaw. Man, he was giving my coffee a run for its money.

"How'd you sleep?" He rubbed the towel hanging from his neck over his dark hair. The hints of red in the waves were muted.

"Umm..." I forced my mouth and brain to engage even as heat hit my cheeks. "Okay," I lied, not wanting to get into why I'd had another restless night.

He dropped the end of the towel and folded his arms over his distracting chest, his eyes narrowing.

My gaze dipped, but I yanked it back up. *Bad, Megan. No staring.*

Unfortunately, based on the light of amusement in his eyes,

I hadn't looked away fast enough. I bit my lip and looked back at the fridge. "Would you like breakfast? I was going to make eggs and toast."

"Sure. You want help?"

Did I want him invading the already small kitchen with his presence, which might lead to me setting the kitchen on fire? "Nope, I've got it." I grabbed the eggs and butter and turned away from the attractive male behind me.

Wood scraped over tile as he pulled out a barstool and took a seat.

I let out a silent breath. *Good.* As long as he stayed over there, I should be fine. Pulling out the frying pan, I asked, "How do you like your eggs?"

"Scrambled works."

Fortunately, my culinary skills were up to his request. I concentrated on the demanding job of whisking eggs in a bowl. It didn't take long for the quiet to get to me. "Did you sleep okay?"

"Yeah. Sorry if I woke you."

"You didn't. I was already up." The quiet beep of the coffee maker sounded as I poured the eggs into the pan. The barstool squeaked against the tile, and I looked over my shoulder to see Bishop get up and head in my direction.

"Where are your mugs?" Catching my look, he added, "I'll get the coffee, seeing how you have your hands full."

"Um, thanks." I tilted my head to the cabinet just to the right of the fridge. "First cabinet on the left. Spoons are third drawer in. Creamer is in the fridge, and sugar's that red canister by the coffeepot."

"Appreciate it, but I take mine black." He looked at me wrinkling my nose and added, "How do you like yours?"

"Two spoonfuls of creamer, please, and just half a spoonful of sugar." I went back to the eggs, listening to him pour and prep. His hand landed on the small of my back, and I couldn't stop my instinctive jump. He kept his hand in place as he leaned in and set a steaming cup on the counter next to me. "Thanks," I muttered as I divvied up the eggs before I started in on the toast portion of our breakfast. I gave a quick downward check to ensure that my oversized T-shirt was hiding my body's reaction to his simple touch. *Thank you, Lord!*

Instead of going back to the other side of the counter, he took a step back and to the side until he could lean against it. "You normally get up this early?"

Managing a half-hearted shrug, I answered, "Sometimes." The toast popped up, and I got to buttering. After handing him his plate, I took my breakfast to the two-seater bar dividing the kitchen and the front room.

I managed a few bites before he quietly said my name, and I lifted my head to find him studying me. When he had my gaze, he continued, "How much sleep did you get?"

I had no reason to continue my lame evasion. "A couple of hours."

His fork paused in midair. "You can't keep going like this."

His words lit a spark of anger. "I'm highly aware of that, Bishop." I looked at my plate and carefully corralled the last of my eggs onto my fork.

Not put off by my snippy tone, he kept on. "So, are you taking anything to help?"

His question scraped too close to the therapist's persistent, if gentle, suggestion of using pharmaceuticals to sleep. My hand tightened on my fork, but I kept my voice level. "No."

"Why not?"

"Because I prefer not to." My patience was at an end, and my response came out sharper than I'd intended. When he didn't say anything more, I looked up to find him studying me with a frown. A sliver of guilt wiggled under my irritation, and I gave him as much of an explanation as I comfortably could. "Look, I'm sorry I snapped, but honestly, I'm not comfortable with using drugs to sleep." I took the last bite of the now taste-less egg and choked it down.

"I get that." He sounded sincere. "But you need to find some way to sleep."

A very wicked inner voice made a graphic suggestion that had my hormones cheering. Doing my damnedest to ignore it, I set my fork on my plate, pushed it away, and pulled my coffee closer. "Kind of why I'm hoping this meeting today with Wolf works."

"And if it doesn't?"

If it didn't, I was screwed and not in a good way.

When I didn't answer, Bishop sighed, set his plate aside and crossed the kitchen. He put his coffee on the counter across from me and leaned in. He didn't say anything, and even though I refused to look at him, I could feel him watching me as I tried to enjoy my coffee.

Finally, unable to take the tension, I lifted my eyes. "What?"

"If you're worried about Wolf, don't be."

Not quite following, I asked, "What?"

"The reason you didn't sleep last night. If it's because of today—"

I was shaking my head before he could finish. "Last night was just par for the course. It had nothing to do with Wolf or what may or may not happen today."

He didn't look convinced. "Maybe this isn't such a good idea."

Knowing he could easily stop the upcoming visit that threatened to eliminate the only line of hope I could see, I panicked. Before I could think better of it, I grabbed his wrist and held on. "No, it's the only good idea I've had since I got home." My hand tightened as I tried to make him under-stand. "I'll be able to sleep when I'm not worried I'm going to snap."

The sharp edges of his face softened. "You're not going to

snap." Although his tone was gentle, I didn't miss the core of steel running through it.

As much as I appreciated his belief, it was important to be realistic. "You don't know that," I said. He opened his mouth, but I cut him off with a sharp shake of my head. "Don't. Ever since I got out of the hospital, it's about all I can do to keep from screaming. Half the damn time, I'm not sure what's real and what isn't." Watching him, I was sure my plea was falling on deaf ears, so I had to be more direct. "Take you, for example."

Drawn up short, he blinked. "Me?"

Fighting a stupid blush, I let go of his wrist and sat back. "Yes, you."

"What about me?"

There was no way I could share how much he reminded me of my illusionary protector or how he made me feel safe. He'd be out the door like a flash, not to mention how pathetic it would make me sound. Cuddling my coffee cup, I scrambled for a less crazy answer. "You stuck with me yesterday and insisted on staying the night."

His jaw tightened. "No way in hell was I leaving you alone."

I tilted my head and decided to try a different tack. "Be honest. If I hadn't come to the colonel's office, how soon would you have gotten the order to show up at my door?"

Color rose in his cheeks, and something flared in his eyes. "A day or two." He sounded reluctant, but he hadn't lied—a fact I was grateful for.

I gave him a tiny smile to soothe the sting of what I said next. "I've worked with Delacourt for a while. Long enough to understand that she has no problem making ruthless decisions for what she considers the best of her teams." Unable to hold his gaze, I fiddled with my half-empty coffee cup and managed a negligent shrug. "To that end, I'm sure sending you in to get close to me was the next step on her agenda."

"Megan…" he growled.

Worried that he would think I was blaming him, which was so far from the truth, I rushed on. "Don't worry, Bishop. I'm not looking for apologies. I get it." I gave him a half smile. "Boy, do I get it."

He cocked his head, his expression suddenly hard to read. "What is it you think you get?"

I might not have been some super-psychic action heroine, but I was far from dumb. This was Colonel Charlene Delacourt we were talking about. But if he needed me to verbalize it, I could do that. "She needs to know what, if any, kind of threat I pose. I can't ask her, or you, to trust me if *I* can't trust me." Just thinking about that caused a tiny pang of hurt. "At least this way, it's my choice."

For a seemingly endless moment, the quiet stretched. Then he asked warily, "Why aren't you upset?"

Not quite following his question, I frowned. "About what?"

He stared at me like I was some new alien life-form. "Most people wouldn't be so cavalier about being seen as a threat. You don't even blink."

His guarded observation sounded like something my brother Dev would say—a wariness common among those who shed their blood for their country—but I understood Bishop's question. "Why would I? I might work behind a desk, but I'm not blind to what's happening, you know."

He settled deeper on his forearms, leaning in and shrinking the counter space between us. "And what is it you think is happening?"

He was so close that his face became my entire world. His wavy hair was still damp, the tips barely brushing his shoulders. They would shorten and lighten to a burnished amber when they dried. His deep-chocolate eyes were slightly uptilted at the corners and edged with lashes any woman would envy. The close-cropped goatee framed his upper lip and shadowed his chin. I wanted to just cup it and feel it rasp against my palm. Bishop was so close it was difficult to keep my mind away from paths best left untaken. I managed to wheeze out, "Someone is targeting the teams."

Deep in those dark eyes, something lethal flared. "How do you figure?"

That look scared me, but it also intrigued me. I licked suddenly dry lips, wondering when all the air in the room had disappeared. "Before I was taken, Delacourt assigned Kayden and Tag to investigate the deaths of their former teammates who just happened to also be psychic, which was possibly one reason they were targeted. When I was in the hospital, she caught me up with what happened there." Her explanation had also included how the four were killed by a man previously thought MIA who had an ax to grind and a plan for lining his wallet with classified information. Oh, and he liked collecting psychic abilities from those he killed, which left me shaken, considering Bishop's involvement in that situation and what could have happened but fortunately didn't.

"Delacourt didn't go into detail," I continued, "but she shared that Risia and Tag are now an item." That was another story I didn't have the details on, but knowing their history and the fact that Risia had been on assignment in Vegas, I figured it was a doozy. "It's not hard for me to put the pieces together and see that whatever went down had a long reach. Add in my situation, and it seems that if whoever is on the other end of that reach discovered a way to fracture Delacourt's teams, they'd be all over it. So while it freaks me out that I may be what they used to create that crack, I'd rather find out now than later." I lifted my cup of coffee, hiding what I was sure was a cynical twist to my lips. "Besides, I'm not a big fan of being used."

Chapter Six

BISHOP

'm not a big fan of being used. Megan's statement bounced around my mind, and I did my best to hide my instinctive flinch.

"Intelligent and beautiful," I muttered before my brain could lock the observation behind my lips.

Her gaze dropped away as color slid into her cheeks, and she sipped from her mug. They weren't empty words, but part of me wished they weren't so true. Her sharp mind existed behind an understated beauty that deepened with exposure, and there was no denying a good heart beat at her center—a heart that would be easily damaged if Wolf discovered she was someone's weapon. Knowing that and hearing her easy acceptance of the whole fucked-up situation pissed me off and added to my feeling of guilt. In the end, it might not be the faceless enemy she needed to worry about but me. No matter how intriguing she was, if she threatened the team, I'd have to deal with it. I wouldn't like it, but I'd do it.

On the counter near the stove, her phone rang, shattering the tension. Being closer to it than she was, I could see the colonel's name on the screen. Straightening, I picked up the phone and handed it to her.

"Hello?" She moved to the living room as she answered, but with the apartment's open main room and kitchen, there was no way to avoid eavesdropping. "He will? Great." A pause. "Uh-huh." Another pause. "Okay, sure, that should work."

Guessing that we would be heading to Wolf's soon, I gathered up our breakfast dishes and took them to the sink, multitasking by rinsing them off while listening to Megan's side of the conversation.

"Go ahead and text it to me, just in case… okay, right, will do." Her tone softened. "Colonel, thank you… uh-huh. Bye."

I put the plates in the dishwasher, pulled the hand towel from the oven's handle, and turned to find Megan standing at the counter, a small frown on her face as she stared at her phone. I asked, "You okay?"

Her head came up as she focused on me instead of whatever was running through her mind. She gave a forced smile. "Wolf agreed to meet at eleven at his place. Delacourt said you knew his address."

Even though it wasn't a question, I nodded and tucked the hand towel back in place. "Yeah, I know where it is."

She worried her bottom lip.

"Megan?" I waited until she looked at me before continuing. "You still want to do this?" When she nodded, I pressed, "Then what's wrong?"

She wouldn't meet my eyes as she answered, "I thought we'd be meeting at HQ."

It took a moment for understanding to dawn, and when it did, I closed the distance between us and took her hand, phone and all. "If meeting at Wolf's place makes you uncomfortable, I can ask him to meet us at the office." I brushed the underside of her wrist with my thumb, subtly checking her pulse. It was a little fast but not too worrying.

"No, it's fine." Instead of pulling her hand free, she used the other to rub over her face as she blew out a long breath and met my eyes. "It's fine. I don't know why I'm reacting like this. It's not like…" Seeming to regain her composure, she gave me a game smile that held for a second before fading into a worried frown. "Besides, you'll be there."

"Yes, I will, but cut yourself some slack." I squeezed her hand then let her go. "You have every right to be nervous about this." Honestly, I had a few nerves of my own. "If it helps, you won't be the only woman there. Chances are high that Meli will be home."

Her frown eased. "Meli?"

"Wolf's girlfriend. You'll like her. And she'll like you."

I wasn't just blowing smoke to ease Megan's concerns. Unlike the more dramatic and dominant women on our team, Meli was open and accepting. Meli, like Megan, radiated an easy acceptance of others as she tackled what life threw at her without complaint. Wolf adored Meli and not just because her mind was one of the few he couldn't read. And it was crystal clear that Meli reciprocated that adoration.

Megan's small smile eased the lines bracketing her eyes and mouth. "What? You can see the future now?"

Joining her move to lighten the mood, I waggled my eyebrows and intoned with an Eastern European accent, "The winds of fortune indicate good things."

She gave a soft giggle that hit me in unexpected places. "Before those winds change, I'll go get ready."

I watched her walk away, my gaze dropping to her ass, and my inappropriate reaction hardened into unmistakable want. *Damn.* She was under my skin. Forcing myself to turn away from the mesmerizing sight, I braced my hands on the counter and blew out a hard breath. When her door clicked shut, ensuring she wouldn't hear me, I muttered, "Get your shit together, man."

Being around her, I forgot why proceeding with caution was necessary, which made her even more dangerous than anticipated. It took a minute or three before I could move without hurting myself. No matter how much my brain warned that this was the wrong damn time, I couldn't ignore the fact that my need to explore the temptation Megan presented might outweigh the risks involved.

I was so fucked.

⸻ •◆ ◆••

Megan emerged from her doctor's office, waving a piece of paper. I rose from the butt-numbing chair I'd been planted in for the last forty minutes and tossed aside the months-old sports magazine. She came right up to me, stopping only when a couple of inches separated us, and grinned. "I'm free!"

"No more appointments?"

She shook her head, sending her dark ponytail flying. "No poking and prodding for another six months." Based on the happiness lighting her face, I could tell her relief was off the charts. Her hands flattened against my chest, the paper in her hand caught between us, and her nose wrinkled. "If only it was this easy with my therapist."

With temptation so close, resistance was futile. Not even the threat of Wolf confirming that she was a sleeper agent, and the shit that entailed, could stop my fascination with her. My hands went to her hips, and I bent down to press a quick kiss to her forehead. "Hang in there, grasshopper. That, too, will come."

Lifting my head, I discovered a million and one emotions swirling in the blue depths of her eyes. Instead of voicing them, she managed a shaky smile. "Promise?"

I raised my right hand and held up three fingers. "Scout's honor."

The shakiness disappeared, and her smile went full blown as she tilted her head. "You were a scout?"

"Once upon a time." I shifted my hold until I could hook my arm around her waist, gently directing her toward the door. Then I used one hand to hold the door open.

She turned to look at me as she walked through. "Sounds like there's a story there."

There was, but it wasn't pretty. I shrugged. "Not really." As I followed her out of the medical center, I pulled my sunglasses down over my eyes.

She stopped in the shaded overhang of the doorway and pulled out her phone. "Hang on a second." Her fingers flew over the keyboard, then she was tucking it away. "Okay, daily check-in complete."

Taken possession by a green-eyed monster, I tried not to snarl. "Check-in with whom?"

She shot me a look over her shoulder, feminine amusement plain on her face. "My mom."

Relief snuffed out that weird spurt of jealousy. "Cool." Determined to regain my balance, I put my hand at the small of her back as we headed toward the parking garage across the street. "Now that you're free, does this mean we have to flip a coin to decide who's driving?"

That earned me a muffled giggle. "I don't know. I think I could get used to having a driver at my beck and call."

I gave a snort. "Uh-uh. More like you just don't want to deal with traffic."

We hit the crosswalk at the four-way stop. Midmorning on a workweek, the street was quiet. Unfortunately, that didn't translate to available curbside parking. Hence, we had to hoof it to the multi-level parking structure on the other side of the street. At least we didn't have to pay for parking since the gate arms were up. Remembering our odd moment with the selfie guy, I scanned our surroundings for anything unusual but fortunately came up empty.

She kept pace as she settled her sunglasses in place. "Who would want to drive around here? It's a freakin' nightmare."

I couldn't argue with that. We made it across before I changed the subject. "You want to stop and pick up something to eat before we hit Wolf's?" My tension ebbed as we stepped inside the parking garage. Somewhere on the level above us, an engine came to life.

She thought about it for a whole second, maybe two, then shook her head. "No, I'm good, thanks."

We were closing in on the car and I'd fished the keys out of my pocket to beep the locks when the rev of an engine echoed through the dim parking structure. I turned and caught a flash of movement bearing down on us. Headlights seared across my eyes, blinding me for a crucial moment. Wrapping my arm around Megan's waist, I jerked her close and dove toward the narrow space between my Jeep and a nearby sedan. Megan's startled "Eep!" was muffled against my chest as I turned to keep her protected. My hip hit the unforgiving metal of the sedan as I kept twisting, stopping when a side mirror tried to impale itself in my back. I got a hand on the sedan's roof as I tried to focus on the blurry image of the retreating car. All I got was a dark four-door vehicle before the brake lights flashed, and I heard the squeal of rubber on cement as the car hit the exit and disappeared.

"Dammit!"

"Bishop! Are you okay?"

I looked down at a pale-faced Megan, who had my T-shirt clenched in white-knuckled fists. With her in my arms, there was no missing the tremors shuddering through her body. "I'm good. Are you okay?"

She nodded as she turned toward the exit. "What the hell is wrong with people? They could've killed us."

That was their intent. That uncanny knowledge hit the back of my brain like a gunshot, locking me in place.

She didn't wait for my response, which was good because I had no intention of offering a verbal confirmation of her claim when she was already on edge. She let go of my T-shirt and tried to step back. "Are you sure you're okay? It sounded like you hit the car kind of hard."

Not willing to let her loose, I kept my hands at her hips and nudged her toward the Jeep. "I'll probably be the new owner of a few bruises but nothing serious. Come on. Let's get to the Jeep."

She twisted her head toward me as she kept walking. "Shouldn't we report this?"

I steered her around the Jeep's bumper. "To whom?"

"I don't know," she said sharply. "Garage security?"

I opened the passenger door, held it, and guided her in. "No one's here, babe. I don't think it will do us any good. Besides, they're long gone."

She hitched her butt into the passenger seat and studied my face. Whatever she saw left her biting her lip, but she didn't say anything and simply pulled her seatbelt into place. When it clicked, I stepped back but stopped when she called my name. When I met her eyes, she asked in a low voice, "That wasn't an accident, was it?"

Guess my poker face needs work. "I don't know."

Fear seeped back into familiar lines around her eyes and mouth. "What if...?"

I stopped her with a gentle squeeze of her knee. "Don't go there, okay?" When she opened her mouth to argue, I cut her off. "Don't. One thing at a time. We'll get to Wolf's, let him do his thing." When that didn't seem to reassure her, I said, "I'll see if Rabbit can work his magic and find out what the deal was with Speedy Gonzales, okay?"

At her reluctant nod, I let her go, stepped back, and closed the door. I rounded the Jeep, pulling out my phone to thumb through my contacts. Finding Rabbit's cell, I hit Call.

My ass was hitting my seat when he picked up. "Bishop, my man, what's up?"

"Hey, Rabbit." I started the Jeep and waited for the Bluetooth to connect. "Need a favor."

"Name it."

"You in front of a computer?" With an arm across Megan's seat, I twisted to back out, ignoring the protest of my bruised side, then navigated my way clear of the parking garage.

"When am I not?"

That was God's honest truth. Rare was the time when the man wasn't connected to something with an electronic signal. "Need you to access the traffic cams near Henderson Medical off of First."

The sound of fingers flying over a keyboard came through the speakers as Rabbit did his thing. "Tell me what I'm lookin' for since this is goin' to take a few."

"Megan and I just missed getting clipped by some moron in the parking garage." Determined to play it smart, I added, "I want to make sure the moron is just a moron and not someone with an agenda." Maybe, if we were lucky, I'd be proven wrong. You never knew. I joined the traffic and headed to Wolf's place.

"Y'know, city's full of crazy drivers," he said.

"You're not telling me anything I don't know."

"Well, if you're wantin' new information, I'm goin' to need something to work with."

Unfortunately, I didn't have much to give him. "Didn't get a good look since I was busy trying not to play hood ornament. Four-door sedan, dark gray or black."

"Gray," Megan chimed in.

"Older? Newer?" Rabbit asked.

"Based on the headlight shape, I'm thinking an older model." I hit the freeway and added, "Probably five, maybe ten years."

Rabbit muttered a curse that I couldn't catch. "Got anythin' else I can use? Tinted windows? Bumper stickers? A flashing neon light?"

Even though I was far from amused, Rabbit's disgruntlement made my lips twitch. "I'm betting they didn't slow down when they hit the main road."

A derisive snort sounded. "Great. Don' think I have a filter for speed racer here."

From Megan's seat came a muffled giggle filled with nerves and adrenaline.

Rabbit gave an overly loud sigh. "Right. Probably goin' take more than a few, seein' as that's about every third car on the road."

Despite his grim prediction, I had faith he'd find what we needed. "Then I'll leave you to it. We're heading to Wolf's, so call when you can."

"Copy that."

"Thanks," I said.

"Anytime. I'll catch you in a bit." With that, Rabbit hung up.

"Thank you," Megan said with a hint of embarrassment. Risking a glance, I saw that hint reflected in her averted face.

"Nothing to thank me for." I turned my attention back to the road. "Nothing wrong with wanting peace of mind." *For either of us.* "Besides, it doesn't hurt to have Rabbit check it out."

"Regardless, I appreciate it."

"Well, then, you're welcome." Focused on maneuvering through the busy streets, I let the quiet settle between us.

It wasn't until I'd managed to merge onto the death race of the freeway that she muttered, "This sucks."

Taking a chance, I shot her a quick look. "What?"

"This." I caught the blur of her hand waving before she continued with an honesty that hurt. "This was the first time I wasn't afraid to be out of my house. Then that… that jackass almost hits us, and I'm back to being scared." She turned to face her window.

That was exactly why I hadn't shared my belief that it was a deliberate attempt to hit us. Not touching on why she felt safe, I addressed the less treacherous part of her revelation. "I'm thinking that's a fairly normal reaction to almost being run down. Comes with the adrenaline letdown and all that jazz." I went to switch lanes and caught her dismissive head-shake. "Not to mention, your life hasn't exactly been all sunshine and roses recently. I'm thinking you can cut yourself a little slack."

"I just want to get back to normal."

The amount of emotion buried in her voice had me clenching my teeth in frustration. Part of me wanted to take her away from all of this until shit blew over, even though I knew it wasn't even in the realm of possibility—especially considering she was smack in the center of the storm. Even knowing that it was lame, I gave her the only comfort I could offer. "I don't know what you consider normal, but it seems to me you're well on your way."

A soft snort came back. "Glad one of us believes that."

"You don't?"

"This—me—isn't normal, Bishop. I'm so far from normal I don't think I'll ever find my way back. I can't sleep, because every time I close my eyes, I end up in a nightmare. I can't step outside without feeling like I'm being watched. Half the damn time, I can't tell what's real and what's not because I can't shake the fear that all of this"—she waved her hand as her voice rose—"is just another mind game meant to break me. Which is pointless because I'm already broken."

Her unvarnished sincerity managed to sneak under my guard, leaving me with an ache. "You aren't."

"I am," she said, sounding uncharacteristically hard and unyielding. "I'm in so many pieces that there's no way I'm going to be able to find them all. I'm never going to be who I was."

"No, you won't." Determined to drag her out of the well of self-pity she was getting ready to swim in, I hauled her back with a dose of harsh pragmatism. "You can't be. You survived six months of hell, and you'll carry those scars forever. There's no escaping that—it's done. Now you have to choose how you'll move forward—bent and cowed, or head up and fearless?"

"It's not that easy."

"Isn't it?" I shot her a look. "Seems to me, considering where we're heading, you've already made your choice." I turned back to my driving, letting silence fill the space between us and hoping I got through because this fight was hers alone to face.

Chapter Seven

With Bishop's reality check reverberating in my brain, the rest of the trip to Wolf's passed in a blur. It was a struggle to match the way Bishop saw me to how I saw myself, but by the time we pulled up to the curb outside a well-cared-for bungalow, I'd somehow managed to pull enough pieces of myself together to create a credible version of a functioning human. *Yay, me.*

Bishop parked behind a truck with the shine typical of a new vehicle. I had my seatbelt undone, the door open, and a foot to the ground when he came up to my side with a hand out. Unable to resist and doing my best to avoid his gaze, I put my hand in his, finding comfort in his touch, and let him help me out of the Jeep. That was as far as I got, because he didn't back away. Instead, he held his position, trapping me in the open doorway, and squeezed my hand. My gaze flew up.

He asked quietly, "You ready?"

Not trusting my voice, I nodded.

He nudged me to his side and beeped the locks then kept hold of my hand as we walked up the pathway to the porch. The neat yard ended at a riot of colorful flowers lining the front edge of the porch and the bay window. Someone clearly sported a green thumb or two, which didn't quite jibe with my preconceptions of the males associated with Delacourt's teams. Granted, my interactions with them had been limited to the office, but that was enough to show me that they could all be considered *manly men*. And very few manly men puttered in gardens, in my experience.

We'd hit the top step when the door opened. My feet froze as the doorway filled with a huge male.

"Hey, you two." The rough smoker's voice that came out of the linebacker body was almost as arresting as the pale-green eyes staring down at us.

"Hey," Bishop said, crowding in behind me, leaving me no choice but to continue forward. "How's it going?"

"Good." Wolf stepped back, letting us in. "Come on in. Meli's in the office on a phone interview."

"With the convention center?"

Wolf nodded. "Yeah. It's her third one, so we're hopeful." He closed the door and waved us into the front room. "We can chat in here." We headed in as Wolf followed. "I appreciate you guys coming here. I figured it might be best if we had some privacy for this."

With Bishop next to me on the couch and Wolf sprawled in the easy chair just to the side, I had a sensation of being trapped, which opened the door for panic to sneak in. *He's here to help.* Using that reminder, I concentrated on not freaking out. Tucking my hands underneath my thighs, I curled my fingers into the cushion. Bishop must have picked up on something because he crowded close until all I could feel was him. The panic slipped further away, and the weight on my chest eased.

"Megan," Wolf said, a hint of gentleness softening his rough voice. I lifted my head and found him watching me. "You're safe here, I promise."

Okay, poker was nowhere in my future. I was obviously an

open book. Still, there was no missing the sincerity in his voice or his expression, and I managed a jerky nod.

"Just a heads-up," Bishop cut in. "I'm expecting a call from Rabbit."

Wolf's attention shifted to Bishop's face, and he frowned. "What happened?"

"On the way out of Megan's appointment, we nearly got mowed down in the parking garage."

The change in Wolf was immediate. His gaze sharpened, and his body coiled. Even the air in the room sparked with a strange intensity. "Deliberate?"

Bishop's shoulder brushed mine as he shrugged. "That's what I'm hoping Rabbit can find out."

"Huh." Wolf's gaze flicked to me and then back to Bishop.

"Yeah," Bishop muttered as the two men shared a look filled with an entire conversation I wasn't privy too.

This wasn't helping my nerves. "Um, Wolf?"

He broke off his silent exchange and turned to me. "Yeah?"

"What exactly is involved in this?" I blurted.

The hard lines of Wolf's face eased, and his tone softened. "Did Bishop or Delacourt explain what we're going to try to do?"

His compassion threatened to undo my determination to hold it together, so I tried to ignore it and choked out, "A little."

Wolf rubbed a hand over his bald head before leaning forward, his arms braced on his knees. "Delacourt said you were worried someone had messed with your mind. To find out if you have a reason to be worried, I'm going to use something similar to hypnotic regression. Do you know what that is?"

I could guess, but I didn't want to, so I shook my head.

"Hypnotic regression is part of regression therapy, which is an approach to dealing with trauma. It's a way for a survivor to revisit a past trauma so they can understand why they're acting and feeling a certain way."

This did not sound good. "But I can't remember what happened."

Wolf held my gaze. "Not consciously, no, but on some level, you do."

Whatever tiny pieces of calm I'd managed to salvage went up in a puff of smoke. "You're a telepath." It was all I could get out.

"I am."

"So couldn't you go in and see for yourself?" That idea terrified me, but not as much as reliving what I couldn't remember.

Next to me, Bishop stiffened, but he remained silent.

A forbidding shadow drifted across Wolf's face before he regained his calm let's-talk-the-crazy-person-off-the-edge expression. "I could, but I don't think that's wise."

I couldn't read his expression, but I also couldn't look away. "Why?" It came out as a choked whisper as fear left my mouth dry.

Wolf's gaze flicked to Bishop, who was sitting still and stiff next to me, then came back. "Because if you're right about being used, it means you survived six months of being tortured by a telepath, and you're not a vegetable. Which would indicate you have some seriously fucking formidable mental protections in place." The harsh comment delivered in a gentle tone made me flinch, but he wasn't done. "Those types of protections would require me to use my ability in such a way that I would do more damage than good."

His statement reverberated deep within me, and I sensed its intrinsic truth. Darkness rose, filled with mocking whispers of that hated voice, twining through my mind and sucking me back into a nightmare. I didn't realize that I had pushed to my feet until Bishop used his hold on my wrist to tug me into him, crowding me, blocking me. Desperate to escape, I put my free hand to his chest to push him away, but the arm banded at my waist held me in place.

"Megan."

I met his eyes, a metallic taste coating my tongue.

He cupped my face. "Breathe."

I sucked in air as I gripped his T-shirt and forced myself to stop shaking my head. "I don't think I can do this."

"You can." He was unrelenting. "Head up, and breathe. Wolf won't hurt you. Neither of us will let anything hurt you, okay?"

I fought back the sickening fear that left me shaky. I had to suck it up. I was here because I needed to know what was happening, not just for me but for the two men watching me as well. There was no way I could live with myself if I was responsible for destroying Delacourt's team, and the only way to prevent that outcome was to see this through.

"Stick with me." He watched as I managed a nod, and after a few tense minutes, he let me go.

It took a bit before I could fight free of the debilitating anxiety, and I only managed because Bishop patiently waited me out. The fear of looking weak in front of the man who stood strong and silent at my side finally allowed me to get my shit together. I carefully reclaimed my seat on the couch. Bishop settled in next to me and took my hand.

Using his touch as an anchor, I dragged in a couple more deep breaths and met Wolf's eyes. "How do we do this?"

⁓•⦿•⁓

Time lost meaning as I followed Wolf's directions down the mental rabbit hole. I was drifting in a hazy world of nothing when he asked, "Megan, can you hear me?"

"Yeah."

"I need you to open your eyes."

Right. Hanging around whatever this was wouldn't get me the answers I needed. With renewed determination, I opened my eyes.

Gray stone walls stared back. I couldn't stop my instinctive search for the shadowy figure that kept me from slipping over the edge. When the cell remained empty except for me, my heart stopped with a painful punch. For a moment, I couldn't catch my breath. "No." The one word escaped in a harsh whisper.

Wolf's disembodied voice broke through the trepidation shredding my gut. "You're okay, Megan. Remember, this isn't real. It's just memories. Nothing can hurt you."

His words reminded me that although I couldn't feel it, I was sitting next to Bishop on a couch in Wolf's house, not imprisoned in some hellhole of my own creation at the mercy of a monster bent on tearing me apart. Still, it was hard to ignore the skin-crawling sensation of being watched by something or someone malevolent.

Clinging to Wolf's reassurance, I forced my body to move, making a complete turn. *Yep.* I was all alone with just the gray walls covered in faded sketches. I could do this. "Where are you?"

"Better question is, where are you?" He sounded disgruntled, like a man who wasn't used to being ditched. "Because wherever you are, I can't follow."

I rubbed my arms as a chill worked over my skin. "The cell."

"Where Bishop found you?"

"No, the one I made so *he* couldn't get to me."

Something close by growled.

Wolf asked, "He?" He must not have heard the noise, because he didn't mention it.

The miasma of evil pressed closer, squeezing my voice to nothing, so I simply nodded.

A warmth I was beginning to associate with Bishop stroked my spine and loosened fear's ugly hold. "You're safe, Megan. We've got you."

Right, because this isn't real. Maybe if I kept repeating that, I'd eventually believe it. "I'm good. I can do this." *Maybe.* "What now?" There was a pause that lasted long enough to make me worry. "Wolf?"

"Right here." His response was immediate, but he sounded worried. "I'm just thinking."

This did not bode well. "Um, is this how it's supposed to work?"

"Not exactly," he muttered.

"Not helpful," I said before I could stop myself.

"Sorry." There was enough sincerity in the single word to keep me from losing it. "Okay, let's try this. Can you imagine a door to your cell?"

That seemed simple enough. I stared at the wall, imagining a door. Slowly, one took shape. When it was complete, I said, "Done."

Frustration laced the rough slide of his voice. "Since I seem to be stuck in some hedge maze from hell, I need you to open it."

Great. I'm not the only one getting grumpy. Stifling a sigh, I pulled open the door only to suck in a hard breath as my pulse spiked. "Well, that's not good."

"What?" Wolf asked sharply.

"I don't think the door thing worked. There's a wall on the other side." I let go of the doorknob and touched the solid stone wall blocking the entry. No chinks. Nothing but a slab of cold, hard, immovable gray. My heart rate picked up, and panic made my voice rise. "Tell me I'm not stuck here."

"You aren't stuck," Wolf said in a soothing tone. "You're just keeping yourself safe."

Okay, that's good, right? "How do I get rid of this?" I asked, frustrated because I knew what Wolf would say.

"I'm not sure you can. At least, not right now. Let's get you back."

Nerves and anger collided, and the ground rocked underfoot. No, we weren't leaving. Not yet. "I need answers."

"And we'll find them, just not this way."

I slammed my hands against the wall as the ground rolled and the light in the cell dimmed. "Break, dammit."

"Stop it, Megan!"

Wolf's command was sharp to the point of being painful. I couldn't ignore it. I dropped my head between my hands until my forehead rested against the cool wall. Self-disgust rose fast and hard, bringing the hot press of useless, *stupid* tears that threatened to fall. "I need to know what he did to me."

"And we'll find out," Wolf said. "Just not this way."

With no other outlet, I slapped the wall and turned away with a growl, brushing off the moisture clinging to the corners of my eyes. I stood in the center of the cell, arms folded over my chest, glaring at nothing. "Now what?"

"Close your eyes, and count backward from ten."

I had to try twice, thanks to the frustration and resentment playing hell with my concentration. Finally, I opened my eyes, Wolf's living room taking shape around me as I blinked against the late afternoon sunlight. Before long, I noticed Bishop was no longer sitting next to me. Frowning, I rubbed my eyes clear and turned to check the metallic art-piece-slash-clock hanging on the wall. *What the hell?* Stunned, I turned to Wolf, who was leaning forward in his chair, rubbing the back of his neck. "Is that clock right?"

He twisted his head until he could follow where I pointed, then he turned back to me. "Yeah."

"Three hours? We were doing this for three hours?" I was having trouble reconciling this information with the maybe twenty or thirty minutes that had seemed to pass while we were playing around in my mind.

"Time doesn't work the same for stuff like this." Wolf stood up and stretched.

My body decided to chime in with its own complaints about sitting in one position for three hours.

"Wolf." Near the archway, Bishop pushed up off the wall he was leaning against. "What happened?"

Wolf shot me a considering look. "Megan's got some serious self-protections in place."

"This mean you can't help?"

I was grateful that Bishop asked, because I couldn't seem to find the courage to do it myself.

Wolf shook his head. "It means I need to check a couple of things with someone before we do this again."

The fact that he didn't just say no blunted my disappointment, but his answer carried a note that left me worried. "What kind of things?"

"Who?" Bishop's question collided with mine as he headed toward me.

Wolf looked between Bishop and me. "I need to talk to Ricochet."

Stopping at my side, Bishop frowned at Wolf as he offered me a hand. "Ricochet? Why?"

"He may have a solution for how to get through Megan's protections."

My last fragile bubble of hope popped. *Great. Why the hell are we considering bringing someone else into this?* "Someone want to explain how this Ricochet trumps a telepath?" I ignored Wolf's look as I took Bishop's hand and got stiffly to my feet. "Because I'm not sold on hosting a free-for-all in my head." I knew that was really snarky, but I wasn't feeling all that accommodating.

Both men ignored me. *Figures.*

Bishop asked, "Is Rico even available?"

Wolf grimaced. "I don't know, but I think it's imperative we get ahold of him."

Bishop let me go and aimed his question at Wolf. "Why?"

Yeah, why? As much as I wanted to echo Bishop's question, I refrained. Well, verbally at least. Wolf shot me a look, raising an eyebrow as grim humor worked behind his eyes.

"Because what's keeping me out isn't another telepath. It's just you."

"Me?" It was my turn to wince, because I'd forgotten what it meant to be in the presence of a telepath. *I guess he really can read my mind.*

"Yes, you." Those eerie sea-green eyes watched me carefully. "If I remember correctly, your file indicated that your brother and sister are both psychic, right?"

Nodding, I wrapped my arms around my middle, not liking where Wolf seemed to be heading.

"What are their abilities?"

I normally didn't share that information, but considering who I was talking to… I swallowed against my suddenly dry throat. "No one can lie to Dev, like, ever, and Kellie can connect with animals."

"And what can you do?" he prodded carefully.

"Nothing." A building dread made my voice low and rough.

Wolf didn't say anything, just continued to study me. His expression set off all my self-preservation alarms, and I took a step back only to bump into something. Twisting my neck, I found Bishop behind me, his hand going to my hip to hold me in place.

"I'm not." I turned back to Wolf, choking on distress. "I've never done anything remotely psychic."

Wolf's gaze lifted above my head, and he arched a brow at Bishop in silent question. When Wolf winced, I started to twist to see Bishop's face, but his hands tightened, holding me in place.

Wolf turned back to me, sympathy washing through his features. "I don't think that's entirely true anymore, Megan."

I was stunned. When I finally found my voice, it came out a little on the high side. "You can't just turn psychic, Wolf. You're either born that way or not."

"Or," Bishop rumbled against my back, "you suffer a severe trauma that unlocks a latent ability." He kept speaking even as I shook my head. "Being tormented by a telepath for six months is about as severe as you can get."

Okay, this is bullshit! Alarmed by his insinuation, I jerked away from Bishop and paced to the other end of the room. Despite my instinctive rejection of their assumption about me, a worm of truth burrowed deep, creating a crack in my reality. "No, you're wrong." My denial came out hot and hard.

I got to the bookshelves, keeping my back to the men as my mind spun. There was no way I was psychic. I would know if I was, wouldn't I? Hell, I'd spent a good portion of my childhood wishing I was psychic, but after watching Keelie and Dev deal with their abilities, it hit me that the price exacted for such gifts wasn't one I wanted to pay. From then on, I was perfectly fine with being the normal one in our family.

Unable to look at Bishop, I turned and glared at Wolf. "You said that you couldn't get through because I was keeping myself safe. Self-preservation doesn't equal being psychic." *Stubborn, maybe, but not psychic.* Maybe I was grasping at straws, but if straws were all I had, I wasn't letting those suckers go. I could live with being stubborn.

Unmoved by my temper, Wolf said, "No, but the last and

only time I ran across mental protections like yours was with Ricochet."

The certainty in his tone ratcheted my uneasiness higher. "That doesn't make me psychic." Panic crept around the edges of my fraying composure. I flicked a look at Bishop to get his take on this crazy idea, only to find him frowning as he watched me. My panic crested. *Oh my God. He's taking Wolf's conjecture seriously.* "You can not actually be thinking he's right, Bishop."

Wolf cut in. "I don't know if I'm right, which is why I want to talk to Ricochet."

Desperate for any escape, I blurted, "Why Ricochet? Can't you or Bishop just figure it out?"

Wolf shook his head. "Until you let me in, I can't tell for sure. What I do know is those protections you have are damn close to Ricochet's. Not to mention you're having nightmares that you say aren't you. All that means there's a possibility you and Ricochet share the same ability."

I had to ask. "Which ability?"

"Dream-walking." Bishop took a couple of steps toward me. With the bookcase at my back, I had nowhere to go and could only brace as he closed in. He stopped, leaving a small amount of space between us. He stroked my shoulders down to my wrists until he held my hands. "You said you wanted answers, babe. I think we just found the first one."

Chapter Eight

BISHOP

With a half-filled glass of iced tea in hand, I stood at the counter and watched Megan listen to Meli out on the back deck. The two women sat on the oversized patio furniture surrounding the stone fire-pit table, holding court. The setting sun picked up the subtle reds in Megan's dark hair while streaking Meli's natural red hair with hints of gold. Now that Meli wasn't hiding from an asshole stalker, not only was her hair back to its natural coloring, but the dark bruises under her eyes were history as well. As for Megan, the lines of stress from earlier had eased. Meli's interruption was well timed, and I was grateful for it. Once she joined us, any further discussion of Megan's possible psychic ability was put aside.

As anticipated, once Meli was introduced to Megan, it wasn't long before they clicked, and an invitation to dinner soon followed. The move was pure Meli, whose last job had been running a B and B outside of Vegas. Taking care of others and making them comfortable was part and parcel of Wolf's woman. She was working her magic on Megan, who was currently smiling at something Meli said. I had no idea what they were talking about, but whatever it was, I didn't want to interrupt.

"What did Rabbit say?" Wolf put the last of the dishes in the dishwasher.

Not keen on being overheard, I turned away from the open patio door and kept my voice low. "Let's hit your office." I drained the last of my iced tea and brought the glass to the sink as Wolf dried his hands and tucked the hand towel back on the oven's handle. I hid a smirk at his highly domesticated habit.

Picking up on either my expression or my thought, he muttered, "Fuck you."

I followed him down the hall to his office. "Just saying, this playing-house thing suits you."

"You know, Bishop..." He stalked down the hall to his office and stopped at the door, his hand on the knob. He turned to me. "You make that green look good."

"That's not jealousy, brother. That's me OD'ing on the hearts-and-flowers bliss you're emanating."

"Right." He pushed the door open and waved me to one of the leather chairs in front of his desk. "How much you got on the pool?"

At the mention of the team's bet on when Wolf would officially make Meli his, I chuckled. "Because I have your back, I've refrained from placing my bet." Grinning at his disbelieving snort, I added, "Besides, it would be like taking candy from wailing babies."

He took the other chair and eyed me. "You wait until it's your turn."

An image of Megan's face popped into my mind, but I gently pushed it aside. I sat back, stretched my legs out, and crossed them at the ankles as I dropped my head to the back of the chair, my eyes closing as the day's events caught up with me. "Going to be waiting a long damn time."

"You sure about that?"

The level of seriousness in his voice had me opening my eyes and angling my chin down to find him studying me. "You know something that I don't?"

"I watched you with her."

I braced myself and bit out, "And?"

"And she's getting under your skin."

A flare of resentment rose, but I held it back. Wolf didn't say shit just to hear his own voice. He was understandably worried about Megan and her role in whatever was swirling around us. I got it, but… "I've got it under control."

He raised an eyebrow. "You sure about that?"

His constant questions were pissing me off. "Yeah, I am." When he didn't back down, I narrowed my eyes. "Why are you pushing this?"

"Because I get the impression you're considering something you probably shouldn't."

Like getting involved with a woman who could be an unintended enemy? Not ready to examine the surprising pinch of truth, I focused on more important things. "I know what I'm doing." As a comeback, it sucked ass, but it was all I could muster.

Wolf's lips twitched, but fortunately, he switched topics. "So, this almost hit-and-run. Was it deliberate?"

Since it was just the two of us, I gave him the truth. "Yeah."

His face darkened. "Shit."

"Yep."

"What did Rabbit say?"

Taking the reprieve from talking about my personal life, I closed my eyes and shared. "Found the car."

"Stolen?"

"Yep. Even better, about an hour after it tore out of the garage, it was found abandoned and torched in a vacant lot."

"So, no way to identify the who or why behind this?"

I opened my eyes and stared unseeing at the ceiling as

some of the pieces fell neatly into place. The *who* might not have a name yet, but it was easy enough to guess—that looming menace that hovered around the colonel. It was too damn bad my psychic premonition hadn't come with a face or a name. But the *whys* worried me most. They had more holes than Swiss cheese.

"The who may be simpler than the why," I said.

"How so?"

"It's someone close to Delacourt."

Wolf's tone sharpened. "Did you tell her that?"

"Hell no."

"Why not?"

"It's all I've got."

"She'd take it if you offered it," Wolf said.

Digging my heels into the carpet, I braced my arms on my thighs and leaned forward. "Yeah, she would, but then what? If I tell her it's someone close to her, she'll give herself away eventually, and any advantage we had would be lost."

"You're leaving her blind?" Wolf mimicked me, leaning forward, and when I didn't answer, he rubbed his face. "Delacourt's not going to be happy when she finds out." He met my gaze and grimaced. "And she will, you know."

"Yeah, I know." Navigating this treacherous game required maintaining what advantages I could, including keeping the colonel in the dark about certain things.

Wolf had been my friend for years and could follow my logic like no one else, so I wasn't surprised when he said, "You think whoever had Megan is still hunting her."

I shook my head. "I don't think it. I *know* it." I emphasized the word to make my point. My ability, that innate sense of knowing things, wasn't an easy one to categorize, but it was enough to let me know that, much like the colonel, Megan was far from safe. She was being used, and whoever was pulling her strings was far from done.

"Are they part of Falcon?"

I nodded.

Wolf looked away for a minute, and when his gaze came back to me, it carried a cool calculation. "If they're trying to take her out—"

"It's because she knows something, and they don't want to risk her remembering whatever it is she's hidden."

His head tilted, and his eyes narrowed. "You knew what I would find when I took her under."

Sometimes it sucked having someone who knew you so well. As this was Wolf, the brother who always had my back, I shared information that I should have given Megan first. "Yeah. I was hoping I was wrong, but..."

"You're never wrong."

Not about things like this. I dragged my hands over my face and blew out a breath. "I didn't know what ability they might have triggered." But I had my suspicions, and spending time with Megan only strengthened them.

"You just knew she had one." Wolf waited for my nod before continuing, "If she's a dream-walker, she's dangerous not just to us but to herself."

He wasn't wrong. Ricochet never shared much about what he could do, but he'd been part of the team long enough for me to see it in action. Navigating the dreamworld was more than tricky—it was downright lethal. "I know, which is why you still need to bring Rico in, because I don't have a damn clue about how to break whatever it is she's got going on." I also didn't like the fact that she was linked to an unknown in the first damn place—the same unknown who was stalking the colonel. It didn't leave me with the warm fuzzies. And because we didn't know who controlled the link to Megan's dreams, the situation was dangerous.

Following my train of thought, Wolf muttered, "God, I feel sorry for her."

"Don't," I said sharply. It was a knee-jerk response. Shaking my head, I held Wolf's gaze. "Don't. She's a hell of a lot stronger than anyone, including she, realizes."

Wolf studied me for a long moment. "For her sake, I hope you're right, because she's going to need a core of steel to get to the other side."

Fortunately, Megan's spine was a titanium rod. "She came to Delacourt, worried she was being used as a sleeper agent. Even knowing that what she shared might make us send her back to the damn hospital, she came. She didn't try to handle it on her own. She knew she needed help, and she sought it out. Tell me, how many people do we know that would do that?" I needed to make Wolf understand that there was a hell of a lot more to Megan than met the eye.

His gaze took on a knowing glint. "I'm not Risia, but there's no doubt you're choosing a hell of a rocky path, brother."

Again, he wasn't wrong, because if anyone knew what the possible fallout scenarios were, it was me. Threat or not, there was one thing I was certain of—the only one dealing with Megan would be me. I ran a hand over the back of my neck. "Tell me something I don't know."

Whatever faint humor his face had held disappeared, replaced by a grim seriousness. "Just watch your step, because I'm not keen on watching you fall off that cliff you're perched on."

Chapter Nine

Movement inside drew my attention, and I watched Bishop follow Wolf out of the kitchen and disappear deeper into the house. Considering the serious looks on their faces, I thought they had to be going off to discuss their crazy theories from earlier.

"So, you and Bishop…?"

At Meli's gentle teasing, my face heated. I turned to face her. "It's not like that."

Amusement danced in her green eyes. "Then you have more restraint than most."

I rolled my glass between my hands. "It has nothing to do with restraint, believe me."

"Oh?"

I winced. "More like all-around bad timing."

The amusement spread from her eyes to her curving lips. "Yeah, these guys are the kings of bad timing." She leaned forward as if sharing a secret. "But they are so worth it."

Hearing the depth of happiness in her voice, I returned her smile. But if I was being completely honest, I also felt a little jealous. "I'm sure they are, but things are… complicated right now."

Meli settled back in her chair. "Sounds like there's a story there."

I brought my glass up and muttered, "You could say that," then took a drink.

Meli sat there, studying me with those too-old eyes before breaking the quiet. "I met Wolf when I was being stalked by the man who killed my brother."

Stunned by the revelation, all I could do was offer a lame, "I'm so sorry."

"Thanks," she said softly. "I just wanted you to know I understand *complicated,* so if you want to share, I'm all ears."

Her quiet offer reassured me that she was someone who might be able to help me navigate this weird new reality. There was a genuineness about Meli that bridged the distance I seem to have acquired with everyone lately. It was scary but not enough to stop me from taking her offer seriously. It wasn't like I could share this whole crazy situation with my family, no matter how accepting they were of unusual abilities. The minute I did, they'd have me back in the damn hospital.

I stared at the glass in my hands, unable to look at her while I spoke. "I don't know what Wolf told you."

"I know you worked with the colonel. You were kidnapped, held hostage, and the team went in to get you."

Okay, so she had the basics. "I'm not like them."

She considered me, a frown marring her forehead. "In what way?"

Fearless, courageous, I thought, but I stuck with an easier answer. "Psychic."

Her frown cleared, her lips twitched the tiniest bit as if she heard what I hadn't said, and she raised her glass in a toast. "Join the club. Neither am I."

Not the answer I was expecting, but it was strangely comforting. "You're not?"

She shook her head. "Nope. Not the least little bit."

Curiosity edged out my personal drama. "Oh, wow. I guess surprise parties are out for Wolf, then, huh?"

She laughed. "Luckily for both of us, he can't read my mind. Something about a natural barrier making me the equivalent of Fort Knox."

"Huh." I studied her carefully.

"What?"

"You seem..." I frantically searched for the right word. "*Unintimidated* by him." If I was involved with someone who could read my mind, I wasn't sure I could be as accepting as Meli. Which made me wonder what exactly Bishop's ability was.

Before I could chase that passing thought down, Meli shrugged. "Honestly, when I first realized what he could do, it freaked me out."

Even before my brutal encounter with a possible telepath, her answer would have made complete sense. No woman would be comfortable with someone who could poke around in her mind willy-nilly. On top of that, she'd have to trust that same someone not to use that power against her. Yeah, that would make any kind of relationship—romantic or platonic—tough.

Meli's amusement faded as she watched me. "But Wolf is not the kind of man who abuses that power." Her gaze drifted to the fading sunset before coming back to me. "Besides, if he skates too close to the line, I yank him back. I might not be a crack shot or ninja, but I can protect him from crossing his lines and slipping over."

Hearing this serenely composed woman echo my earlier concerns eased my tension. "It's good that he has you, then."

She made a hum of agreement as the early evening settled

around us. The soft hiss of gas-fueled flames dancing in the fire-pit table joined the chatter of a few cicadas braving the cooler weather.

Bolstered by her easy acceptance of what most would consider bizarre, my curiosity got the better of me. "May I ask you something?" When she nodded, I said, "It's personal, so…"

"Ask," Meli said. "If I don't want to answer, I'll tell you."

Taking her at her word, I blurted, "Most people think psychic abilities are a bunch of crap. Why are you so accepting?"

Meli pulled her legs under her. "Do you know Risia?"

Not expecting her to respond with a question, or to even know the name of the seer Delacourt contracted with on various assignments, I stumbled over my answer. "Umm… yes."

Meli's face lightened. "She's my best friend. It's kind of hard to deny that psychic abilities exist when she's proven right time after time." She studied me. "You said you're not psychic, so how come you accept it?"

I set my glass down on a side table before bringing one leg up to brace my bare heel on the edge of the seat's cushion. Shifting to a hip, I tucked my other leg under. "My younger sister and older brother are both gifted." Since she was with Wolf, I decided it was safe to assume she understood the importance of keeping such facts to herself. "In fact, my brother is part of one of Delacourt's other teams."

Sympathy washed across her face. "Must have been hard growing up." Before I could ask what she meant, she said, "Not being psychic like them."

"At first it was." I gave her a self-conscious half grin. "Especially since my childhood goal was to grow up into the world's best wizard or a kick-ass queen of a secret kingdom. I was not thrilled my siblings had the abilities I could only dream of." My self-directed amusement faded. "As we got older, and I watched them struggle to deal with what having these gifts really meant, I was secretly grateful that the psychic fairy passed me by."

"I get that."

Somehow, I thought she just might. I looked at my toes, unable to hold her gaze as I gave her the rest. "Now it seems that maybe the psychic fairy is getting hers back."

"What do you mean?" Meli asked gently.

Against the backdrop of normality, her quiet acceptance unlocked my tongue. "Wolf and Bishop think I might be psychic now." Saying it out loud made the theory seem more real.

When I couldn't get anything more out, she asked, "What do you think?"

"I don't know." Pressure grew in my chest, making my voice raspy. "But I want them to be wrong, because if they're right..."

She waited until I looked at her before she finished what I wouldn't. "Then you're no longer normal, and you're just like your sister and brother."

God. Hearing the truth out loud meant I couldn't dodge it. Uncomfortable, I rubbed my chin over my knee.

Meli leaned forward, compassion clear on her face. "Wolf didn't share details, just that you were hoping he could help you find some answers. If they are right about this, it may not be what you wanted to hear, but it is an answer. Doesn't that count for something?"

Does it? Or does it just add more weight to the fact that I might be the loaded gun aimed at the team? Doubt kept me mute.

After a few moments, Meli sighed and sat back. "I wish I could be like Risia and give you something solid to hold on to, but honestly, if anyone could see you through a tough situation, it would be Bishop and his team."

"I know." That wasn't a lie. I'd gone to the colonel because I knew if my fears held any grain of truth, she and her teams would stop me before it was too late. I counted on them doing that. What worried me was who or what waited on the other side if I slipped through the teams and managed to do some real damage. "I just don't want anyone to get hurt."

Meli had opened her mouth to reply when she suddenly looked up and broke into a smile. She was uncurling her legs and getting to her feet as the sliding door opened. I twisted in my seat to see Wolf and Bishop step out onto the deck.

Wolf headed straight for Meli, but my attention stayed on Bishop, who held my gaze as he came up behind my chair. He moved with a flowing grace. Watching his big body walk my way made me feel as though a predatory cat was stalking me. Caught between thrilled and mesmerized, I kept my neck craned back as he stopped and brushed a hand down my hair. "We should probably head out soon."

As he played with the ends of my hair, I kept my reaction to his touch confined to an internal shiver. He was right—we'd been here much longer than anticipated, and while I enjoyed getting to know Meli, what I really wanted was to retreat somewhere so I could consider what he and Wolf had dropped in my lap before determining my next move.

Grabbing my empty glass, I got to my feet, turned to Meli, who was standing under Wolf's arm, and offered her a small smile. "It was wonderful to meet you, and dinner was lovely. Thank you."

She stepped away from Wolf and gave me a hug. "I'm glad I got a chance to meet you, too." She kept her hands on my shoulders but pulled back enough to see my face. "When you can, we need to do lunch or something."

"I'd like that," I answered with complete honesty.

Meli and Wolf led us to the door, where we spent a few more minutes exchanging goodbyes under the porch light. The sun had disappeared, and evening was settling in as Bishop gave a final wave. His hand landed on the small of my back, making the heat spread up my spine, as he guided me down the walkway to his Jeep.

We were halfway down when Wolf called out, "See ya tomorrow!"

I stutter stepped, but with Bishop's hand in my back, I could only move forward as he twisted his head back and said, "Till tomorrow."

I waited until I'd climbed into his Jeep before asking, "Tomorrow?"

He braced a hand on top of the frame, trapping me in the car. "We called Ricochet, and he agreed to see us tomorrow."

"Excuse me?" I squeaked as I struggled to figure out how I felt about the impending meeting with the mysterious Ricochet and what it meant.

Bishop's dark eyes flashed with irritation, and his voice gained an edge even as it stayed low. "Let it go, Megan."

Turning into a shrew in the middle of a quiet street wasn't on my agenda, so I snapped my mouth closed and gritted my teeth. Calling him on his high-handedness required privacy.

Amused, he said, "Thank you."

Giving an annoyed sigh, I fastened my seatbelt as he closed the door and rounded the Jeep's hood. He settled behind the wheel, started the engine, and navigated through the neighborhood. Brooding, I let the quiet stand and simmer.

Once we cleared the neighborhood, he spoke. "You okay?"

Knowing that a lie would be pretty damn pointless, I answered, "Not really." I winced, recognizing how unfair it was to take my crazy emotional roller-coaster ride out on him. Nor was it fair to be pissed because the visit to Wolf hadn't fixed everything the way I thought it would. *Stupid Megan. What's next? Chasing freakin' rainbows to find the pot of gold? Dammit.* I cleared my throat and tried for something less likely to start an argument. "I like Meli. She's a sweetheart."

Fortunately, he took my conversational switch in stride. "Yeah, she's perfect for Wolf. She can out stubborn him like you wouldn't believe."

Remembering the deep love wound around the core of steel in Meli's voice when she spoke of Wolf, I had no trouble believing that. "I can see that."

"I figured you two would get along."

"Why?"

Bishop drummed his fingers on the wheel. The passing streetlights chased shadows over his face, morphing it from fascinating to intimidating and back. "You two are a lot alike."

Confused, I blinked and blurted, "We are?" Granted, it hadn't taken Meli and I long to bond over our shared love of books, but she was worlds beyond me. She exuded a quiet strength, while I was busy playing fifty-two-card pickup with my sanity. Heat hit my cheeks. "Sorry." When he shot me a questioning look complete with raised eyebrows, I kept going, digging my hole a little deeper. "That question sounded like I was fishing for compliments. I'm not."

"So why ask?"

"I guess I'm stunned that I'm faking it so well."

"Faking what?"

"Having my shit together."

Bishop's quiet chuckle took me off guard. "Babe, I hate to break it to you, but everyone fakes it at some point."

"Even you?"

The grin that curved his lips was wry. "Yeah, even me."

Strangely, his easy admission eased the chaotic mix of feelings plaguing me. As I stared out the window from the cocoon of the darkened interior, my whispered confession slipped free. "I wanted Wolf to fix me."

His answer was equally soft. "I know."

I rubbed my forehead and sighed. Gathering my wispy courage, I cleared my throat and asked in a reasonably normal tone, "Do you really think Wolf's right?"

Bishop shot me a look then turned his attention back to the road. He answered solemnly, "Yeah, I do."

The unshakable certainty in his response triggered a series of internal tremors. The last of my fragile hopes that Wolf's guess was horribly wrong began to collapse. I clutched the shoulder strap of my seatbelt with bloodless fingers as if it would keep me grounded.

Bishop reached over and squeezed my knee. "It's going to be okay."

"Glad one of us thinks so." The words came out unmistakably bitchy because I was struggling not to scream in frustration. Logically, I knew it wasn't fair to take it out on Bishop, but after having my hopes of ending my nightmares dashed by Wolf, I wasn't all that keen to rebuild them on another slim possibility. "Are you sure this Ricochet will be able to help?" A small part of me was scared to death that if this didn't work, I'd slip, screaming, over the edge and be lost.

Bishop's jaw flexed. He was probably not thrilled with my snippy response. *Oh freakin' well.* Sure enough, when he spoke, there was an edge to his tone, but he didn't remove his hand from my knee. "If I didn't, I wouldn't have made the call."

Still feeling resentful, I asked, "What if he can't?"

"He will."

"You sound awfully sure."

"Because I am." Before I could snap at him, he continued in a hard tone, "Chances are damn good that those nightmares you're having are because you're linked to the asshole who took you."

His explanation was like a brutal fist to the gut. "Me?" Panic filled me. The idea of being connected in any way to that monster coated my mouth with the sick taste of fear.

"Yeah, you."

I stared at him as terror churned and kicked my pulse up until the beat throbbed in my temples. "If there's a link, can Ricochet destroy it?"

His hand on my knee tightened, and the hardness in his voice eased. "I don't know, and neither will he until he sees what he's working with."

Swallowing against my tight throat, I choked out, "What if he can't break whatever connection exists?"

"Megan, stop." His tone was both commanding and gentle. "There's nothing more we can do tonight." He lifted his hand and put it back on the wheel as he exited the freeway.

I stopped myself from reaching out to bring it back, and instead, I tucked my hands between my thighs and stared out the window. Right, it didn't do me any good to sit and stew about what would happen. Tomorrow would be here soon enough. I needed to focus on how I would get through the night because there was no way in hell I could even contemplate sleeping—not when the chances were so damn high that another nightmare lay in wait. I tried to drag in a breath without making noise, not wanting to clue Bishop in to the fact that I was, once again, falling apart. When I was sure my voice would work, I asked, "What time are you picking me up tomorrow?"

"Excuse me?"

Leaning my head against the window, I said, "For the meeting with Ricochet. What time will you be by?"

"I'm not leaving you alone tonight, babe."

Relief seared through me, and I closed my eyes, cursing how needy the situation made me feel. "You don't have to."

"Yeah, I know that," he said gruffly. "But I'm going to."

"Okay," I said. If he thought I was going to argue, he was sadly mistaken. I was too busy trying to pick my way through the emotional fallout that left me with a familiar numbness. I lifted my head and rubbed at the ache in my temples. "Thanks."

All I got was a grunt in reply as he turned into the apartment's parking lot. He parked in a visitor's slot and shut the engine off. Moving on autopilot, I reached for my seatbelt only to stop when his hand covered mine. When he didn't say anything, I looked up to find him bracing his other arm on the steering wheel as he studied me.

Caught in his gaze, I froze in place as awareness hit me. The heat, gentleness, and determination with which he stared back at me slipped past my encroaching numbness, and I felt an ache. Involuntarily, my hand twisted under his until I could lace my fingers with his, finding solace in his touch.

His hold on my hand tightened. "I'm not going anywhere until this is done."

I struggled to stay ahead of the avalanche of my tumbling emotions and couldn't make sense of his words. "What?"

"You're not doing this alone."

It was nothing short of a vow, and it sank deep until the hot press of tears rose behind my eyes. To keep them from falling, I widened my eyes and said, "Okay."

He lifted his hand from mine only to cup my face, and my breath stalled in my lungs. His gaze dropped to my mouth, and my lips parted as his thumb brushed over them. My pulse picked up, and my focus narrowed to the slow, seductive slide of his thumb. His eyes darkened, and the skin along his cheekbones flushed as his head lowered. I tightened my grip on his hand, trying not to drag him down to me even as I leaned in to meet him. His hand left my face to slip to the back of my head, and I angled myself for the kiss I desperately wanted. But before our lips could meet, light flooded the interior, breaking the moment and making us both wince. I found my forehead pressed against his hard chest while a curse rumbled above my head. Relearning to breathe, I listened to the car drive by. We sat there for a moment, our breathing loud in the quiet.

"We should go up." It came out as a whisper because that was all I could manage.

"Yeah." The hand cradling my head drifted down my spine.

I pulled back slowly until I could see that he was still thinking of our almost kiss. Hell, so was I. I wanted to know what he tasted like and get lost in his heat for just a little bit. And as selfish as it was, I wanted an escape from the mess.

So do something about it.

Heeding that internal voice, I held his gaze and reached up with both hands to cup his jaw. He didn't pull back—in fact, he angled his head against my palms. His goatee rasped against my skin, the soft brush lighting up nerve endings. I felt it in other, much more sensitive places, too. Carnal thoughts danced through my mind, and my breath stuttered. Unable to talk about my wants, I did the next best thing. I leaned in, despite the shoulder strap, and brushed my lips against his. When I pulled back, I gave him a shaky smile and dropped my hands. Before I could do more than that, he growled. It was the only warning before his hand was back in my hair, holding me in place as he took my mouth in a heated rush.

Chapter Ten

BISHOP

There was no way to resist Megan's unspoken invitation. Hell, I wasn't even going to try. Instead, I took what she offered, teasing along those lush lips until they parted, letting me in. My hand tightened on her ponytail when she didn't shy away but met my advance with one of her own. Her tongue danced with mine as we fed the fire racing between us. Her taste—heated spice and traces of tea—seared through my bloodstream like a lit detonating cord, triggering an explosive hunger that left me hard and aching.

With the hand that wasn't holding her in place, I stroked her neck then moved downward until I could brush my knuckles over the warm skin of her upper chest. I kept my touch gentle as I traced a path down the soft material of her scoop-necked shirt and over the slope of her breast.

She tore her mouth free, and her quiet whimper filled the space between us. The very feminine sound made my dick twitch, and her hands fisted my T-shirt as she tried to pull me closer. Happy to accommodate, I leaned in and laid a line of open-mouthed kisses along her exposed neck. As much as I wanted to keep going, the Jeep's interior wasn't exactly comfortable. It took every bit of my hard-earned discipline to pull back from the temptation. Somehow, I managed to do it without inflicting serious bodily harm.

Her lashes lifted, revealing blue eyes dark with feminine hunger. That, along with her flushed face and lips reddened from our kiss, created a picture that would fuel my fantasies for a fucking long time. The urge to finish what I'd started rode me hard and left me harder, but the gentleman my mama had tried to encourage managed to rein in my baser instincts.

God, I am in so much trouble here.

She blinked, and the flush crept up along her cheeks as she pulled against my hold. Not wanting to hurt her, I let her go and moved my hand to her back. Instead of drawing away, she dropped her forehead against my sternum until it rested above her hands, which were tangled in my T-shirt. "Okay," she murmured on a breathy exhalation. "Well, wow."

Yeah, that was one way to put it. Hiding my satisfaction at her comment, I pressed a kiss to the top of her bent head and made a noncommittal sound. She took a shuddering breath but didn't look up.

Since staying in position might leave me crippled, I finally said, "We need to head up."

"Right." She pulled back and let go of my shirt. When she ran her hand over it, carefully smoothing the material out, I wanted to smile. It was obvious she was trying to get her bearings.

I let her go and undid her seatbelt, waiting for her to open her door before I made my exit. Getting out with a hard-on wasn't easy, but by the time I made it to her side, I could at least move without imitating the hunchback of Notre Dame.

We moved through the parking lot, passing through the pools of illumination cast by the scattered lights. We were roughly halfway to Megan's building when the hairs on the back of my neck stood on end. Considering the fact that we were in a well-lit complex in a fairly upscale neighborhood, my reaction was highly unusual, but I would have been beyond stupid to ignore it.

Letting Megan move ahead of me, I scanned our surroundings, trying to pinpoint the threat. The parking lot was full, the cars dark. An older couple was walking a small fur ball, and some kids on bikes were shooting the shit.

Megan headed to the bank of elevators tucked between two buildings and hit the button for her floor. Coming in close behind her, I continued to scan as the itch at my neck got worse. The elevator dinged, and the doors slid open, revealing an empty cage. Ushering Megan in, I hit the button, and once the doors closed, the aggravating itch eased a bit.

The warm weight of Megan's hand landed low on my back. "Bishop?" I craned my neck to find her studying me with a small frown. "What's wrong?"

The quiet ding as we bypassed floors chimed. I shrugged. "Maybe nothing."

"But?"

I rubbed the back of my neck. "Just an itch."

She bit her lower lip and dropped her hand as her gaze shifted away. "Got it."

Not missing the stiffening of her shoulders, I caught her hand and held it. "We're good, Megan. We'll just play this smart, so let me go first, okay?"

She gave me a doubt-filled side look and a careful nod but didn't say anything.

The final ding sounded, and I let her go. Stepping through the opening first, I did a quick assessment of the hallway. Empty both ways. Despite the soundproofing, I could hear soft murmurs from behind the closed doors of the other occupants. I moved aside, keeping a hand on the elevator door so it wouldn't close, and motioned Megan out.

When she moved into the hallway and turned to her apartment, I followed, the persistent itch making me uneasy. Busy monitoring the hall, I almost ran into Megan when she stopped short. My hands closed on her rigid shoulders. Following her fixed gaze, I realized she was staring at her door, which wasn't fully closed.

I pulled her back and to the side and put a finger to my lips. Her throat worked as she swallowed, but she wrapped her arms over her stomach and nodded, keeping quiet and still.

Since I wasn't currently carrying, a fact I'd remedy as soon the opportunity presented itself, I put my back to the wall on the hinge side of the door. Before I pushed it open, I visualized the layout of Megan's apartment, cataloguing angles where her possible intruder could be situated. Thanks to the open floor plan, the possibilities were restricted to the couch, the kitchen, and a hall to my left.

Not keen on getting plugged full of holes, I dropped into a crouch. My focus narrowed to surviving the fatal funnel of the doorway and clearing the apartment. Using the flat of my hand, I shoved the door wide and braced.

Fortunately, there was no welcoming hail of bullets, so I rushed into the room, staying low to present a limited target, my head on a swivel. Light from the patio painted broad strokes through the apartment, but a quick scan didn't reveal anyone lurking in the shadows. I stayed closed to the walls near the door as I took in the no-longer-neat living room.

My instincts were grumbling that I was late to the party, but I wasn't ready to risk letting Megan in until the entire apartment was cleared. Praying she'd stay put, I made quick work of the task. I hit Megan's room, and my anger spiked, threatening to breach my control. The violation of her personal space was unmistakable. Drawers were partially open, their contents spilling out and onto the floor. A few bottles of whatever feminine shit she had on the dresser were leaking across the top of it and clogging the air in a sickening mishmash of odors. Books had fallen to the floor in a haphazard pile by the end table, and torn sheets of paper were mixed into the mess. When I flicked on the light in the walk-in closet, I found more of the same.

I stalked out of her room and over to the one that belonged to her sister. The previously closed door was open in invitation. In that room, I noted fewer signs of a search. Either the intruder hadn't been too interested in that room, or Megan's sister was a lax housekeeper.

By the time I retraced my steps back to Megan, I had no doubt that whatever this was—threat or warning or both—was aimed at her. Stepping through the door, I barely had time to brace before a pale-faced Megan rushed at me. I held her back by not moving out of the way. "Hold up."

She rocked to a stop, rolling up onto her toes before dropping back to her heels. Her hands landed on my chest, this time not to pet but to push me away. "Move, Bishop."

I had to give her credit—she almost pulled off making her words a command if I ignored the slight hitch at the end of my name. "Not until you take a breath and agree to stay at my side."

I didn't think she could get much paler. I was wrong. "Oh God."

Realizing she'd taken my advice the entirely wrong way, I pulled her hands away from my chest. I held onto one of them just to ensure she'd stay at my side. "It's a mess, but that's probably the worst of it."

It was a lame attempt at reassurance, but it seemed to work. She stilled, and watching her pull it together, I couldn't help but admire her inherent strength as she faced another violation. It might not be as bad as the one she'd already endured, but it was another shitty addition to the already craptastic pile she was dealing with.

"Ready?" I asked.

After getting her nod, I led the way inside, taking time to

turn on the hall light. Behind me, she gave a small gasp, and the hand in mine tightened and pulled free. "Holy shit."

"Hang tight." Leaving her frozen at the edge of the living room, I closed the front door and came back to her side to survey the mess. Her reaction was justifiable. At first glance, it looked like someone had torn through the room with a vengeance. Only on closer inspection did the destruction's pattern become clear.

"Keelie is going to be pissed." Megan sounded angry, which made me happy.

"I'm assuming you two have renter's insurance."

She toed a torn-up couch cushion. "We do, but we'll need a police report."

"I'll call Delacourt and let her handle that." I had no intention of spending the next couple of hours dodging questions I couldn't answer.

"Sounds good." She spun in a slow circle, taking in the stuffing scattered like snow. "What on earth did they want?"

Instead of answering, I gave her something else to focus on. "Why don't you check out your room and let me know if anything's missing."

She gave me an absentminded nod and headed down the hall alone.

I made the call to Delacourt, who promised to have someone come by to take the report. Of course, she then demanded I catch her up on what had happened with Wolf. By the time I finished, Megan reappeared.

Hanging up with Delacourt, I asked, "Anything missing?"

"Not that I can tell." She leaned against the wall, arms wrapped over her stomach, and stared at the living room. "What the hell was the point of this?"

In the short time I'd spent with her, I'd learned not to sugarcoat my answers. "To rattle you."

She switched her gaze to me. "Well, they succeeded. I'm not sure I can sleep here tonight."

She said that as if staying had even been an option. "We won't be. We'll get a room after we talk to Delacourt's police contact."

"I should call Keelie," she murmured, wan and drawn with defeated exhaustion.

"Tomorrow's soon enough. For now, let's see what we can salvage." Noting the fear creeping back into her shadowed eyes, I decided it was time for a distraction. In the kitchen, a little poking around netted me a broom and dustpan. After a little more digging, I struck gold, locating a half-full box of garbage bags.

I turned to find her standing there with her hands out. "Here, let me."

Recognizing her need for action, I handed over the broom and dustpan then moved into the living room. Picking up one of the couch cushions, I noted the long rip. I stacked the rest of the cushions in a pile. A judicious application of duct tape would be enough for most. "Got any duct tape?"

From the kitchen came the sound of her rummaging, then she returned with the familiar gray roll. "Here."

I took it from her and went to work on taping the cushions back together. We worked in silence, the quiet broken by the rough rasp of tape and the dull clink of shattered dishes being dumped. With the last cushion temporarily repaired, I started restuffing.

"Bishop," Megan called.

I looked up.

She was shaking her head. "What are you doing?"

"What's it look like?"

"Okay, *why* are you doing that?"

Because it keeps me busy and keeps me from stewing in my temper. "Might as well salvage what we can."

She stood there, broom held like a staff, the dustpan forgotten in the hand at her hip. "Should we even try?"

"Why not?"

"Well, not that I'm familiar with filing police reports, but should we have left things alone until they got here?"

She was probably right, but I knew what an impending panic attack looked like, and Megan had been a hairsbreadth away. "I'm sure sweeping up the broken dishes and doing a patch job on the cushions won't undermine their investigation." I was betting that there wouldn't be much to find by way of fingerprints. This toss job held too many professional markings.

A knock sounded, followed by Rabbit's distinctive drawl. "Y'all home?"

I took a step to the side until I could see Rabbit coming through, Jinx on his heels. "You beat the police."

"We were nearby when Delacourt called." Jinx picked her way around Rabbit and moved to Megan. "Hey, Megan, sorry about your apartment."

Megan managed a half-hearted smile. "Unfortunately, it's my sister's."

"Even worse."

"Yeah." Megan blew out a breath. "Bishop, if we're not staying, can I go grab some stuff while we wait?"

I gave her a nod and shot Jinx a look. "I'll come help," Jinx said.

"Thanks." Megan turned and led the way down the hall.

As the two women disappeared, Rabbit stopped next to me. "Quick-and-dirty job." He eyed the intact TV and electronics, and his hazel eyes grew cold and turned serious. "Scare tactic."

"Yeah."

He dropped his voice. "What the hell does she know or have that's got someone runnin' hot?"

I grimaced. "Hell if I know."

"Any luck with Wolf?"

Since Megan was having a hard enough time coming to terms with the idea that she might have joined the psychic brigade, I kept that theory to myself. "Not much, but we're meeting with Rico tomorrow."

Rabbit's eyes narrowed. "'Not much,' but you're bringing in Rico?" He folded his arms. "What ain't you sharin'?"

"It's not mine to share," I muttered. Then, so he'd stop pushing, I added, "not yet."

Before he could continue, a brisk knock announced the arrival of the authorities.

Chapter Eleven

Filing the report with the officer didn't take nearly as long as it would have if the colonel hadn't thrown her weight around, tapping a grizzled detective she knew to step in. Then there was brooding, impatient Bishop, whose attitude probably helped speed things along, too. Either way, a little more than an hour later, Bishop herded me out of Keelie's apartment, leaving Rabbit and Jinx to stick around until the police were done.

Bishop didn't say much during the ride, which worked for me as I took advantage of the unexpected break offered by his quiet and tried not to think or feel. It wasn't as hard as it sounded to accomplish.

By the time we pulled up a hill and turned into a drive ending in a two-car garage that fronted a mid-century ranch, my eyes felt like they'd been scrubbed with a Brillo Pad. As the Jeep slowed to a stop, my brain decided to kick into gear, providing an increasing whirlwind of questions and worries that, despite my exhaustion, guaranteed there would be no sleep that night.

The engine went silent, and Bishop said, "How are you doing?"

Instead of blurting out the obligatory "Fine," I poked at my response. The cautious optimism I'd woken with was long gone, extinguished by uncomfortable possibilities and surprise attacks. Fortunately, what replaced it wasn't the familiar numbness but was, instead, gut-churning frustration and an annoying collection of unanswered questions. "You know what sucks the most about all of this? Say we manage to get through and unlock my memories. Maybe we get a face, and if we're really lucky, we might get a name, but what then?"

He shifted in his seat until he was facing me, one arm resting on the steering wheel. "What do you mean? We follow up."

Caught up in a bout of cynicism, I waved a hand between us. "Right, but then what?" I dropped my arm and made fists in my lap as I stared out the window, my voice tight. "You confront them with a kidnapping accusation, and they play dumb. It'll come down to their word against mine." I turned my head and met his gaze. "There's no proof, and even if you found something, it still would come down to the crazy chick with PTSD versus whoever did this. Whoever is behind all of this is damn smart with seriously deep pockets, because it takes money to hide someone that deep for that long. Money and brains versus amnesiac me. There's no way to make that work."

"You're not giving yourself, or us, much credit." There was no judgment in his tone.

He might have been right, but... I forced my fists to relax and looked away. "It's not that."

"Sure sounds like it."

I kept my attention on the fading light drifting across the front yard, knowing I wouldn't have the courage to share if I looked at Bishop. "I can't shake the feeling we're being..." I trailed off, unable to find the right word.

"Played?" Bishop supplied.

Sliding him a side look, I nodded.

His mouth opened then closed, and he looked thoughtful. He tapped the steering wheel twice with his knuckles. "Do you know what my ability is?"

Not sure where he was going with his question, I shook my head.

"I know things." Picking up on my confusion, he continued, "The official label is claircognizance or 'clear knowing.'"

That word triggered the memory of a long-ago conversation with my siblings about how perceived psychic abilities were categorized. Anything with "clair" attached to it fell into one of the four major intuitive groups. "So you're like Risia? You can see the future?"

He shook his head. "Not quite. Think of Risia as a pre-cog on steroids with an accuracy rating that's off the charts. She gets sucked into visions, but what she sees can change because the future is fluid, altered by individual choices." He looked away with a grimace. "I don't see things. I feel that something is going to happen, and then it does." His gaze came back to mine. "It's knowing things beyond a shadow of a doubt. There are no triggers, no bad feelings, just *knowing* something will happen or why it will happen."

"Okay." I drew out the word, feeling my way around his explanation. Rubbing my palm over my knee, I tried to figure out the difference between knowing and seeing the future.

He must have read my confusion because he added, "Rabbit once described my talent as a psychic data download."

It was such a strange image. I asked, "So you're a psychic computer?"

That earned me a half laugh. "Maybe. The theory is that it

is a mix of precognition and telepathy, like a combination of instinct, mind reading, and thought transference. Let's just say that considering the advantages I tend to have in most situations, I'm not the one you want to play games with."

There was a familiar arrogance in his claim, one I'd heard with my brother, Dev. Since no one could lie to Dev, it not only left him cynical, but it also blinded him to the truth that no one could outrun the odds—that despite his gifts, someone would eventually manage to slip a lie past him. Maybe I was too tired to make his explanation work, but I wasn't sure how it helped. "Are you saying that you know we're being played with?"

He looked away, his jaw flexing, before he turned back to me. "There's no doubt we are. I just don't think they understand who they're playing against."

"And you do?" The question escaped before I could stop it. I raised a hand, half in apology and half to stop whatever answer he'd give me.

He ignored my hand, the line of his jaw tightening. "When information came in on where you might be held, the colonel wanted to hold off on going in until she was certain it wasn't a false lead. I knew it wasn't, and I knew we had to act immediately."

Something in his tone made me brace myself. "Why?"

"Because if we didn't get you out within forty-eight hours, you would be dead." He paused then dropped another revelation. "It's also how I know that your suspicions are right."

I stilled, like a rabbit in the presence of a wolf, as a sense of dread settled like a stone on my chest. Arguing was futile against the utter conviction in his voice. Working against the heaviness in my chest, I wheezed, "What?"

In the shadowy interior of the Jeep, it was hard to read his expression, especially when he quickly locked it down as if prepping for an explosion. "You're worried you're being used against the team, a tool to destroy us."

Even though it wasn't a question, I managed a nod.

He gripped the steering wheel. I was so focused on that telling reaction that it took me a moment to register his gentle, "You are." Then I jerked at the impact.

A soundless wail tore through my mind, threatening to spill out, but a combination of pride and denial refused to give it voice. My tenuous belief that I hadn't broken under the relentless mental torture shattered, and for a breathless moment, my world stilled, waiting for the approaching storm. Shame and fear rose, only to be sucked under by a tidal wave of fury and resentment.

"No." My denial came out as a whisper but then rose to a scream. "No, no, no, no!"

Hard hands cupped my face and dragged me forward, and then my words were cut off by a hard kiss. The shock of it snapped me out of my hysteria and forced me to focus on breathing—not an easy task with Bishop sharing my breath. When he finally lifted his head, he left me breathing hard, my emotional storm momentarily held at bay.

Staring into his dark eyes, I shared the only truth I had. "I need to leave."

"No."

"Yes." Unable to hold his gaze while I struggled to get a handle on my feelings, I closed my eyes, but it didn't help. "I won't be the reason you get hurt." Hurriedly, I tried to cover my slip by saying, "You or your team."

The hands on my jaw tightened then relaxed. "You won't be."

My bitter laugh hurt my ears. "You just said differently."

"No, I said they wanted to use you as a tool, not that they would succeed." His utter conviction made me lift my eyes and pull back, but Bishop didn't let me get far. He waited until my gaze met his before he said, "Six months, Megan. They had you for six months and couldn't break you."

I sneered. "You're so wrong—they sure as hell did. Otherwise, this discussion would be moot."

"God dammit, woman," he growled, his dark gaze bright with frustration and anger. "You were the one who came to us. You're the one who agreed to let Wolf do his thing. If you'd broken, we wouldn't be having this fucking conversation because you'd be under lock and key."

The need to hold on to what he was telling me was so strong it hurt, but I—we—couldn't afford for him to be wrong. Not to mention that paranoia was a hell of a head trip. "You don't know that. Maybe it's part of their plan." As he held me in place, I wrapped my hands around his wrists and squeezed. "You're not infallible, Bishop, no matter how much you know things. Haven't you ever been wrong?"

His expression closed down suddenly. With a sharp twist, he freed his wrists from my hold and pulled away. Stunned, I twisted in my seat and scrambled for the door, my mouth moving ahead of my brain. "Right, sorry, not my business." Hurt joined the myriad of other feelings vying for my attention, but before I could make my escape, he spoke.

"Once. I was wrong once. Years ago."

No matter how neutral he kept his voice, I could tell I had tripped a trigger. My frantic movements stilled, but I didn't dare to look back at him. Instead, I rested my forehead against the cool glass. "Bishop, you don't—"

"It was just after graduation. I took a road trip with my best bud, Austin. He never came home."

I didn't want to hear this, didn't want to add his pain— lying under his oh-so-rational tone—to mine, but I'd chosen to open my big mouth, so now I would deal with the damage I'd caused. Lifting my head, I turned back, but he wasn't done.

"There were four of us—Austin and his girlfriend, Terri, me, and Austin's twin, Becca." He turned to the windshield with its uninspiring view of the garage doors, a muscle jumping in his jaw, his hand tight on the steering wheel. "We were heading to Seattle to spend a week messing around before Austin and I were to report for basic. We had a cabin rented at Lake Sammamish. From our home in Montana, it's a straight shot along I-90. But just as we passed the Snoqualmie Casino, I told Austin to take an alternate route because I *knew* if we kept going, we'd end up in an accident. By the time I realized we were on the same route I'd tried to avoid, it was too late." He stopped, the silence spilling into the tension-filled space.

I resisted the urge to touch him, hard though it was, because something told me it would do more harm than good.

"When the semi in front of us swerved and lost control, Austin managed to avoid it, but we ended up in a ditch. The car rolled three times despite the heavy foliage. The girls and me, we were banged up, had a couple of broken bones, nothing serious, but Austin..." He stared at his hand then flexed his fingers with a pained deliberateness. "A branch came through the driver's-side window, sliced right along his neck. He bled out before EMS got there." He finally turned to look at me. There was a world of guilt and grief in those dark eyes. It hurt to look at them—and it hurt even worse to hear the remorse in his voice. "So yeah, I've been wrong, but it only took once to ensure that I don't ever make a similar mistake again."

"Okay," I said quietly. There was nothing I could say to assuage the guilt he carried, even if he let me. "Okay." I looked away, not sure I could hide my doubts from him. However, I needed a way to guide him back from the nightmare I'd inadvertently awaken him. Since he was certain that I wasn't the threat I feared I was, there was no use arguing any further. Instead, it was time to focus on what I could do to help.

Floundering, I tried to determine exactly what that was. I settled for changing the topic. The terrifying possibility Wolf had raised about my possible psychic ability drifted to front and center, and I chose to tackle it. Swallowing hard, I did my best to keep my voice from shaking. "You believe Wolf's right, don't you? About me being a dream-walker?"

It took a few moments before he rumbled, "Yes... with Rico's help, you should be able to regain control of your dreams. Once you manage that, we can turn the tables on whoever this guy is." He paused, and I could feel the weight of his gaze on me. "If you take control of the dreamworld, it'll be our turn to get the answers we need to nail whoever's behind this."

And that doesn't sound dramatically dire or daunting at all. Suppressing a shiver, I sought comfort in the fact Bishop was offering the possibility of gaining some control over this mess. If he was right, I might be able to stop the nightmares. I wasn't as sure as he was about my ability to turn the tables, but arguing would accomplish nothing but prolong an argument I couldn't win.

"Guess we'll find out tomorrow." Pulling in a deep breath, I raised my head, taking note that many of the streetlights had fallen dark while we sat there. A few nearby houses had turned on their porch lights, but Bishop's house remained unlit. "We should probably head in before someone decides to call the cops because they think we're casing your place." My attempt at humor fell flat—Bishop just nodded and got out.

I used my few seconds of alone time in the car to gather my wobbly composure. Unfortunately, the best I could do was stand there as a formidable avalanche of change bore down on me. I just hoped I could keep my balance as chaos made the ground under my feet buckle. When this was done, maybe I would look into a career as a bull rider. It might be easier—and safer. That off-the-wall thought warned me that I was closer to hysteria than I wanted to admit.

I scrubbed my hands over my face. "Buck up, buttercup," I muttered.

I reached for the door, but it opened before I could touch it, and Bishop was there. "Come on, before you fall asleep on your feet."

Not bothering to tell him that sleep wasn't on my radar, I took the hand he offered. We were partway down the curving walkway when I remembered my bag. I came to stop and tugged my hand out of his hold. "I forgot my bag."

"I'll get it."

I waited, taking in the neighborhood. Lights flashed over Bishop as he leaned in to grab my bag from the back seat. A car drove by and turned into a drive a few houses down as the nearby streetlights flickered back to life.

The neighborhood was an eclectic mix of bungalows, ranch houses, and renovated mid-century homes. The jumble of architecture added a unique charm to the area. Plus, it was quiet, which wasn't a surprise since it sat up in the hills. It was not exactly the place I expected Bishop to call home, but I liked it.

I was caught up in my musing, and when Bishop's hand landed on my hip, I let out a startled yip.

He stared down at me with a frown. "Hey, you okay?"

"Yeah, sorry. Just spaced for a moment."

The lines in his face eased as he nudged me along the walkway toward the door. "Understandable. It's been a hell of a day." We trudged up the short steps, and his hand disappeared as he unlocked the door and held it open. "Make yourself at home."

I stepped into an open entryway to be greeted by the warm oak tones of the floor and the professional two-tone beige wall common in rentals. I moved to the side so Bishop would have room to pass. He hit a switch, and the light in the overhead ceiling fan burst into life, illuminating an oversized leather sectional and a squat, cluttered coffee table facing a large wall-mounted flat-screen TV. Over by some bookcases housing music, books, and stereo equipment was a stack of boxes.

Seeing the crumpled newspaper huddled inside the top box, I asked, "Did you just move in?"

He set my bag on the end of the couch. "A couple of months ago. Haven't really had time to unpack." He skirted the couch and headed into the kitchen. "You want something to drink or anything?"

"No, I'm good, thanks." I slowly followed him. "So it's just you and Rabbit?"

He opened a cabinet and pulled down a glass. "Jinx tends to be around, but otherwise, yeah." He went to the fridge, and the rattle of ice dropping into the glass took over. When it was replaced by the glug of water, he continued. "Tag was Rabbit's roommate, but once he and Risia hooked up, they wanted their own place. Unfortunately that meant Rabbit needed a new place and a new roommate." The glass filled, he turned and came to stand with me by the pub-style table. "The lease on my apartment was up, the buddy I was rooming with was planning on relocating, so I took Rabbit up on his offer."

"It's a cool neighborhood."

"And quiet, which is more than I can say for my apartment down by the base."

Yeah, I bet it is. With the tourists and the density of buildings over by Coronado, it was hard to find a quiet place in a reasonable price range. Heck, nowadays, it was hard to find anything *affordable* in San Diego, period, a fact I wasn't looking forward to when it was my turn to go apartment hunting.

"Well, you got lucky."

"Yeah, I did." He set the glass down. "Want a tour?"

"Sure."

It didn't take us long to go through the rest of the house. Besides the open kitchen-living room, there were two bedrooms, both with en-suite baths, a half bath located just off the hall for guests, and a third room that I assumed was meant to be an office, based on the lack of a closet, but was currently cluttered with boxes, a weight set, and a couple of bikes. And that was just what I could see from the door.

After following Bishop back to the living room, I flopped onto the couch. Sinking into the surprisingly comfortable cushions, I stretched out and sighed, exhaustion sweeping in. My eyes drifted closed. I just needed a minute.

Warmth wrapped around my ankle, but I couldn't find the energy to open my eyes.

"Hey, you falling asleep on me?"

"Mmm," was the best I could manage.

His hand lifted from my ankle, and the cushions under me shifted—not much but enough to register. I drifted in a half-awake state, grateful when nothing lurked in the corners. The cushions under me shifted, and I lifted my eyelids enough to see Bishop crouched next to me.

When he caught me watching, he smiled. He leaned in, and thanks to my drowsy state, nothing stopped me from reaching out to pet the burnished shadow along his jaw. He caught my hand with his, holding it still as he turned and pressed a soft kiss to my palm. The tenderness of his action eased that aching fear I couldn't shake.

I curled my hand closed and pulled it down, holding that small bit of comfort close. My position suddenly shifted as he lifted me from the couch and cradled me against his chest. I managed a mumbled, "What are you doing?" even as I curled into his chest.

"I need a shower." His voice was a quiet rumble under my ear. "And I'm not comfortable leaving you sleeping out here. You can crash in my bed."

Mmmm, that sounded like a great idea. To share my appreciation with his idea, I pressed a soft kiss against his throat. His arms tightened and he carried me out of the living room as my eyelids rose, fell, rose, and fell again.

When I opened my eyes again, I wasn't moving and he was tucking my hair behind an ear. "Sleep, Megan. You're safe."

Exhausted and reassured, I curled deeper into the comfortable bed, unable to fight the pull of sleep.

Chapter Twelve

BISHOP

Standing under the pounding spray of the shower, I dropped my head onto my arm, which was braced against the tile wall, and tried not to think about the woman sleeping on my couch. Hunger, bright and vicious, spiraled through me. Not just the normal lust-filled want I was used to, this was something sharper, deeper. Hell, I didn't even need my ability to understand that Megan had stolen a piece of me that no one else had managed to find. It didn't matter that it had only been two fucking days. Even before I'd rescued her, she'd teased me with possibilities. It started back when the colonel had me investigate her disappearance. The more I delved into her life, the more real she became to me, more so than any other woman I'd spent time with. Then she started haunting my dreams.

Once I had gotten her out of the hellhole, it was all I could do to limit my time at the hospital to once a day. Even Wolf had raised an eyebrow at my routine visits. Now that she was in my house, there wasn't a chance in hell of me walking away. In fact, I was hiding in the shower because as much as I would have enjoyed curling up with Megan, it wasn't going to happen anytime soon, at least not if the itch under my skin was any indication. That itch was a good indicator that we couldn't stay here. It wasn't a *knowing* but a common-sense knowledge based on experience.

I might not be able to hide Megan from whoever was stalking her dreams—something I hoped to change once we had a sit-down with Rico—but I sure as shit could keep her physical location on the q.t. I had no doubt that Falcon was using someone close to the colonel to hunt Megan and, by extension, the teams. They had to be close enough to know how and when to strike, which meant they probably had access to each team member's basic information, such as home addresses and contacts. That would have required a high-security clearance, which would explain how they knew to wait outside Megan's doctor's office and then to hit Keelie's apartment. Megan might no longer be employed by the colonel, but Delacourt would have kept tabs on her and her schedule.

I had to hope the more sensitive information, such as what each team member could do, was buried deep enough to keep our hunter blind. It was bad enough that Falcon had enough of their own set of psychic skills to draw accurate conclusions about ours, but keeping the specifics hidden would be our only advantage in this game. The longer we stayed in my house, the more we ran the risk of being cornered, so we needed to disappear that night.

Of course, that wouldn't help once I got Megan somewhere safe and she could actually sleep uninterrupted. It had been a risk to leave her sleeping, considering that Falcon's hunter could slip in and out of her dreams, but she was dead on her feet and barely able to keep her eyes open. Hopefully, her exhaustion would be enough to keep her dreamless. She wasn't the only one who was tired—exhaustion was riding my ass like my old gunny sergeant—but there'd be no stopping until I had Megan somewhere relatively safe.

Washing my hair, I evaluated a couple of options, leaning more and more toward an old friend's condo out on the beach. He still had another month on tour, so the place would be empty, and I had a key since he'd asked me to do an occasional drop-in to make sure it stayed standing. Since it wasn't easily linked to me or Megan, it should work.

I started a mental checklist of things we'd need as I rinsed then stepped out to towel off. I was about to hang up my towel when I realized I had forgotten to bring clothes into the bathroom. Well, shit. Normally I'd just waltz into my bedroom, but that might not be the smartest thing to do with Megan curled up in my bed. Not that I expected her to be awake or aware, but a man could hope.

My overly-optimistic imagination triggered a hunger that had nothing to do with food and everything to do with indulging, no matter how unwise. Shaking my head at both my imagination and even more enthusiastic dick, I wrapped the damp towel around my waist and hit my bedroom, taking care to keep my movements quiet. Seeing her curled up on my bed softened something in my chest. Damn, I had it bad.

Even understanding the threat that Megan posed, it was hard to remember it when watching her struggle to her feet, hit after hit. The depth of her courage and determination snuck under my caution and found a hidden spot. It didn't help that she appealed to my tarnished white-knight side in a huge fucking way, even though she didn't need me to fill that role. How she'd managed to hide all that strength of character while working for Delacourt was beyond me. Then again, when I was in the office, I wasn't really paying attention to paper pushers. More fool me.

I hit my dresser, grabbed a pair of boxer briefs and tiptoed into my walk-in closet. Once safely inside, I slid the door almost closed. I tossed the damp towel to the laundry basket and then quickly donned clean jeans and a T-shirt. Dressed, I gathered a couple more T-shirts and pairs of jeans and left the closet. I dumped them on the far side of the bed and went back to my dresser for socks and briefs, adding them to the growing pile. With clothes for the next few days taken care of, I focused on the next item of importance—protection.

Crouching in front of the squat but solid gun safe tucked at the back of the closet, I let it do its thing with my fingerprints, and when it popped open, I collected what I would need. First up, my HK USP, followed by two extra-detachable box magazines, each holding sixteen rounds of .45 ACP, which had a heavier impact than a regular nine-millimeter. Overkill, maybe, but I'd rather be certain than sorry.

Dropping the extra magazines into the small weapons bag, which contained a few key items in case I found a need to hit the road quickly, I stood up and snagged my concealed holster off the top shelf. After clipping it to the waist of my jeans at the small of my back, I left my T-shirt untucked for easier access. Primary firmly in place, I sank back into a crouch and snagged my backup, the small fourth-generation Glock 19, and added it to the bag. No way was I leaving Megan unarmed with so many unknowns floating about. I didn't plan on leaving her side, but it was better to be safe than sorry. She needed to be able to defend herself if I wasn't around.

With protection set and bare feet now covered with well-worn combat boots, I took the bag over to the bed and set it next to the pile of jeans and T-shirts. It took me ten minutes to toss my clothes, toiletries, and weapons bag into a faded pea-green duffle showing the wear and tear of multiple trips around the globe. Shouldering it, I snagged a hoodie from the chair and left the bedroom.

Halfway down the hall, a noise at the front door brought me to a standstill. I set the duffle bag and jacket on the floor, taking care to keep as quiet as possible. Straightening, I pulled the HK free and brought it up, barrel aimed at the door.

As the door swung open, a familiar voice called, "Don't shoot. I'm not the biggest fan of Swiss cheese, *mon ami.*" Rabbit's dark head popped around the door, and his hazel eyes marked the gun before lifting to meet mine. Despite the teasing tone, his expression remained serious. "A little jumpy, are we?"

Before I could answer, Jinx's miffed voice ordered, "Move it, Cajun boy." She forced Rabbit to take a couple of steps forward as I holstered my gun and picked up my bag and jacket.

Rabbit glared over his shoulder as he moved out of the doorway. "Watch where you're poking that finger, sugar."

"You moved, didn't you?" Breezing by him, Jinx headed into the living room and gave a small finger wave. "Hi, Megan!"

I turned to find a heavy-eyed Megan coming up behind me.

She stopped at the mouth of the hall. "Hey, Jinx." She changed course and met Jinx at the couch.

Rabbit closed and locked the front door, waiting until I set my stuff down inside the entryway. "Not plannin' on sticking around?"

I shook my head. "I think it's better to keep Megan tucked out of sight tonight."

Rabbit stayed at my side as we headed into the living room, where the two women were talking quietly. "Probably for the best," he agreed.

I bypassed Jinx, who had claimed the corner of the couch, and aimed for a seat close to Megan, the germ of an idea taking root. "Hey, Jinx."

"Hey, Bishop," the tawny haired woman shot back as Rabbit plopped down next to her and wrapped an arm around her shoulders. She shot him an exasperated look before turning back to me.

When I went to sit, Megan drew her legs up, making room

for me. I settled in and let her tuck her bare toes under my thigh. "You think you can do your thing on Megan and me?"

Jinx studied us both, her brown eyes calm but critical. "Do we have eyes on us?"

I shrugged. "Not sure, but I'd rather be safe than sorry." That seemed to be my theme for the night.

"You wanna be safe, you might want to consider catching some z's, my man." Rabbit played with the end of Jinx's hair.

"I will as soon as we get under cover."

"Did something happen?" Megan asked.

I patted her leg. "No, and I'd like to keep it that way."

She studied my face, her brow creased as she bit her lower lip.

"What are you thinking?" Jinx asked, pulling my attention away from Megan.

I shared my suspicions with her, concluding, "So, I want to hole up somewhere with no link to any of us. If they're watching the house, I don't want them to know we're leaving."

All sense of Rabbit's earlier playfulness was gone. "This is not good."

"No," I agreed. "It's not, but there's not much we can do about it tonight. For now, Megan and I both need some sleep. Once we meet with Rico, we should have a better idea of what we're dealing with."

Jinx studied Megan as she tapped her fingers on the couch's arm. "If she uses my hoodie, I can cover her from the front door to the car." She turned to me, and her lips curved. "But making them think you're Rabbit is a little more involved."

"But it can be done?" Jinx's ability to weave illusions wasn't just cool as shit—it was also a critical weapon in our team's arsenal. While it worked, for the most part, the success of her illusions tended to depend on the assumptions of the audience. If they expected to see Rabbit and Jinx leaving, then that was what they would see. Of course, if they were tailing us, all bets were off because Jinx had to be in visual range for the illusion to hold.

She raised a brow. "With a few adjustments, yeah." She shifted her attention between me and Rabbit. "You got something like that?" She waved a hand at Rabbit's navy zip-up hoodie.

Thinking of the hoodie sitting on top of my go bag in the foyer, I nodded. "Yeah, it's black, not navy, though."

"That'll work, because no way is Rabbit's jacket going to fit you," Jinx said. Since Rabbit was built along the lines of lean and mean and I had heft to my shoulders, her concerns were valid. She leaned over, snatched Rabbit's battered baseball cap off his head, and threw it at me. "Here."

"Hey!" Rabbit tried to rescue his hat but missed. "Don't be such a mean woman, Jinx," he whined, his southern accent rolling in heavy. "That's my lucky hat."

Unmoved, Jinx just raised a brow. "If I'm going to pass Bishop off as you, I need a little help."

I turned the cap around, my lips twitching at the manically grinning crawfish that decorated it. "Only Rabbit would wear this."

Rabbit flipped me off. "Doncha lose my hat."

Jinx gave a delicate snort as she stood up and shrugged off her hoodie, ignoring Rabbit's theatrics. "Come on, Megan. Let's hit the bathroom."

Megan gave me a wide-eyed look of confusion but shoved the blanket aside and followed Jinx down the hall. I waited until the women disappeared into the bathroom before turning back to Rabbit, who was still watching them. When his attention came back to me, he asked, "How good are the odds they'll hit here tonight?"

"High." I braced my arms on my knees as I lowered my voice. "You and Jinx need to ghost as soon as you can."

Rabbit grunted as he dug a hand into his pocket and pulled

out a set of car keys. "You're going to need these." The keys flew threw the air, and I caught them. "You take care of my pretty girl, yeah?"

"Yeah." I closed my hand around the keys to Rabbit's beloved Dodge Charger. There was no use arguing. We needed wheels to get out of here, and taking my car was out of the question—to pull this whole illusion off, my Jeep had to stay in the driveway. It left me worried for Rabbit and Jinx, who would be stuck in the house like sacrificial lambs. "You got access to other wheels?"

He nodded. "Don't worry about us. We'll be fine. Just get your woman undercover, man. I don't like how hard they've been hounding her."

"Yeah, me either."

Rabbit was quiet for a long moment. "I'm not keen on having my privacy violated." He met my gaze, and there was no missing his determined ruthlessness. "Think it might be time to turn the tables."

After having shared my suspicions, I didn't find his comment unexpected. We needed to switch from defense to offense because defense sucked ass. Poking around might rattle some bones, but if anyone could dig through the electronic shadows without ruffling feathers, it was Rabbit. Still... "Watch your step. Got a feeling we're about to step into some serious shit."

Rabbit's grin was all teeth. "I'm thinking we're already knee-deep and sinking fast, *mon ami*."

Before I could respond, Jinx's voice came from down the hall. "All right, ready to get this show on the road?"

I put Rabbit's hat on and stood up. "Ready when you are."

Turning, I watched the two women come down the hall. Megan wore Jinx's pullover, the hood up and shadowing her face, the ends of her unbraided hair peeking around the edges. When Jinx stopped, Megan kept coming until she stood across from me with the couch between us, her hands buried in the hoodie's front pockets.

She shot Jinx a worried look. "You sure they'll think I'm you?"

Jinx gave her a genuine smile. "Yeah. We might have a couple of inches and few pounds of difference, but as long as you remember to keep your face away from the light, we can totally pull this off."

Megan didn't look convinced. Then again, short of her witnessing Jinx's ability firsthand, skepticism was to be expected. I stepped over Rabbit's legs and headed toward the foyer to get my jacket. I was shrugging into it, listening to Jinx give Megan pointers—"Keep your back to the street, head tilted downward, don't talk, just wave, let Bishop take the outside position"—when Rabbit called my name.

"You got a contact number?" he asked.

Dropping to a crouch, I dug through my go bag and pulled out two burner phones. "Here." I tossed one to Rabbit, who wasted no time powering it up. "Hit 1. That's me."

"Got it." He tucked it into his back pocket. "Check in tomorrow once you touch base with Rico."

I straightened and, following one of Jinx's suggestions, pulled my duffle on like a backpack. "Copy."

Jinx flicked off the main foyer light, leaving us backlit by the living room, before stopping at Rabbit's side. She did a quick top to toe before dipping her chin in a little nod. "Right, time to move."

I went over to Megan, who stood awkwardly off to the side of the front door, her smaller backpack cradled against her stomach, holding herself stiffly. Wrapping my free arm around her waist, I gave her a quick hug. "Hey, relax. Jinx has us covered."

She bit her lip, opened her mouth, then closed it again and just nodded. Her shoulders relaxed fractionally.

"Watch your six, Bishop," Rabbit said softly.

Meeting his dark eyes, I said, "Intend to." I turned to Jinx. "Tell me when."

She took a couple of deep breaths, her gaze focused on Megan and me. The only tell that Jinx was doing anything was the emergence of gold flecks in her brown eyes. They looked like miniature fireflies.

Next to me, Megan sucked in a startled breath, but that was all I caught before my ears filled with the cotton of an abrupt altitude change. By the time they cleared, Jinx's eyes were back to their normal color. She brushed her hands together as if dusting them off. "Done."

Megan looked at me, a frown marring her forehead, then told Jinx, "I don't think it worked."

Jinx laughed. "Do me a favor and close your eyes." Once Megan's lashes drifted down, Jinx continued. "Okay, now, before you open them, I want you to imagine Rabbit is standing next to you and Bishop is next to me." She paused. "Got it?" When Megan nodded, Jinx said, "Good. Open your eyes and look."

Megan looked at me, and her eyes widened. "Holy crap!" She blinked rapidly, frowned, and turned to Rabbit. When her attention went back to Jinx, she said, "It's like some weird optical illusion. If I look straight on, I'd swear Bishop is there," she pointed to Rabbit, then turned to me, "And this is Rabbit. But"—she turned back to Jinx—"standing like this, if I try to look without really looking, I can see bits and pieces of them."

"That's because you know on some level who's who, but if you were just passing by or didn't know for sure, you'd think—"

"That they'd switched places." There was a bit of awe in Megan's voice, and based upon the color rising in Jinx's cheeks, she caught it. Megan gave Jinx an embarrassed smile. "That's really freaking cool."

"Umm, thanks."

"No time to lollygag. Let's get a move on," Rabbit cut in and moved to the door. With his hand on the knob, he shot Megan a wink. "Showtime!"

In a matter of minutes, Megan and I were out the door, down the walk, and at Rabbit's gray Dodge Charger. I popped the trunk and dumped the bag in it as Megan closed the passenger door behind her. My neck itched, a confirmation of my suspicions, but I didn't look around as I went to the driver's side and got behind the wheel.

Once we were behind the safety of tinted windows and backing out the drive, I scanned our surroundings in an effort to pinpoint our watchers. No luck. Looking back through the side window, I caught a disconcerting glimpse of my body turning and ushering what looked like Megan back into the house. *Damn, Jinx is good.*

I concentrated on getting out of the neighborhood while Megan sat, tense and silent, in the passenger seat. As we merged onto the freeway, I reached over and squeezed her knee. "You okay?"

"Yeah." It came out shaky, but her next words were stronger. "Just trying to wrap my head around all of this."

From the corner of my eye, I caught her movement as she lifted her hands to the hoodie, but when she stilled, I said, "Go ahead. I think we're in the clear."

She dropped the hood back and ran her hands through her hair, her tension easing as she resettled in her skin. "What Jinx did was…"

When she stopped, I offered, "Weird?"

"Cool."

I smiled as I switched over to the middle lane. "Yeah, she's damn impressive."

It didn't take long for Megan's curiosity to get the better of her. "I've never heard of an ability like that."

Figuring it was better to keep her distracted by the wonders of Jinx, I decided to elaborate. "You have, but most people pass it off as being good at disguises. The thing is, most of her abilities depend on the willingness of those watching to believe what they're seeing, so she's careful to work with expectations. She's a hell of a mimic too."

"Mimic?"

"Next time you get a chance, ask her to do her impression of Rabbit." I shook my head. "She's hell on wheels when she's doing accents."

Jinx could master more than accents. Given a chance to study a target, she could mimic vocal inflections and mannerisms with an uncanny precision. It might have been part of her ability, but it was also just her.

"It must come in real handy when she's working undercover."

It sounded like Megan's imagination was running a mile a minute, which was better than worrying. She didn't say anything more, and it wasn't long before her curious quiet turned to a pensive quiet.

Since she wasn't talking, I figured I'd better find out what rabbit hole she was wandering down. "What's wrong?"

"Will Jinx and Rabbit be okay?"

Hearing the concern in her voice, I gave what reassurance I could. "They'll be fine. They can handle themselves."

I could feel her watching me, but I kept my eyes on the road. Finally she said, "That's not really an answer."

I risked looking away from the road to meet her gaze. "It's the best I can give you." Turning my attention back to driving, I tried to find something more to give her.

She finally sighed and changed the subject. "Can I ask where we're going?"

Unfortunately, that was the one subject I wanted her to avoid. "You can ask."

Her next question carried an edge. "Are you going to give me an answer?"

"Probably better if I don't." I wasn't going to lie to her. "Megan, look, it's better if you don't know."

"Because if I don't know, then he can't find out, right?"

I winced. Hearing my logic explained aloud didn't make it any better. Nor could I miss the pain in her voice. "Until we can ensure that you can block him, it's better this way."

That explanation didn't seem to help much either, because she turned away and faced her window. A few minutes later, I snuck a glance her way and wished I hadn't. Silver streaks trailed down her cheeks.

The visual landed like a horse's kick to my gut. My hands tightened on the wheel as I tried to concentrate on driving instead of my urge to strike out. The last thing I wanted to do was hurt her, but whoever this sick fuck was, his game left me no choice. I had to keep her safe. One way or the other, I'd make him pay for this, too.

Chapter Thirteen

As grateful as I was that Bishop didn't sugarcoat our current situation, it didn't lessen the sting of hearing, yet again, that I wasn't to be trusted. Closing my eyes, I drifted as Bishop drove us to his secret safety spot. Under the hurt, anger stirred, and I was grateful for it. I was sick and tired of being the weak point.

So stop.

That snarky inner voice sounded remarkably like Keelie, which was no surprise considering that she rarely, if ever, backed down from a fight. If she were here now, witnessing my pity party, she'd be in my face, telling me to put on my big-girl pants and get my shit together. And younger sister or not, she'd be right.

A quote from a favorite childhood story drifted up in my beleaguered brain: *You can't go back and change the beginning, but you can start where you are and change the ending.* Since I agreed with C. S. Lewis, starting now, I'd change the ending to one I wanted.

The truth was, to survive this, I needed to take an active part in my own damn rescue. That meant no more crying *Woe is me* because that got me nowhere and simply added to the weight everyone else was carrying.

If both Bishop and Wolf believed I was the proud new owner of a psychic ability, it had to be true. Although I'd made the choice to reach out for help, I had to be honest with myself and admit that I'd hoped I could turn this over to the colonel and Bishop and walk away, letting them handle the resulting mess.

I could no longer pretend that was an option. Bishop was right—it was time to shift the balance of power in this nerve-wracking game of hide-and-seek. So tomorrow, Ricochet was going to get a star pupil, and if I needed to play the part of the bait, so be it.

Lost in my thoughts, I totally missed Bishop coming to stop, until I felt his hand on my shoulder. "Megan, we're here."

I blinked my eyes open and lifted my head. When the muscles in my neck protested, I bit back a groan. "I'm awake."

I was still waking up when he pulled back and opened his door. The unique scent of salt water, sand, and the nose-wrinkling odor of sea critters drifted inside the car. Following his example, I opened my door, grabbed my backpack, and got out. Fortunately, Jinx's hoodie protected my skin from the chill of the cool night breeze.

Curious as to where we'd ended up, I looked around. We were in a midsize parking lot populated with a mix of family vehicles and the larger masses of homes on wheels for the seasoned travelers. Just behind those, I could make out the darker lines of roofs of what appeared to be small cabins clustered under trees that better fit the Northwest than San Diego's coast. Completing my circle, I saw masts and hulls bobbing on the far side of the lot, while somewhere in the distance, the tide rose and fell against an unseen shore.

The nearby marina seem to be home to more modestly priced boats, not the sleek high-end beauties of the more popular marinas like Embarcadero and Mission Bay. Near the small buildings that probably housed the marina offices was a sign illuminated by two lights perched on top. Before I could read it, the muffled thump of the trunk closing brought my attention back to Bishop.

He slung his duffle bag over a shoulder. "Ready?"

Nodding, I turned toward him, and by my second step, realization struck me through my half-awake fog. I muttered a curse and dropped my gaze to the ground. Bishop hadn't shared where we were going for a reason—the same reason that I needed to not be noticing things that would make this place easy to identify.

The toes of his heavy-soled boots came into view but didn't move. I found my head being directed upward with a finger under my chin.

"What's going on?" he asked.

There weren't many lights out here, but there was enough to see his frown as he studied my face. Adjusting the slipping strap of my backpack, I said, "Nothing. Why?"

His lips thinned, and he said, with a hint of command, "What's with the hangdog routine?"

Understanding dawned. I waved a hand. "Honestly, noth-ing, Bishop." I stepped back, away from him, and did my best to put his mind at ease. "I just remembered why I shouldn't be playing tourist and figured it was safer to keep my mind on something less specific."

The hovering storm of displeasure dissipated, and his face cleared. "Shit. I hadn't thought of that." He offered me a small grin. "Glad to see one of us is thinking clearly."

Heat hit my cheeks at his causal compliment, but I ignored it. Instead, I returned his grin and curled my hand over his upper arm. "Lead on, good sir."

He started walking, and I fell in beside him, my gaze back on the ground. We left the asphalt of the parking lot and moved on to the smoother terrain of cement pathways. Light and shadow played tag as he steered us along.

Needing a distraction, I pondered out loud, "Why is it, when you're trying not to notice something, that's all you can see?"

He chuckled. "It's called the Baader-Meinhof phenomenon."

Not expecting that answer, I shot him a look. "Seriously? That's a thing?"

He looked down at me, humor easing the normally stern lines of his face. "Yep, but it's also known as a frequency illusion. It happens because your brain is excited about the challenge, so now it's on the lookout for exactly what you're trying to not to see."

Shaking my head, I went back to my concentrated study of the ground. "You are just a font of information."

That got an honest-to-God chuckle. "Want more?"

Enjoying the momentary respite, I bumped his shoulder. "Let your brilliance shine forth, oh wise one."

"The name—Baader-Meinhof—didn't come from a researcher."

Happy to follow his lead, I played along. "Okay, I'll bite. Where did it come from?"

"It's actually named after a militant West German terrorist group from the seventies."

"Now you're making it up." I shot him a look, trying to determine if he was screwing with me or not, and managed to trip over a crack in the sidewalk. He caught me before I could do a face-plant and left his arm around my waist. I went back to focusing on the ground.

"Nope, cross my heart." He made an X over his heart that I caught from the corner of my eye. "I think it was sometime in the nineties on some Midwest online chat room that somebody heard Baader-Meinhof referenced twice in, like, a day, so the frequency illusion became the Baader-Meinhof phenomenon." He came to a stop.

I lifted my head enough to note that we were in front of a tidy one-story cabin. I deliberately bypassed the numbers half-hidden by shadows and focused on the dark windows. *That's bland enough, right?* I let go of Bishop's arm so he could move up the two steps to the narrow porch.

The rattle of keys preceded the snick of the lock sliding free. He leaned inside and hit a switch near the door. Yellow light spilled free, leaving me blinking. When my vision cleared of little white spots, he was holding the door open. "Welcome home for now."

I stepped inside to find a clean but dated interior. Despite the fact that most of the furniture had to be close to ten years old, it still managed to give a homey impression. There was even a picture of some marina stretched above the couch—a sure sign of a beach home—but there were no impersonal rental motifs, and comfort trumped style.

The living room, eat-in dinette, and galley kitchen took up the front of the house. A hall disappeared toward the back, where I assumed the bedrooms and bathroom were located. Remembering how small the house looked from the outside, I hoped it led to more than one bedroom but knew I might be reaching.

Keys danced across the laminated counter, making me jump, as Bishop stepped around me. "There's a bedroom back there." He dropped his bag near the two-person table. A rush of images hit me, all revolving around Bishop and a bed, but before they could gain strength and get me in trouble, he added, "It's all yours."

I shrugged off my backpack and dropped it on the seat of the easy chair next to the couch before turning to Bishop. "You take it. I think I'll stay up for a bit."

His gaze drifted over me, and I got the sense he saw more

than I was comfortable with, but he finally shook his head and said, "You need to sleep."

Actually, sleep was the last thing I wanted to do at that moment and not just because of the possible threat lying in wait. After the catnap in the car, my brain was wide-awake. I wanted some alone time. I lifted my chin. "I'm good."

Bishop frowned and rubbed the back of his neck. "Look, Megan, about what I said earlier—"

Nope, we are not going back to that. I cut him off. "Don't!" It came out sharper than I'd intended. Not wanting to spur an unnecessary argument, especially when it was obvious to me that the one who needed sleep was the man trying to protect me, I closed the distance between us until I could pat one of his arms, which was folded over his chest. "Look, Bishop, you're right to be cautious."

When his tense stance didn't soften, I turned to study the couch. Well-worn it might be, but it also invited a person to drop in and stay awhile. Since all I wanted was a spot to curl up in for a bit, it would work. "You take the bed, and I'll take the couch."

"You can't stay up all night."

God save me from overprotective males. "I won't." Turning back to him, I had no doubt he'd keep arguing with me until he was blue in the face, so I admitted, "I need some alone time, okay?"

He didn't look convinced. His gaze drifted over my face, and he relented, albeit reluctantly. "Fine. I'm leaving the door open. You need anything, just call."

Channeling my younger sister, I held my position, folding my arms over my chest and raising a brow in challenge. "Good night, Bishop."

His coffee-dark eyes held mine, and I hid my amusement at his hesitation. Ultimately, necessity beat manners as he stalked to his bag, snatched it up, and headed toward the bedroom. I held my position as he moved into the bedroom. I dropped my attention to the carpet as he walked from the bedroom to the bathroom.

Only when the bathroom door closed with a soft click did I let out a full breath. "All righty, then."

Even though Bishop wasn't happy, I was. For the first time in what felt like forever, I was alone. I hadn't been joking when I told Bishop I craved some alone time. Too much had happened in too short a time, leaving me reeling. I needed time to process it. Staying out on the couch with Bishop down the hall would work. He was close enough to make me feel safe but distant enough for me to try to work through all that had happened.

While Bishop did his thing in the bathroom, I dug through my backpack and pulled out the oversized T-shirt and yoga pants I used for pajamas. I set my clothes on the counter along with toiletries for my nightly routine. Since the rest of the night was all about taking a break from reality, my choices were limited to my Kindle or my sketch pad. My brain was spinning like a hyperactive hamster on a wheel, and bolstered by my recent decisions, I decided to brave my sketch pad. The choice made, I set the pad and pencils on the side table. A quick visit to the kitchen netted me a can of soda and glass of ice. That, too, went on the side table.

"Bathroom's free," Bishop called.

Gathering my clothes and toiletries, I claimed the bathroom. I managed to complete my nightly routine in less than fifteen minutes. On the way out, I shot a glance at the bedroom, but the partially closed door showed only darkness.

Back on the couch, I found a neatly folded blanket topped by a pillow. I checked the front door, making sure it was locked, even though I knew Bishop would have taken care of that already. Safely locked inside, I turned off all the lights but the one by the couch and settled in. I flipped open the sketchbook, and it hit me that the last time I'd drawn was before I was kidnapped. As I bypassed the first few pages filled with random images—a dog and a toddler at the beach, a close-up of an older woman's face, a surfer riding a wave—I hit the more detailed panels of a story I'd been working on before... before my life went off track.

Done in graphite, the images were stark but clearly showed the first steps into a wild adventure. Once upon a time, I'd considered pursuing a career in graphic arts, but life and bills had sent me in another, more responsible direction. Studying my creations, I started rethinking my future. It wasn't like I'd be going back to work for the colonel. If this whole screwed-up situation taught me anything, it was that life was too short not to go after what I wanted.

Caught up in my thoughts, I was soon lost in the stroke of the pencil over paper. There was something therapeutic about watching the lines come together to morph into the images clogging my brain. Fortunately, it wasn't just the twisted nightmares spilling from my hand but a mix of everything, as if I was purging my subconscious.

I had no idea how deep I'd fallen into my work until Bishop's hand wrapped around my ankle. The unexpected touch caused my hand to jerk, marring the shading I was working on. I swallowed a noise of protest when I caught sight of the bare-chested man with sleep-tousled hair crouched in front of me.

Okay, that's an image I can definitely get lost in. I dug my toes into the cushion as I thought about that.

"Megan, what are you doing?"

It took an embarrassing moment for his question to pierce my dazed appreciation. I looked at the sketch pad propped against my thighs. "Sketching." Then I realized why he was asking. The images I'd been drawing filled a couple of pages. On the current one was his face, done in starkly defined lines.

Not keen on sharing, I tried to casually pull the pad closer to my chest.

That turned out to be a huge fail when he caught the top edge of the pad and pulled it free of my grip. I white knuckled my pencil as he studied my drawings. It was hard to read his face. After what seemed like forever, he lifted his eyes from the pad. "You're really good."

Based on his tone of admiration, he meant what he said. Heat hit my cheeks, but I managed to say, "Thanks."

Instead of handing back my sketch pad, Bishop rose and settled into the cushion next to me, using the small table to prop his feet up. He was so close his thigh brushed my hip and his shoulder rubbed against mine. It wouldn't take much to give in and lean against him. And boy, did I want to, but I somehow managed to resist, despite the enticing scent and warmth that seemed to follow him wherever he went. I tried to convince myself the rush of unsettling emotions was nothing more than hormones, but I knew better.

Oblivious to my near lapse in self-control, he continued to study my renditions of his face. "How long have you been doing this?"

His continued focus on the images made me nervous because those sketches carried a depth of emotion I wasn't ready to admit to. Nor was I sure if he would even welcome them. Needing an outlet for my nerves, I fiddled with my pencil. "Since high school. I had an art teacher who was really into manga and comics." I managed a shrug. "I got hooked and found I enjoyed it, so I use it when I need to decompress."

He shot me an unreadable look. "You ever thought of doing it professionally?"

Surprised by how closely he was mirroring my earlier thoughts, I gave him a half grin. "Once upon a time, but making a living from it isn't easy. Besides, I worry that if I had to do it as a job, it might not be as much fun."

His attention went back to the sketches, and his brow furrowed as he brushed a thumb over the paper. "Maybe you should give it a shot," he said thoughtfully. He looked at me and held my gaze. "Talent like this shouldn't be hidden."

There was no missing his sincerity. Feeling it settle deep inside, where I allowed very few people, I swallowed around a sudden lump in my throat. "Maybe, when all this is done, I just might." In an effort to dial back the seriousness, I added, "Especially since I think a career change may be imminent."

Following my lead, Bishop smiled. "The colonel would rehire you in a heartbeat."

I wasn't sure it would be her decision to make. "Maybe she would, but my security clearance is shot at this point. Besides, I'm not sure I'm ready to come back."

When those dark eyes roved over my face, I dropped my gaze and reached for the sketch pad.

His hand tightened, refusing to let me take it away from him. When I looked back up, he was staring at the paper. "Is this how you see me?"

I looked at the sketch I'd been working on when he interrupted me. Hard, grim, and determined, Bishop's face stared back in stark black and white. The expression was burned into my mind because it was the one he'd worn when he found me. It was the same image I'd held onto when I woke in the hospital, scared out of my mind that I was still trapped in hell and reality was just some fragile dream.

Start as you mean to go. With that reminder whispering in my ears, I gave him the unvarnished truth. "It's who I see."

A weighted silence fell, filled with unspoken things and broken only by our breathing. I didn't dare look up. I was too afraid of what I'd find. He had to know that what lay on that pad was more than just my artistic talent. It was Bishop who steered us around the invisible elephant taking up space between us. He flipped through the pages backward until he came to a sketch of the stone cell I'd created to hide from the monster in my mind. He stopped. "And this?"

My eyes were locked on the detailed sketch, and my stomach did a slow pitch and roll. Walls stretched fantastically high, disappearing into the unseen horizon, while up out of reach was a small window providing the barest glimpse of an approaching storm. Swallowing hard, I answered, "Where I hid."

He tipped my chin up, holding my gaze. His jaw tensed. "When I joined Special Ops, there was an operator who managed to bank almost a decade on the teams. We were at a dive bar in some hot spot after a mission went sideways—intel was shitty, and we were outgunned and outnumbered." His face clouded. "We lost a couple of us, and I was second-guessing our actions until he said something I've never forgotten."

I waited while his thumb brushed over my chin.

"He said, 'You can't win every battle, son. When the odds are against you, your best option is to hunker down and survive to fight another day.'" His thumb stopped, and the shadows lifted from his face. "You did what you needed to do to survive. There is no shame in that."

He let me go, and while I was feeling his words smooth the ragged edges of my pride, he turned to the next page and stilled, a frown creasing his forehead. "What?"

I turned to look at the page. When I saw the hint of a face staring back, my head swam, and I reached to snatch the sketch pad from Bishop. Wrapping one arm around my shoulders and pulling me to his side, he held the pad out of my reach. "This is him, isn't it?"

The vague profile was wreathed in shadows, which added a palpable menace to it, taunting me. My hand curled into a fist against Bishop's chest as fear squeezed my voice into nothing, leaving my throat aching. I gave a barely perceptible nod.

He murmured, "You can almost see him."

I tried to suck in a breath without being obvious about it. The tight band around my throat eased, and I was able to get out, "Not enough."

He set the pad down on his other side and turned to me, his arm tightening around my shoulders. When I finally lifted my eyes to his, he promised, "We'll get him."

Stifling an automatic denial, I tucked my doubts away because they served no purpose. Instead, I dropped my head to his shoulder. He didn't say anything more, and I sank into the quiet, enjoying the comforting feel of his hand stroking my spine.

My lids drifted closed, and my fist relaxed until the beat of his heart pulsed against my palm. Every breath was filled with the clean spice scent I associated only with him. The combination of heat and strength under my hand was hard to resist, and soon, I was absentmindedly petting him. I wasn't sure how long I wallowed in being close to him, but the tension our discussion had generated slipped away, leaving me to enjoy the sense of safety I found in his arms.

In no rush to lose that, I burrowed into him, rubbing my face against his shoulder, brushing my nose against the base of his throat. As close as I was, I couldn't miss the hitch in his breath or the way his hand stalled mid-stroke. The chest under me flexed, and I felt him drop his head on top of mine, his groan nearly silent. My pulse slowed, going molten as a creeping tide of hunger, need, and want slipped in, changing that safety into something much more tempting and definitely more dangerous.

Chapter Fourteen

BISHOP

I ran my hand through Megan's silken strands, my attention caught on the sketch of my face staring back from her sketch pad on the coffee table as her delicate fingers trailed down my chest, stirring the hungry beast lurking outside my control.

Is this how you see me?

It's who I see.

There was something in her voice that made my chest ache, but instead of having the balls to follow it through, I'd changed the subject. I was probably being stupid, but I wasn't sure I wanted to brave those treacherously deep waters yet. I was still struggling to stay above the damn waves. In order to keep her safe, I needed to keep my mind clear, but it was so fucking tempting to just let go and sink with her, into her.

Closing my eyes, I pressed my lips to the top of her head, taking in the flowery fragrance of her hair. Keeping my eyes closed, I wallowed in this moment out of time, when she was safe and here with me. Those whispery strokes slowed, becoming longer, dipping lower as she rubbed her face along my chest. Fire licked over nerve endings, and I swore I felt her tongue take a quick taste, but it was so fast, so light that I couldn't be sure. Unable to resist, I opened my eyes to find Megan's flushed face raised to mine, and I knew I was fighting a losing battle.

My arm tightened, pressing all those soft curves against me. I stroked her hair, moving downward until I could capture her chin, my thumb rasping over her damp lips. Holding her darkening blue gaze, I gave in and took those lips that had infiltrated my dreams. As I kissed that sweet mouth, drowning in the honeyed heat and spice, I couldn't hold on to the reasons for not doing this—for not taking what she offered and feeding the hunger clawing through me.

As she'd done earlier in the parking lot outside her apartment, she met my hunger with hers, no hesitation in those sexy little caresses as her tongue tangled with mine. The kiss went supernova in seconds as the heat of her palms ran down my chest, leaving aching trails of need in their wake. I drank down her feminine taste, gorging on her as she twisted and her hands slid up my shoulders until her nails could curl into my neck, holding me close as she all but crawled on top of me, almost as if she was worried I'd pull away. *Fuck that.* I was right where I wanted to be, diving into the fire and heat that wrapped around us.

As I kept her mouth captive, my hands went to her hips, helping her find her position until the heated center of her settled over my aching dick. I let her lips go to suck in much-needed air. "Fuck," I groaned.

She pulled back. Not about to let her escape, I ran my hand up her spine, over the thin cotton of her shirt and sank my fingers into her hair. With a gentle tug, I took advantage when she dropped her head back, exposing the long elegant lines of her neck. Using my lips and tongue, I kissed my way down to the hollow of her throat. The arc of her spine pressed the luscious unbound curves of her breasts against me as the heated scent of a summer storm wrapped around me. The smell and feel of her had my dick jerking with anticipation.

"Bishop." My name came out on a husky moan as her hips began to ride me.

Holy shit. If I didn't regain some control, I was going to come before I could get her where I wanted her—namely, under me, naked, wet, and wanting. Tightening my hand on her hip to still her sexy ride, I shifted my hold, dropped my feet, and lifted her enough to take her to her back on the couch. Something fell to the floor, but caught in the carnal storm, I couldn't give a fuck. Short of a damn house fire, I wasn't leaving the delectable feast in front of me.

The change in position pushed her shirt up, baring the soft skin of her stomach. Not about to miss out, I smoothed my hand over all that silky warmth, inching the material higher until my fingers could brush the curves hidden beneath. I wasn't the only one intent on touching. Her hands drifted down my chest, making me eternally grateful I'd decided against a shirt. Those clever, devious fingers slipped low until they could trace along the elastic edge of my sweats.

Nipping her lower lip in punishment, I whispered against her mouth, "You're playing with fire."

Those fingers continued to taunt even as she lay under me, her hair an alluring tangle, her eyes dark with hunger, and a flush riding under her skin as her lips, reddened from our kiss, curved into a purely female smile of wickedness. "I know." It was the only warning I got before she hooked a leg around my hip, pulling me closer.

"Megan!" I hissed, tormented. God, she was breathtaking. Unable to resist, I ground my aching length against her heated center. Her moan echoed mine as I took her mouth in another carnal dance. Our clothes didn't do anything but irritate me. Determined to change that, I stripped off her shirt in a quick pull, leaving her bare from the waist up. There was no way to stop my groan at what met my eyes.

Her luscious curves were topped by rigid berry-red nipples that made my mouth water and my hands itch. It was like revealing a feast to a starving man. Unable to resist assuaging my hunger, I captured one beautiful breast and traced her curves with fingers and tongue until she writhed under me, piling sensation on top of sensation. Only when I'd managed to map every delectable inch and she was panting my name in a soft pleading tone did I go for dessert, drawing her breast deep into my mouth as I continued to stroke and pet the other.

She called my name in a husky wail, and her spine arched as she offered me more. Not one to turn down a good thing, I took it. As her hands delved into my hair, her nails scraping against my scalp, I switched to her other side. I didn't want any part of her feeling neglected. The leg at my hip tightened as she rolled her hips against mine. The feel of her, hot and damp, seared through me like lightening, and I lifted my head, eyes closing, as I could do nothing but follow her.

Holy hell. I needed to slow us down before we spontaneously combusted. Fighting for control, I gritted my teeth and forced my hand to brace against the sofa cushions next to her. As I lifted my chest, my hips pushed tighter against hers, which made my dick twitch like a damn anxious puppy. *Pull your shit together, man!* I didn't want to take her in a mindless lust-filled rut—I wanted to take my time. I wanted to lose myself in her taste, in her touch, in the feel of her until she knew who held her, who fucked her, who needed her. I dropped my forehead against hers, keeping my eyes closed as I tried to get a grip.

"Hey." Her voice was soft as she cupped my face in her palms.

"Hey." I lifted my eyes to find myself caught in a sea of worry and need.

Those blue eyes held mine even as a small frown lined her brow. "What's wrong?"

I rubbed my jaw over her palm, relishing the feeling of her skin. "Nothing." *Except I want to fuck you so bad you won't consider walking away. Nope, not saying that out loud.*

She dragged her hand along my jaw then traced my lips with a finger. "Do you want me?"

The doubt in her voice cut me to the quick, and I winced. "God, yes." A small frown marred her brow, and the finger at my lips paused. Unable to fight the temptation, I drew it into my mouth in a blatant suggestion. She gave a small gasp and tugged it free, but in case she still hadn't understood, I nipped her chin and growled, "Hell yeah, I want you."

She swallowed hard, but her eyes drifted over my face. "Then why'd you stop?"

A world of vulnerability was held in her question, and my need to protect rose fast and strong. "I don't want to hurt you."

"Hurt me?" Her lips twitched. "If you think you were hurting me, I'm not doing something right."

Her playful tease had me smiling. I shifted to the side, trapping her between me and the back of the couch. "Oh, you were doing everything right. Too damn right, woman."

Her hands braced on my shoulders as she moved until she was facing me, her back against the couch, our legs tangled. "You want this, right?" She slid her hands down from my shoulders, and her fingers curled into my chest.

I tucked a strand of hair behind her ear and drew my finger down her jaw until I could hook it under her chin. Angling her face upward, I dipped my head and took her mouth in a hungry kiss. Only when breathing became necessary did I stop. Those long lashes fluttered, and a flush of hunger and lust colored her face. "I want this, but..."

She bit her lower lip as she cupped my face, waiting until my gaze met hers. "But?" When I didn't answer, she dove in with a courage that left me weak. "I don't understand how you think you're going to hurt me. I know what I'm doing, Bishop. I'm a big girl. I want you. You want me. That means there are two consenting adults here." She let me go, and her fists rested against my chest.

Unable to stop touching her, I stroked her shoulder, her arm, and the curve of her hip. "And when this is over?" I inwardly cursed the fact I couldn't play the typical male-female games and pretend I wanted nothing more than a casual relationship. Megan was too important to me, too necessary. That was a first for me. I'd spent my life flirting but refusing to let anything more than a good time develop. But this woman, with her quiet courage and loyalty, had managed to wiggle her way into my heart. I wanted to hold her close, protect her from what lay ahead of us, but that wasn't in the cards. As much as I wanted to promise her a happily ever after, I couldn't.

As if reading my thoughts, she gave a smile of sad resignation. "I'm not looking for forever here."

But what if I am? That resentful thought left me off balance and wondering when the hell I'd managed to lose my mind. Even worse, why did it piss me off to hear her say she wasn't looking for a long-term relationship? Did she have no sense of her worth? She was exactly the type of woman a man would be blessed to have standing at his side. She wouldn't bail when shit got hard—her loyalty was hard-wired to those she loved. *And I want to be one of those.* I tried to ignore that childish thought, and frustration made me speak sharply. "You deserve it."

Her gaze dropped from mine as her hands uncurled and pressed against my chest. "No, I don't, because we both know tomorrow it could all change."

Reading the guilt in her voice, I snapped, "You won't betray us."

An edge of humor lightened her face. "Why? Because you said so?"

Battling the urge to shake her until she stopped spouting shit, I hooked an arm around her waist and pulled her close until mere inches separated us. "No, because that's not who you are."

She stiffened, her gaze burning into mine. "And who am I?"

"Mine." It was an asshole thing to say, but the truth of it reverberated through me with a startling clarity. There was no way I could walk away from this woman, no matter what happened.

Her expression darkened, and her tongue came out to swipe over her lips, disbelief clear in the azure depths of her eyes. "Maybe for tonight."

I let the topic go, knowing it was an argument for another time. For the moment, there were other things I wanted to talk about. "Are you offering?"

She studied me before finally giving me a slow nod. "I want to do something I know comes from me, not what someone wants me to do. I want you."

"Works for me." I decided to move us to another room, where I could make the most of what she offered and convince her to take a chance on whatever this was between us.

I got up and stood in front of the couch, holding out a hand. She shifted until she was sitting in front of me, looked up through those long lashes, and took my hand. My fingers curled around hers as my mind took in our respective positions and offered some highly erotic images of what we could do. *Hmm, maybe later.* My dick twitched, and her gaze dropped to it and darkened. If she kept looking at me like that… "Bedroom," I growled, tugging her to her feet.

Not trying to hide her partial nudity, she led the way to the bedroom as I kept my hands on her hips. There was something about following that sexy strut that made walking hard. We stepped into the bedroom, where moonlight seeped through the blinds and joined the faint light from the front room, leaving the bed wreathed in shadows. She stopped at the foot, her back to me. Even in the murky light, I could make out the line of her spine and shoulders. Her yoga pants clung to the curve of her hips. I came up behind her, closing in until the brush of her warm satin skin against mine was a seduction in itself. This close, her ass cradled my dick as I ran my hands down her arms and tangled our fingers together. I laid a line of soft open-mouthed kisses along her shoulder until her head fell to the side, and she gave a soft moan. Not about to miss out, I kissed my way up her neck as I let go of her hands and caressed her stomach until I could capture the warm weight of her breasts in my palms. She shackled my wrists, not to pull them away but to hold on as I used my thumbs to stroke and tease.

"Oh God, Bishop." She melted into me as she turned and met my mouth with hers.

"Megan." All I could manage was her name, as I wanted nothing more than to eat her alive. Leaving the wonderland of her breasts, I sank my hand into her hair, holding her where I wanted as I kissed her. Slowly, with destructive accuracy, I ran a hand down her stomach, dipping under the edge of her pants. Lace and warmth met my fingers. I traced patterns over the material, circling closer to the damp heat that waited.

The hands at my wrist tightened but held it in place as she turned to face me. Her move forced my fingers lower until slick fire coated them in silky wetness. My knees buckled, but I managed to stay standing as her husky moan joined my groan. The feel of Megan, hot and damp, blew apart the last of my control. Lust, desire, want, and need collapsed into an inferno, wiping all but instinct away.

In a sensual blur, her hands and mine clashed as we got rid

of our clothes and tumbled into the waiting bed. Mouths, tongues, nips, moans, and groans... the need to touch, taste, devour, take, and give drove me. Her cries spurred me higher as she arched and writhed under my hands and mouth, like a beautiful flame. I wasn't alone in my hunger—her mouth was a wicked weapon of destruction as her hands caressed and reshaped me until I was wholly hers. Those fingers wrapped around my dick and stroked with a sexy ownership that stole my breath as her thumb spread my wetness along my sensitive tip. I thrust into her hold with more instinct than finesse. Only when one more stroke threatened to set me off did I capture her hands, drawing them above her head and locking them in place. "No touching."

She pouted, and when she opened her mouth to argue, I gave her a hard kiss. Without let her hands go, I raised my head and stared into her dazed eyes. "Keep them there."

She stared back with wild hunger, but she followed my directions, so I rewarded her by kissing my way down her chest and not letting her pretty breasts distract me as I moved down her stomach, where the musky scent of her filled my mind and left me ravenous. Drawing her legs open, I didn't go gently but covered her, using my tongue with carnal precision, feasting until her body danced under my mouth as her cries filled the room. Only when her muscles began to stiffen, heralding an ending I didn't want, did I lift my head.

Frantic and lost in our shared passion, she clutched at my hair, trying to hold me in place. "Don't stop, Bishop."

I pressed a kiss against the inside of her thigh before resting my chin above where that honeyed garden waited. "You taste like fucking paradise." I stared up her body to find her watching me, her lips parted, face flushed, eyes glittering as those fingers pricked my scalp. I crawled up her body, sliding my skin over hers as her hands brought me closer and her legs rose to wrap around my hips. I braced myself above her, dragging my dick against the hot, wet center of her. The feel of her against me held me in a momentary vise. As much as I wanted to sink into her, skin to skin, the need to keep her safe intruded. With a mild curse, I shifted and managed to nab my wallet from the nightstand. My fingers fumbled as I freed the two condoms tucked inside. I dropped the wallet and used my teeth to open the package.

Before I knew it, she was there, taking the package from me as she licked her lips. Those clever, wicked hands rolled the condom over my aching length as she nibbled on my chin. Her hands stroked once, twice. "Do I get a turn?"

The image of her on her knees, those red lips wrapped around my dick, just about finished what her clever hands and spicy taste had started. I dipped my head until my lips barely brushed hers. "Next time."

"Promise?" she asked on the softest breath.

"Fuck yeah," I groaned as I took her mouth and sank into paradise.

Chapter Fifteen

I was in the colonel's office, my arms filled with files, when the top one jumped out of my grasp and tumbled across the floor. I set the pile down on the colonel's desk and crouched to pick up the escapee. As I held out my arm, it scooted just out of reach until I was engaged in an awkward game of tag. The fact that I found nothing odd about an inanimate object doing something distinctly animate should have been my first clue about what was happening, but I was so focused on capturing that elusive file that I didn't even give it a second thought. Stupid me.

When the file did another hop, I lunged forward and ended up on all fours. Slapping my palm on it, I trapped it against the cool linoleum. "Gotcha, you stubborn little—"

Voices drifted down the hall. Scrambling to my feet, I tucked the runaway file on top of the others I was holding. A quick glance down revealed blurry lettering, making it hard to read. Okay, maybe I was tired. I rubbed my eyes with a knuckle and tried again, and this time, a familiar name caught my eye—Jacob Archer. My heart skipped a beat as recognition hit. Jacob Archer was Bishop's legal name.

The thought acted like a switch, and the rest of the file names snapped into sharp focus, searing my vision. As I scanned them, dread built because each name belonged to one of Delacourt's operators, including Devon Rouser, my brother. *What the hell?* Panic scrambled at my brain as I tried to figure out why the information was stored like this—on paper, unsecured—when policy required secured access.

The voices in the hall got closer, triggering an anxiety I didn't bother to fight. Instead, heeding instinct, I gathered the folders and frantically searched for somewhere to stash them. No one could see these, no one. I needed to hide these names before anyone saw them, otherwise... my thoughts refused to cross that dark line. I didn't want to tempt fate. Moving behind the desk, I tried the drawers. Locked.

Dammit. Scanning the rest of the office, my pulse raced as the voices got progressively closer, riding the tide of foreboding, making my hands shake. Other than the desk, there was a filing cabinet, but I dismissed it. *Too obvious.* The bookshelf under the window held a mishmash of books and binders, offering a quick-and-dirty solution. I could hide the files in plain sight. I rushed over and grabbed one of the thickest binders, taking note of the label designating it as a collection of archived order forms. *Good enough.* I tucked the files inside the binder and shoved it back in place. I managed to get back to the colonel's desk and sat there, pen poised over a sticky note. When the door opened, my heart was pounding so hard I worried I would pass out.

Trying for casual, I glanced up. My stomach dropped, and my vision narrowed on the face wreathed in unsettling shadows. The oddity of a shadowy figure in a well-lit room barely made a dent because I was more focused on his speech. He was in midsentence: "... don't think it's necessary."

Something in that voice held me in an icy grip.

"That's not your decision." The colonel swept through the

door, totally oblivious of the threat standing at her side. Catching sight of me, she pulled up short. "Megan, what are you doing here?"

Somehow, I tore my eyes away from the shadowed man and met the colonel's gaze. Offering a smile I hoped looked more real than it felt, I managed a passably steady, "Just leaving you a note about my leave request. Lydia in HR mentioned she couldn't find your previous approval."

The colonel was not the biggest fan of duplicating paperwork, so I wasn't surprised by the annoyed frown marring her brow. "I'll resend them and copy you."

"Thank you." I set the pen down and moved out from behind her desk. To make sure I hid my unsteady hands, I brushed them down my hips. "I'll make sure I've got everything tied up before I leave tonight."

She gave me a distracted smile. "You enjoy that vacation."

"Yes, ma'am." With no option left but to move forward, I braced and approached the man standing near the door. With difficulty, I managed to step around him without flinching. It was hard not to shiver at the heavy sense of menace clinging to him, especially when it seemed to reach out with greedy fingers. Hell, I barely breathed, trying to avoid it. I was almost free when he caught my wrist in a merciless grip that ground my bones against each other. Swallowing the impulse to make a pained sound, I failed to hide my wince.

He chuckled as he leaned in, and the colonel, her office, and everything else disappeared until only the shifting shadows of his face were left. "I see you, Megan."

That hated familiar voice echoed through my skull, tearing through my flimsy composure and turning my blood to ice as my pulse skittered. Soul-deep fear left a metallic taste in my mouth, and the overwhelming need to escape triggered years of self-defense training. Ignoring the pain of his hold, I twisted my wrist, angling for the break point to pull free. When it didn't work, I gritted my teeth to hold back a scream of frustration and fear.

"You're not going anywhere until I get what I want."

I kept my mouth shut, not bothering to argue, because my previous horrific experience taught me it was useless.

"Where are they?"

Even as my brain screamed at me to fight, to get away, I was frozen in place, shaking my head. Ignoring the fire of pain streaking up my arm, I pulled against his grip, my breath coming out in panicked gasps.

He dragged me relentlessly closer until those nightmarish shadows enclosed me in an icy shroud. "Give me the names."

The horrifying sensation of fiery fingers clawing through my brain, trying to tear through my thoughts left me with the urge to scream, but under my paralyzing fear, a spark of fury found fuel. "No." The word came out as a whisper, but the next one was stronger and fiercer as I tried to shove away the fingers on my wrist and in my brain. "No!"

Those dizzying shadows obscuring his face stilled, and for a moment, I could almost see him. Then the dark wings of menace swept in, hiding all but the malevolence burning in his eyes. "Give me the names, or your brother comes home under a flag."

The threat aimed at Dev managed to do what the ones aimed at me had failed to accomplish. Fury roared through me, sweeping the fear under, until only the need to keep my family safe remained. "Fuck you!"

Instead of trying to escape, I stepped in close, forcing his arm to twist out. I wasted no time sinking a fist into his kidney just the way Dev had taught me. I didn't hold back but channeled all my riotous emotions into the punch. When the shackle on my wrist disappeared, I struck up with the heel of my palm, aiming for his nose. He jerked his head to the side, and I missed the mark but managed to nail him just above his eye. He bellowed and stumbled back.

I broke free and ran, but not down the familiar office hall. Instead, I stumbled through a cluttered alley caught between two looming buildings. There was something familiar about it, but as frantic as I was, I didn't stop to figure it out. Wind whipped down through the narrow opening, carrying the crisp scent of an approaching storm. The rumble of thunder overhead drowned out any sounds of pursuit. Since I had no intention of doing the too-stupid-to-live heroine thing and looking back, I focused on my end goal—getting the hell out of there.

It didn't take me long to realize that no matter how hard I ran, the end of the damn alley stayed out of reach. A frustrated scream ripped free, and the looming storm broke, dumping torrential sheets of rain. Blinded by rain, I tripped and landed hard. The skin on my knees and palms tore.

"God dammit, no!" I sobbed. I dropped my head and, ignoring the pain in my hands, pressed against the rough ground, determined to get back up. I didn't get far. Hard hands grabbed my arms and yanked me to my feet. From somewhere in the distance, I heard my name, but the howling winds tore it away.

Fear, fury, and panic reduced me to nothing but blind instinct. I struck out, using every dirty move I knew, my entire being focused on getting the hell away. Lost in that terrifying haze, it took a few seconds before I recognized Bishop's rough voice calling my name. "Megan! Megan, stop."

As much as I wanted to believe it was him, the monster had tricked me before, using the voices of the ones I loved. I wasn't going to fall for it again. Unwilling to stare into that monstrous face, I kept my eyes closed and increased my struggles. From above me came a curse, and then something heavy covered me and caught my face in a smothering hold. I tried to scream, but no sound emerged.

The startling taste of Bishop—spice and heat—filled my mouth, chasing away the metallic tang of fear. The sensation of his lips against mine felt real, too real. Then came the sharp, punishing nip, and I forced my body to still even as small involuntary jerks continued. That enticing heat retreated, and my breath came out in hard gasps.

"Open your eyes, Megan."

I forced myself to comply and found myself staring into Bishop's eyes. Concern darkened his eyes as he held my gaze, giving me something to hold on to as the world reshaped around me. There was no alley, no rain, no storm, just him braced above me, pressing me into the soft mattress under my back. He was so close, with the heavy beat of his heart against my chest and his breath whispering over my mouth. My tongue swept out nervously and caught a lingering trace of his taste.

"Bishop?"

Relief swept over his face, easing the concern. The shackle on my wrist disappeared as he cupped my face, the heat of his hand sinking into my skin. "Are you awake now?"

My pulse still raced, and the muscles in my legs felt like I'd run a marathon or tried to outrun a monster. Using the sensation of his weight and touch to fight back the panic, I swallowed and nodded, only to stop with a wince at the soreness of my throat. "Yeah, I'm awake."

He let me go and dropped his forehead to the side of mine, resting it in the pillow. Strands of his hair fell over my chin. "Holy hell, woman." The words were muffled. "What the hell was that?"

Now that my arms were free, I wrapped them around his broad shoulders and hung on. "Nightmare." I could feel the hot press of tears as tremors started up. Burying my face against his neck, I concentrated on taking his scent deep into my lungs as I reminded myself I was safe.

His arm wrapped around me, holding me close as he turned and rubbed his chin over the top of my bent head. "No shit."

His disgruntled tone made me smile, which was not my normal reaction after a nightmare. "I did warn you." My words came out choked.

He grunted and shifted his weight, taking me with him. I ended up like clinging ivy, half on his chest and curled tight into his side. Only then did it hit me that we were both naked. A different kind of tremor erupted. Fortunately, he ignored it, keeping one arm locked around my waist while the other gently stroked my hair. "Tell me about it?"

Even though he posed it as a question, he sounded insistent. Under his touch, I calmed down a bit, but it took a few minutes before I could talk without my voice shaking. "I was in the office, chasing a runaway file," I started, but then he moved his leg, which meant the leg I had curled around it moved up higher on his thigh. Heated muscle settled against me in a not-so-subtle reminder of what we'd been doing prior to falling asleep. My breath stalled. With nothing between us but skin, I nearly groaned. *Holy hell!* I forgot what I was saying as goose bumps broke over my skin.

"A runaway file?"

I lifted my head to find him watching me with a mix of humor and male awareness. *Dammit.* He knew what he was doing to me. Without thinking it through, I narrowed my eyes and nipped his chest in reprimand.

"Hey!" The hand in my hair gripped the strands until he held my head still. "What was that for?"

He knew damn well what that was for. Arching a brow, I set my chin on his chest just below the small red mark I'd left. "Are you going to let me finish?"

"I'd be happy to let you finish."

Not missing the double entendre, there was no way to stop the heat rising under my cheeks.

He let go of my hair and brushed a finger along my cheekbone. "You were chasing a file."

I nodded and turned to rest my cheek against his chest. "In the colonel's office. There was a stack of them, and I don't have a clue why I had them. Once I got the one on the floor, I realized they were files on each of the team members. The one I caught was yours."

The hand brushing along my spine, stilled. "Mine?"

Glad that I didn't have to look at him, I drew an abstract pattern over his skin under my hand. "Yours. It had your name on it—Jacob Archer."

"What else was in the files?"

"I don't know, and I didn't get a chance to find out because there were voices coming down the hall. One of them was the colonel's, and the other…" My heart began to race as the fear crept back.

"The other?" he prompted.

Memories and nightmares collided while I tried to remember that last day before I'd left the office. I'd been trying to get everything tied up, including the resubmission of my hours. That aligned with the damn dream, but that voice with the colonel… there was something familiar about it, but the knowledge hovered just out of reach, and as I reached for it, it slithered away.

The arm at my waist tightened. "Who was the other voice, Megan?"

I stared unseeing into the night-shrouded room. "Him." I spoke barely above a whisper as if saying it any louder would invite him into the bedroom. I tried to pull away, but Bishop's hold locked me in place.

"You recognized him?" he pushed.

I managed a nod. "He's the same one."

Tension swept through Bishop, his body under me hardening. "The same one as the one in your dreams?"

"Nightmares," I snapped, glaring at him. "They're nightmares."

"Okay, nightmares, then."

"Yeah, the same one." I tried to bring that niggling sense of familiarity into focus.

"What?"

At the growled question, I met Bishop's gaze. "I know that voice."

"Well, if we're right about your dreams being invaded, that would make sense."

I was shaking my head before he finished. "No, I mean I heard it before I was kidnapped."

His gaze sharpened. "You're sure?"

My sense of certainty grew. "Yeah, I'm sure."

"Where?"

Where? I tried to navigate the jumbled mess of broken memories. "The office. He's been to the office a couple of times." I kept digging until pain sliced behind my eyes, making me wince.

Not missing my reaction, Bishop gentled. "Shh. Okay, let's go back to the dream. You were in the colonel's office, they were coming in, and you had the team's files…"

"I didn't want to be caught with them, so I hid them."

"You were trying to protect the identities of the teams," he guessed.

I nodded, ignoring the pounding in my temples. "Something warned me that if he came in and found me holding them, things would not end well."

"Makes sense." His hand drifted along my spine. Watching his face, I could practically see his mind working. His gaze dropped to mine. "After you hid them, then what?"

"The colonel came in first, and he was right behind her, but

I couldn't see his face. It was covered in shadows." I rubbed my temple and looked away. "It was freaky."

Bishop's hand shifted from my spine to the back of my neck. I dropped my forehead to his chest as he gently kneaded the tight muscles. At his soft, "Hmm," I looked up and caught a flash of recognition in his eyes. "What?"

He studied me with a grim intensity. I knew that look—it meant he was trying to decide if he wanted to tell me something. I held his gaze, silently waiting him out.

Finally he sighed. "Something similar happened to another team member a few months back."

"And?"

He grimaced. "And it adds weight to our suspicions about a telepath being involved."

Well, shit. Doesn't that just figure.

He didn't let me dwell on it. "It's not new news, babe, so keep going."

No, it wasn't new news, but it still made my stomach clench. Anxious to get this over with, I summarized, "He tried to stop me—told me he could see me and that I wasn't going anywhere until he got what he wanted. I told him no and tried to get away. I was running through an alley in a storm when you woke me."

"That's it?" Bishop pressed. "He didn't threaten you or hurt you or change the dream in some way?"

As if it had been waiting for that question, the hated voice echoed in my mind. *Give me the names, or your brother comes home under a flag.* I stiffened in Bishop's arms. *Oh God, how could I have forgotten?* I pushed at Bishop's chest, trying to get out of his hold as renewed panic swept through me. "Dev. He threatened Dev. Oh God. I need to get ahold of my brother!"

Bishop managed to roll me under him, ignoring my attempts to get free. "Stop, Megan. Take a breath."

Hard as it was, I managed to lock my panic down, stilling myself as my breath came in heavy spurts.

"You good?" Bishop didn't shift off of me until he got my nod. Only then did he ease back, his gaze holding mine. "Okay, what did he say about Dev?"

"He said he'd send him home under a flag." I repeated the threat verbatim because the word choice was telling. When Bishop's face darkened, I knew he understood. Desperation had me digging my nails into his shoulder. "Please, Bishop. I need to get ahold of Dev. I can't lose my brother!"

Chapter Sixteen

BISHOP

As much as I wanted to promise Megan her brother was safe, it wasn't the smart choice. Instead, I gave her what comfort I could. "He's on assignment. Getting to him won't be easy." I hid my wince at telling her a half-truth. If the bastard hunting Megan could access secured information, there was a slim chance Dev's current assignment could be jeopardized if Megan contacted him. "I'll have Rabbit reach out and get a heads-up to Dev," I added, although how much help that would be was up for debate. If orders came down forcing Dev or his team into a compromised situation, it wasn't as if Dev could refuse. Not without losing his career.

Her gaze searched mine as she bit her lower lip. "Wouldn't it be faster to have the colonel reach out?"

Tucking her hair back behind her ear, I shook my head. "In this situation, no."

"Because whoever he is, he knows the colonel." She said it as if the concept had just occurred to her.

I realized then that I hadn't shared my suspicions on just how close the threat could be. But at least she was putting the pieces together. "Yeah, so it's better to let Rabbit work his magic than accidentally give ourselves away." *Safer too.*

Her fingers tightened on my shoulder then relaxed. "Now? Can you call Rabbit now?"

Panic hovered in her dark eyes, adding fine lines around her mouth. Reminding her that it was barely four in the morning wasn't going to work. My hands settled on her hips. "Yeah, I'll call him now."

She looked relieved and grateful. I rolled her under me and dropped my head to take her mouth in a gentle kiss. I didn't rush it but took my time, indulging, until the tension-filled curves softened under me. Only then did I leave her and the bed.

I grabbed my phone from the nightstand. A glance at the screen revealed three missed calls—all from Rabbit's burner number—in the last twenty minutes. How the hell had I missed those? On the bed, Megan shifted to her side and propped her head on one hand as she watched me. The sheet settled at her waist, leaving her luscious curves bare except for the tangle of dark hair. The sight sucker punched me. *Oh yeah, that's why I wasn't paying attention to my phone.* Turning away from temptation, I flicked a thumb over the touchscreen, noting that at some point, I must have silenced the damn phone. *Fuck.*

I hit the number then snagged my sweats, pulled them on, and moved out of the bedroom and into the hall. It rang once before Jinx's voice came on, edged with urgency. "They hit us as we left the house, but we're good."

Biting back my anger and frustration, I stuck with the immediate concerns. "What the hell happened?"

Rabbit snapped something I couldn't make out, but Jinx ignored him. "We were heading out, but someone forgot that your neighbors were in the midst of redoing their damn yard, and we got bogged down in all the dirt and construction. So while we were trying to figure out how to get out of there, half of the four-man team tailing us caught us bailing, and we were forced to engage. We disabled them and barely managed to ghost out on the other two. We're in the clear for now, but we need to go to ground."

Son of a... Reading between what Jinx wouldn't say on the open line, I understood that, cornered in the neighbor's torn-up yard, Rabbit and Jinx had been forced to engage in a fire-fight. That meant the police had to be crawling all over my neighborhood—bad news for whoever was watching the house, and worse for Rabbit and Jinx. They needed some place to lie low.

I gave Jinx the address as I hit the front room. There was no way in hell I'd let those two blow in the wind with shadows on their asses. "Make sure you don't bring visitors along."

"Copy." Jinx hung up, leaving me with nothing but a dial tone.

"Bishop? What's wrong?"

I turned to find Megan standing at the edge of the hall, dressed in nothing but my T-shirt. Overly large for her, the shirt slipped off of one shoulder, leaving it bare except for the curling ends of her tousled hair.

Unable to resist, I went back to her, wrapped an arm around her waist, and pulled her close. "Rabbit and Jinx are on their way."

Her hands flattened against my chest, but other than pulling back to see my face, she stayed put. "What happened?"

"They tripped over the team on the house." Her eyes widened, and her mouth opened, but before she could ask, I added, "They're okay."

"Good. That's good." She studied my face, the shock disappearing under that damn ugly fear. "Are we still safe here?"

"So long as they manage to shake their shadows, we'll be fine."

"They followed us to your home—"

"Or they have access to each of the team's residences, which means they either hit the most logical one first, or someone dipped into deep pockets to post eyes on each resident." Either way, it didn't bode well. As much as I enjoyed having her in my arms, there were more urgent matters to address. I used a hand on her hip to nudge her back to the bedroom. "Come on, let's get dressed. Once they get here, we'll figure out our next steps."

⸺ ◦•◆•◦ ⸺

By the time Jinx and Rabbit knocked, Megan and I were both dressed but still barefoot. Heeding the sharp one-two summons, I opened the door, interrupting a heated dispute between a grim-faced Rabbit and an exasperated-looking Jinx.

"What were you thinking, woman?"

"I was thinking I wanted to make sure you didn't get your idiotic head blown off," Jinx snapped as she brushed by me and stormed into the house.

As they entered the house, I scanned the outside to ensure that their arrival hadn't gained any early-morning witnesses. Everything remained quiet and dark, but the argument behind me showed no sign of ending.

"I was fucking fine," Rabbit growled, not in his usual accent, as he all but threw a backpack on the dinette table.

"You were fucking not," Jinx shot back.

Megan cut in, looking concerned. "Jinx, you're bleeding."

"No shit," Rabbit muttered.

Jinx shot him a death glare and turned to Megan. The biting edge in Jinx's voice disappeared, replaced with wry humor, as she said, "'Tis but a scratch."

"Let me guess—it's merely a flesh wound, and you plan to bleed on me."

Jinx laughed. "Nice to find someone else with an appreciation of the greatness of Monty Python."

Despite the worry on her face, Megan managed a grin. "Come on. There has to be a first aid kit around here, let's get you cleaned up."

As if corny movie quotes met the admission requirements of sisterhood, the two headed down the hall.

"That woman's going to be the death of me," Rabbit snarled as they disappeared into the bathroom.

Ignoring the familiar indicator of one of Rabbit's Jinx-related rants, I demanded, "Tell me what happened."

"I was taking Jinx out through the Mallory's backyard, since they're on vacation. What I didn't realize was they decided to add a damn obstacle course back there. I tripped over a fucking pile of pavers."

That explained the torn knee of his jeans and the gray dust he sported.

Rabbit grimaced. "Do you know how loud stone is?" He shook his head, not waiting for my response. "They tried to cut us off, but we forced a change to their plans and got out."

Of all the stupid, dumb luck… but it failed to explain one thing. "Why the hell were you two still there?" They should have been long gone.

Rabbit shot me a look indicating that it was none of my damn business. "Because." When I didn't comment, he added, "They were targeting Jinx."

Reading between the lines, I ran a hand through my hair and paced to the kitchen. "They thought she was Megan." Not really thinking about it, I opened the fridge and stared at the scant offerings, my mind churning.

From behind me, Rabbit said, "No fucking doubt about it." Closing the fridge, I turned to find Rabbit sprawled at the dinette table, his face grim as he studied me. "Not sure how long you can put off clueing in Delacourt, Bishop."

Leaning against the counter, I folded my arms. I knew he was right, which left me feeling frustrated and cornered. "Did you leave any bodies?"

He shook his head.

"Then what the hell can I give her?"

"Maybe the fact she's got a rat snugglin' up close like?"

"I do that, and you and I both know she'll want what we don't have."

"Proof," he acknowledged grimly.

"Exactly—proof. Until we have that, we're dead in the water."

"I'm not feeling good about keepin' her in the dark."

"Yeah, neither am I," I said, but I knew Delacourt. If I couldn't give her something definitive to work with, she'd try attacking the problem head-on, and that approach was not going to work here. In fact, it would only make it worse.

With nothing more to say, we both fell silent. I could hear the murmurs of Megan and Jinx in the bathroom. I looked at Rabbit. "I need a favor."

He tilted his head as he studied me. "*Mon ami*, you rackin' up points."

Yeah, I was, but I'd promised Megan. "I need you to get a message out to Dev Rouser."

"Megan's brother?"

I nodded. "Tell him to watch his six."

Rabbit's eyes narrowed. "Gettin' a little vague there. You goin' give me more than that?"

I checked to make sure the women were still in the bathroom. Then I shared the high points of Megan's dream. When I was done, Rabbit let out a low whistle.

"This is not good, not good at all." He sat up and braced his arms on his knees as he leaned forward. "Your meetin' with Ricochet?"

I glanced at the clock by the fridge. "It's in four and half hours." That struck me as being four and half hours too long.

Seeming to understand, Rabbit rubbed his chin. "Any chance of movin' that up?"

"To do that, I'd have to reach out to Wolf, and if they're watching all of us—"

"You don't want to give things away."

"Right."

Rabbit nodded. "You want me to try to tag Rico on the q.t., maybe see if he can meet you here?"

His suggestion eased the tightness in my gut. "Think you can do that?"

"Wouldn't offer otherwise."

"Yeah, that'd be great."

"Right, then," he said. "I'll work on getting those messages out."

"Without alerting Delacourt."

He shot me a shit-eating grin. "I'll do my best, but I ain't makin' promises, especially where her brother's concerned. Hacking military communications channels is not for the faint of heart."

"And why are you hacking military channels?" Jinx crossed the kitchen. When she was within reaching distance, Rabbit snagged her wrist, turning her until he could inspect the gauze pad on her upper arm. He was so focused on her wound that he missed the flash of gentleness in Jinx's face as she watched him. It disappeared under a teasing grin as she used her free hand to ruffle his hair. "Don't worry, Cajun man. It's all good."

Rabbit gave her a long look then let her go. She took the other chair while Megan came over and stood next to me.

Jinx looked between Rabbit and me. "Spill."

Catching Jinx up took all of two minutes, and by the time I finished, she was tapping her fingers against the table, a familiar expression on her face. "What are you thinking?" I asked.

Instead of answering me, she turned to Megan. "The colonel's calendars are electronic, right?"

"Unless she's changed things, most of them should be," Megan said. "But if you're looking for personal appointments, you might be out of luck. She tends to keep those on her phone or in her head."

"The phone might be tricky, but if we start with her work calendar, we can narrow down who's been through the office."

"And then do a deep dive to see who connects?" Rabbit asked. "That might actually work. Accessing her calendar is doable, and I'm betting I can finagle her phone records while I'm at it."

Megan wrapped her arms around her stomach. "Rabbit, if you get caught…"

Rabbit flashed her a grin as he sat back, cockiness wafting around him like a noxious cologne. "Not gonna happen, sugar."

When Megan looked as if she wanted to argue, I gave her a slight shake of my head. "Don't bother." She gave me a gimlet eye, so I added, "When it comes to electronics, they all give it up to Rabbit."

While Megan didn't looked convinced, she at least backed down.

Jinx knocked her knuckles against the tabletop, drawing everyone's attention. "Okay, so we're agreed? Our plan is to reschedule Ricochet, get word to Dev, and sneak into the colonel's electronic life?" Getting a round of nods, she grinned. "Good. Now that that's out of the way, who's making breakfast?"

Chapter Seventeen

Rabbit didn't waste time reaching out to Ricochet, and while we waited for his response, Bishop managed to find enough ingredients to make biscuits. Sipping my coffee, I listened to the three team members joke around despite the gravity of the situation. It wasn't hard to join in, and for a little while, I was able to tuck away my insecurities and worries. But once breakfast was demolished to a few crumbs and dregs of coffee, Jinx and Rabbit dove into their electronic skulking, and everything I'd shoved aside crept back in.

Needing space, I left Bishop finishing up the last of the kitchen cleanup and wandered into the living room. My sketch pad peeked out from behind the coffee table. Seeing it, the memories of how it had gotten there crowded in, leaving my cheeks hot and other, more personal places bothered. Thank God my back was to the others, or my flaming cheeks would have resulted in uncomfortable questions. As casually as possible, I gathered up my fallen sketch pad and pencils and escaped to the bedroom.

Once inside the dubious safety of the bedroom, I let out a quiet breath. I skirted the tangle of covers piled on the floor at the foot of the bed, crouched in front of the chair where my bag sat, and tucked the pad and pencils away. There was no way I'd leave it out for curious eyes. The lightest scent of spice and male, the one I associated with Bishop, tickled my nose. Lifting my eyes, I found my impromptu pajamas—Bishop's T-shirt—discarded on the chair in front of me. Before I could check the urge, I caught up the soft material and buried my nose in it, inhaling deeply. That tightness in my chest eased as I carefully folded the shirt. *Stealing a man's T-shirt, Megan? What are you, twelve?* Neither the chastising inner voice nor the discomfort it brought stopped me from tucking the shirt out of sight.

"You okay?"

Bishop's quiet question tripped a flash of guilt, and I twisted around to find him closing the door.

Uh-oh. That didn't bode well.

"I'm good." My mouth went on autopilot, letting the lie escape. I wasn't anywhere close to *good.* But it wasn't worth getting into when there was nothing I could do about it. "I'm just putting my stuff away." I zipped the bag closed, hiding my newly stolen security blanket, and stood up. Turning, I found Bishop dragging the blankets back over the bed. I reached for the edge closest to me and straightened it.

Together, we got the blanket back on the bed. Although my hands were busy, my mind slipped into a downward spiral. The worries and doubts joined forces with rising uncertainties, leaving me adrift in misgivings. Was I doing the right thing by insisting on working with Bishop and the team, or was I just making things worse? Jinx had already gotten hurt —maybe not seriously this time, but what about next time? My paranoid delusions could get Bishop or the others hurt, like, the dead kind of hurt. That would be on me, just as I would be to blame if my unsubstantiated claims damaged their careers—which was a very real possibility, especially as they were determined to leave the colonel in the dark. This would not get any easier before everything was said and done.

Am I willing to risk their lives, their futures, on my broken mind? That answer was simple. *Not a chance in hell.* That meant I needed to call all of this to a halt.

Lost in my thoughts, I nervously smoothed the blanket only to freeze when Bishop's hand caught mine. He tugged me closer. "Hey, what's going on?"

I avoided his gaze and muttered, "Nothing."

"Uh-huh, right." His comment served as proof that he was highly familiar with female subtext. Without letting me go, he sat on the edge of the bed and pulled me between his thighs. The position—what it implied and where it could lead—left me struggling between anxiety and anticipation. Once he got me where he wanted, his hands on my hips blocked any chance of escape and held me still. "Look at me, Megan, please?"

My hands landed on his shoulders as I bit my lower lip and did as he asked.

"Let's try this again." His dark-brown eyes drifted over my face, his thumbs brushing absentmindedly at my hips. "What's wrong?"

With nowhere to hide, I held onto him and waded in with the truth. "I'm worried."

His lips twitched. "Yeah, I kind of figured."

I dug my fingers into his muscles. "It's not funny."

His faint traces of humor disappeared, replaced by the familiar steadiness I was getting used to depending on. "No, it's not. What exactly are you worried about?"

For the briefest moment, I hesitated, but then I pushed past my stupid insecurities. "I'm going to ruin your life and your teams' lives. I shouldn't have dragged you into this."

One of his dark brows rose, an inherently sexy move. "You didn't drag me or the team into anything." Before I could challenge him, he said, "We've known for over a year that Falcon was targeting the teams. Even before you were taken, we had theories that they had someone on the inside. Unfortunately, without proof, we were left playing defense. Which means if anyone owes anyone an apology, it's us to you."

Floored, I said, "No one owes me an apology."

"Don't they?" For the first time, he dropped his eyes, a grimace creasing his face. When he looked back up, his remorse and determination were clear. "I warned the colonel if we weren't careful, Falcon would target someone close to her, someone we wouldn't expect. Do you know why she refused to stop the hunt for an MIA administrative assistant?"

I licked suddenly dry lips as my heart started to pound. "Because she thought I was the leak."

"No. Because she knew Falcon had you, and it was her fault."

The absolute truth of what he said arrowed through the mess in my mind and lanced a hurt I hadn't realized I carried. I'd spent years working alongside the colonel, and while I logically understood why she might have considered me a traitor, I hadn't realized how deep the wound went. As the days drifted into months, I began to believe no one was looking for me, that not even the colonel, who I'd worked beside for years, considered me important enough to search for. It hurt—that perceived lack of faith. Not that I had room to cast blame. Hadn't I given up on anyone coming for me?

Bishop said softly, "You are as much one of hers as any member of the team, Megan, and she did the best she could at the time. Unfortunately, in our world, taking action requires proof, and that's something we didn't have."

"You still don't—not really. My sketchy memory and paranoia do not count as evidence, Bishop. You must know that, or we'd be sharing with Delacourt."

"I'll give you that," he conceded, "but because of you, we

have a starting point, a damn good one. Once Rabbit's able to narrow down the names, we'll start putting those to faces and working on motives."

"And while you guys turn up the heat, they're going to try to take you out." *Possibly through me.* That thought scared me the most.

The hands on my hips tightened. "We know that. It's part and parcel of the job, Megan."

His casual acceptance of danger worried me. "Again, your job sucks."

"Sometimes, yeah, but the end results are worth it." Then he demonstrated just how psychic he really was by saying, "You think you're going to get us killed."

My throat closed, making it impossible to answer, but I curled my fingers around his arms as if I could hold him in place.

Reading my silent answer, he wrapped his arms around my hips and pulled me in until there wasn't much space between us. "You won't."

The change of position put his face just below mine. Unable to resist, I looped my arms over his shoulders. One hand went to his hair and played with the ends. Swallowing hard, I found my voice, husky though it was. "You don't know that."

"Yeah, babe, I do." Rock-solid belief came through in his tone and expression.

"How?" I needed something more than his innate knowing. This was too important.

"Because I won't let you."

Why his vow made me feel better, I couldn't say, but knowing he wouldn't let me hurt him or anyone else gave me the strength to wrangle my worries back into their dark little box while my balloon of panic slowly deflated. "Okay."

"Okay," he repeated softly. A long moment ticked by as we

held each other. He broke it with an unexpected question. "Do I need to apologize?"

Confused, I pulled back and looked at him, but he wasn't giving me any clues. "For what?"

His gaze drifted moodily over my face. "That's what I'm trying to figure out."

Something in that look finally clicked. All that had happened the night before came in and took a seat, demanding that I give it some attention. *Guess it's time for* that *discussion. Eek.* "No, I wanted what happened."

He said, "But...?"

Shifting a little, I countered, "But what?"

That managed to pierce his blank mask, because he smiled the tiniest bit. "There's always a *but* after a comment like that."

I watched myself twist a piece of his hair around my finger. "Uh, I guess you're right."

"So what's the *but*?"

Was that nervousness in his voice? I looked at him, really looked at him, taking in the fine tension riding under my hands and his stoic expression. Then it hit me. I wasn't alone in the insecurities department. We both knew this might not end well. Strangely, that realization gave me the strength to admit how I felt.

"I like you." Hearing myself give that lame description made me wince, and honesty had me adding, "Really, really, like you. Any other time, I'd be on cloud nine about exploring this with you."

"Sounds like a plan to me."

His sincerity stung because I wanted to bask in it but couldn't. "But"—there was that damn word—"there's a high chance I'm compromised. It's a little hard to build something if you can't trust the foundation, right?"

He didn't answer right away. Instead, he reached up and pulled my hands down until he was holding them between us.

I stood there, caught in his gaze, a humming silence falling between us. Finally, he asked, "Do you trust me?"

That was not the question I was expecting, but my answer was immediate and filled with startling truth. "Yes."

"Good to know." He brought my hand up and pressed a kiss to the back of it. "Let's work with that and worry about the rest when we have to, okay?"

Before I could answer, there was a knock at the door. We both turned to look, and Bishop said, "Yeah?"

The door opened, and Rabbit stuck his head in. "Ricochet will be here in forty."

Bishop lifted his chin. "Thanks."

Rabbit propped a shoulder on the doorframe, a speculative gleam in his eyes, followed by a wicked grin, but before he could start something, Bishop cut him off. "Did you reach Dev?"

"I'm good, my friend, but I'm not that good. It's next on my list."

"Thank you, Rabbit," I said. The simple phrase didn't cover how much it meant to me, but I hoped he could hear the depth of emotion behind it.

Rabbit's amusement disappeared, replaced by compassion. "No thanks needed, *chere*. We protect our own." He turned to Bishop. "Once Ricochet gets here, Jinx and I will head back to the office and start combing through the colonel's calendars."

That didn't sound smart to me at all. Confused when Bishop didn't argue about Rabbit's announcement, I asked, "You're going to the office? Is that a good idea?"

Rabbit's grin came back in full force. "Doncha worry none there, darlin'. We'll be jus' fine."

"And if you're caught hacking the colonel's calendars?"

Rabbit clutched his chest in mock injury. "Caught? Don't utter such blasphemy. Have a little faith."

"He's right," Bishop said. "The last place anyone would try for them would be at the office."

"Plus," Rabbit added, "accessing her files is easier when I can mask my searches from an internal source."

That made absolutely no sense to me, but arguing with the computer genius would be pointless. Hopefully he was right, because if he was wrong… that didn't bear thinking about.

"Megan," Bishop said, and I turned to him. He squeezed my hand. "It's okay."

Jinx called Rabbit from the kitchen. "Comin', sugar," Rabbit called back. He pushed off the frame. "I'll leave you two alone now." With a flash of a leer, he was gone.

I watched the empty doorway as all my doubts and worries reconvened. Each move the team made sucked them deeper into this mess, all because Bishop trusted me. What the hell was up with that, anyway? *I* didn't trust me. Behind me, I felt Bishop stand up. Bracing myself, I turned. "Bishop—"

That was as far as I got. His mouth took mine with a sweetness that almost hurt and definitely took my breath away. When he was done, he lifted his head, clear determination etched in every line of his face. "Whatever this is, it's something I want to explore, so I'm not giving up on you. Do me a favor and don't give up on you either, okay?"

With the heady taste of him on my tongue and a lump in my throat, I gave in. "Okay."

Chapter Eighteen

Standing in the kitchen, working on my second cup of coffee, I tried hard not to think about my conversation with Bishop or the more frantic ones with both my mom and my sister via one of Bishop's many burner cells. While I had no choice but to share about the break-in, I avoided talking about my concerns about Dev. Still, by the time I hung up with both of them, I wanted to crawl back into bed and pull the covers over my head.

When the knock sounded, the casual atmosphere in the condo went wired as Rabbit rocked his chair back to peek through the blinds. He dropped the chair back to all four legs. "It's Ricochet."

Bishop went to the door as Rabbit and Jinx began packing up the rest of their stuff. Bishop let Ricochet in while I hung back by the sink. The newest arrival dropped a duffle bag on the floor next the door and exchanged manly one-arm hugs with Rabbit and Bishop before pulling Jinx into a quick hug. Now that the team's most reclusive member was here, the apprehension I'd managed to ignore all but slapped me in the face.

Trying not to be obvious about it, I studied the man who was probably going to upend my world. He wasn't as tall as Bishop but was closer to Rabbit's height, which put him just under six feet. Like Rabbit, he ran toward the leaner side, but where Rabbit was like a live wire, Ricochet moved with a mesmerizing grace his jeans and T-shirt did little to disguise. Straight dark hair brushed his collar and framed a face with an intriguing blend of Native American and Asian traits as he scanned his surroundings.

When he caught sight of me, I found myself in a staring contest with a wild tiger, his focused patience made more lethal for its intensity. I only realized I'd frozen in place and was holding my breath when he finally looked away. Dropping my eyes to my cup, all I could do was thank whoever was listening that he was on our side.

My musings were interrupted by Jinx. "Megan?" She stopped in front of me, a worried frown on her face. "You okay?"

Setting my cup on the counter, I gave her a small smile. "Sorry, just spaced out for a second." I lifted my chin at the backpack on her shoulder. "You guys heading out now?"

"Yeah, but I wanted to let you know that as soon as we get ahold of your brother, we'll let you and Bishop know, okay?"

I wrapped my arms around my stomach. "Thank you."

She studied me, and before I could brace for it, she gave me a quick hug. "Trust Bishop, and things will be okay, all right?" She pulled back and waited for my nod before turning to follow Rabbit out the door.

Once the door closed behind them, Ricochet turned his attention to me, and it was all I could do not to fidget like a toddler being caught with a hand in the cookie jar. That feeling made no sense, since I had nothing to feel guilty for, at least not that I knew about. While there was nothing in his expression to indicate otherwise, I couldn't escape the feeling that

Ricochet had judged me and found me lacking. That impression did more to rile my battered pride than anything else had in a while. But hard as it was, I held his gaze and lifted my chin, refusing to give ground.

"Ricochet, this is Megan." Bishop crossed the kitchen to me, breaking the strange staring contest. "Megan, Ricochet." He got to my side and stood next to me, leaning back against the counter, one arm behind my back, his hip brushing mine as we faced the quiet man studying us. Bishop leaned into me, his voice low, his breath brushing my ear. "Play nice."

His unnecessary warning ruffled my temper, and I jerked my gaze to his face. "Me? I'm not the one you need to worry about."

Ricochet's rough chuckle broke through the room. "She's got a point, Bishop."

Bishop turned back to his friend. "You know why you're here?"

Ricochet folded his arms over his chest and held Bishop's gaze without any hint of concern. "Falcon's got someone embedded close to the colonel, and Wolf thinks Megan's a dream-walker." He turned to me. "If Wolf is right, we've got quite the day ahead of us."

Some little devil made me ask, "And if Wolf is wrong?"

"Then I ensure that you're not a threat." He spoke without any inflection.

While his answer should have left me shaking in fear, it actually reassured me. Not so for Bishop, who stiffened at my side. Undoubtedly, he understood better than I what Ricochet would do to keep his team safe. As for me, so long as I couldn't hurt anyone, I was okay with that. To make sure Bishop understood my position, I asked Ricochet, "Promise?"

A flash of compassion or pity, I wasn't sure which, came and went before he gave me a solemn nod. "Yes. I won't let you hurt any of us."

"Thanks." It seemed to be my word of the day.

He inclined his head in a respectful nod.

Next to me, Bishop shifted, some of the tension draining away. "Did you pick up any shadows?"

Ricochet shook his head. "After Rabbit filled me in, I made it a point to look."

Bishop frowned. "Nothing?"

"Nothing," Ricochet repeated.

"Isn't that a good thing?" I looked between the two men. Clearly, I was missing something.

It was Ricochet who answered. "Maybe, maybe not. There's not enough information to know." His gaze went back to Bishop. "The colonel wasn't expecting me back for a few more days. Plus, my ride landed in a private airfield, so chances are good if they are watching, they have no clue I'm stateside."

Bishop looked relieved and muttered, "Gives us at least one ace in the hole."

Worry knotted my stomach as I read between the lines. "Wait, will you being here get you in trouble with the colonel?"

Ricochet smiled just the tiniest bit. "I'm on official leave. There's nothing for her to get upset about."

"Except the fact that we're all plotting behind her back." The snippy comment slipped free before I could censor it. Heat rushed to my cheeks, and I turned away and put my empty cup in the sink.

Bishop touched my shoulder, waiting until I looked at him. "She might get pissed, but she'll understand that we're doing our job."

Maybe she would, but I'd worked with her long enough to know she did not deal well with being kept out of the loop. There was a quiet warning in Bishop's dark eyes to let it go. Heeding it, I bit my lip instead of pursuing an argument I had no hope of winning.

"Any chance there's something besides coffee around

here?" Ricochet asked, breaking the underlying tension between us.

I pointed to the cabinet above the coffee maker. "Tea. There was a tin or two up in that cabinet. Not sure how old or how good it is, but…" I waved him to it.

"Thanks." Ricochet crossed the floor and began rummaging in the cabinet.

While he worked on his tea, I finished rinsing my cup and dried my hands. Leaving Bishop and Ricochet to their small talk, I escaped to the living room and curled up on the couch. It didn't take long before both men joined me. Bishop sat close while Ricochet took the chair nearby.

Once everyone settled, Ricochet got straight down to business. "What do you know of dream-walking?"

"Pretend I know nothing." I didn't want to admit that my knowledge of dream-walking was more likely to be found in the pages of a book than in reality.

Ricochet explained, "Dream-walking is a form of telepathy. It's the power to enter and control others through their dreams and thereby influence their waking lives."

Bits and pieces of the research I'd dug through trying to understand Dev and Keelie's abilities came to my rescue. "So, it's another term for lucid dreaming?"

He balanced his cup of tea on the armrest of his chair. "Being aware that you're dreaming is just one part of it. Dream-walking is a psychic ability that tends to combine lucid dreaming, astral projection, and telepathy. Put all of that together, and you basically have the ability to turn someone's dreams into reality."

"Or a nightmare," I muttered, thinking of the images that haunted me.

He nodded. "Or a nightmare."

And I was supposed to let Ricochet, an admittedly powerful dream-walker, waltz into my head and poke around?

Panic and dread crawled over my bones, giving me the sickening willies. "As a telepath, shouldn't Wolf be able to tell if I have this ability?"

A shadow flickered over Ricochet's face as he shared a look with Bishop, but his voice remained even and calm when he answered me. "Control is crucial for Wolf. It allows him to live with his ability's demands."

His answer made me stop and think of what it really meant to be telepathic and all that it would entail. What would a lifetime of being bombarded by the thoughts people kept buried in the dark be like? I'd only suffered through horrific nightmares for the last few weeks. The hell of seeing that all the time… a shiver crawled down my spine. "Poor Wolf."

Ricochet winced. "It's not an easy ability to carry."

"None of them are," Bishop added.

The two men shared a grim look of commiseration. Hearing the acceptance in Bishop's tone and watching the haunted look in his face, it wasn't hard to guess that he was back on that road with his best friend. Not wanting him to slip back into the dark, I changed position until I was under his arm. "No, but you do the best you can. That's all anyone can ask."

He blinked, and his expression cleared.

I turned back to Ricochet. "Okay, so Wolf didn't want to break my mind trying to figure out what was going on. So how do you plan to do this?"

Ricochet didn't answer right away. Instead, he studied us, and whatever he thought about what he saw, he didn't share. "I'm going to bring you into my dream and see if you can alter it."

Taken aback, I blinked. "That's it? It's that simple?"

He shrugged.

I narrowed my eyes, not about to let him get away with the mute-male shtick. "That's not an answer, Ricochet."

Those dark brows rose, but he said, "It's the best I can give you."

Okay, time to try a different tack. "How dangerous is this?"

Bishop stiffened next to me, but Ricochet just tilted his head and frowned. "I won't let you get hurt."

"What if I hurt you?" Granted, that was probably a long shot—like, seriously long—but with the way things were going, I had to ask.

Instead of being insulted or worried, he ducked his head, which did nothing to hide his grin. When he looked back up, even though he maintained what I was coming to think of as his teacher voice, that grin lingered in his eyes. "How about I promise you won't hurt me?"

"You can do that?" My fingers did a nervous dance on Bishop's thigh. This dream-walking stuff didn't sound like an ability that played nice with others.

Ricochet's expression softened. "My dream, my world."

His reassurance did jack all to ease the sense of horror crawling along my skin, or maybe that was just nerves. "What happens if we get in there, and I freak out and screw something up?"

Instead of brushing me off, Ricochet took a moment before answering with equal gravity. "I've been doing this for a long time, Megan. Even if you are a dream-walker, you couldn't match me. Not yet and probably not ever." He leaned forward, his arms braced on his knees. "It takes years of practice to master dream-walking. Not only do we not have years, but we have maybe hours—at most, days—to get you to a point where you can become the bait we need."

The word *bait* bounced around my mind until it drowned out everything else. For some reason, hearing the plan from Ricochet instead of Bishop made it more real, more frightening. If it turned out I could do this, I would have to find the strength to turn the tables on my nightmares. While a part of me fiercely hoped I was a dream-walker and that I would have a chance to take my life back, the thought of facing what haunted me scared me to death.

My fingers bit into Bishop's thigh as my heart picked up speed. The familiar metallic taste of fear coated my mouth, and it was suddenly hard to breathe. Refusing to look away, I held Ricochet's hard gaze and found the strength to say, "Let's do this, then."

Chapter Nineteen

"Open your eyes."

I opened them, squinting against the brightness. The light faded back to tolerable levels and left me standing in the stark beauty of the desert at sunset. Off in the distance, I could see the smudge of mountains. "Where are we?"

"Consider this a testing ground."

Turning, I found Ricochet sitting tailor-fashion on a boulder behind me. Other than him and his rock, there was nothing but dirt and scrub bushes. "Okay," I drew the word out. "So now what?"

"Now I want you to imagine holding a walking stick."

An image flashed through my mind. Between one breath and the next, a white staff, as described by Tolkien and immortalized in an epic film, appeared in my hand. Stunned, all I could manage was, "Holy crap!"

"Really? Gandalf's staff?" Ricochet shook his head, sounding exasperated. "We're not here to fight orcs, Megan. You're going to need a walking stick."

The staff in my hand started to shift, the edges slipping away like a watercolor, but I wasn't done geeking out. Besides,

I liked this staff much better than some boring walking stick. The image stilled then snapped back to the white carved staff.

"Well, guess that answers our first question."

Startled, I spun to find a frowning Ricochet at my shoulder. "A little warning next time?" When he didn't bother responding, I asked, "What answers our first question?"

He nodded at my nifty staff. "That tells me you're a dream-walker." Before I could stutter out a pointless protest, he folded his arms over his chest. "Okay, let's see how strong you are."

An eerie howl rode through the air, and a dark shape broke free of the horizon, growing larger and more distinct as it stormed closer. Recognition hit me, leaving me speechless as I stared at a charging huge snarling wolf straight out of the worst Little Red Riding Hood story. "Holy sh—"

I stumbled back as instincts as old as time kicked in with a vengeance. Turning to run, I realized that Ricochet was nowhere in sight. "Ricochet? Where the hell are you?" I darted behind the boulder. It sucked as cover, but it was the only thing available. There was no way I could outrun a wolf. Behind me, the wolf's snarls grew louder, and I swore I could hear its paws hit the earth like an ominous drumroll.

Back pressed to the boulder, hands white knuckling the staff, I tried to think beyond my panic. This might be a dream, but something told me that getting hurt here was not a good idea. Not keen on being eaten alive, I scrambled up the boulder, which seemed to have grown while I was huddling behind it. Or maybe that was just my fear-spurred imagination—not that I cared, because it got me off the ground and that much farther from becoming the rabid wolf's chew toy.

I managed to get to the rocky top without losing the staff and scraped only a couple layers of skin off my palms. Standing there, chest pumping, I flinched as the wolf lunged. There wasn't much room on the uneven surface of the boulder, but I inched back.

Somehow, I found enough air to yell raggedly, "Ricochet?"

Canine snarls were my only answer. The wolf below lunged again, claws scrambling for purchase. When he managed to get his head and shoulders above the edge, pure adrenaline had me swinging the staff like a long baseball bat. It hit with an impact that reverberated up my arms, but the wood didn't break. Fortunately, the wolf yelped and dropped away.

Think, Megan. Ricochet believed I was a dream-walker, and dream-walkers controlled the world around them, which meant that I should be able to get out of this. He also said something about seeing how strong I really was. To determine someone's strength required testing, which meant... *This is a freakin' test?*

My mental gymnastics were interrupted when a snarl came from below, followed by the overly determined wolf popping his head back up. This time, he must have found a stronger foothold because I could see the feral glow in his amber eyes and his shoulders were above the edge of the boulder.

Finding another half inch to retreat, I snarled under my breath, "I swear I'm going to kill you." And it wasn't the wolf I was talking to.

"Got to get past the wolf first." Ricochet's voice echoed around me, but he was nowhere to be found.

Fine. Keeping a wary eye on the animal in front of me, I couldn't miss the baleful light in his eyes. Test or not, he was determined to get to me. Even knowing this wasn't real, I couldn't convince my body of that fact, nor could I find it in me to cause serious damage to the wolf. Which left me between a rock and hard place—no pun intended.

Even as my mind spun through options, I struck out with the staff, hoping that by knocking the wolf off, I could discourage his hunt. I hooked the staff under one forepaw, twisted it, and shoved. Ricochet was right—a walking stick would have been better. Still, the move worked, forcing the wolf to abandon his hold on the rocky surface. Without that support, the furry head disappeared, and a pained yelp soon followed.

I inched toward the edge and found that the drop to the ground had grown from inches to feet. Pacing below, favoring a back paw, was the wolf. When he saw me, his lips peeled back from menacing teeth, and he began to scramble up the boulder again, using the uneven surface to work his way back toward me, which should take him longer than before, considering that the ground now appeared to be farther away.

The unusualness of that realization stalled my mental tailspin, and it hit me that boulders did not spontaneously grow. So if my desire to stay out of reach equaled a growing boulder, then… concentrating on the boulder's surface, I imagined the rough sides smoothing out. Before doubt could creep in, I found myself lying on top of a smooth column of stone and the wolf restlessly prowling below.

"I guess that's one way to do it."

Ricochet's wry tone had me rolling to my back to find him crouched beside me. He held out a hand. I took it and let him pull me up. He didn't let me go until I had the staff planted on the column's weirdly smooth surface and found my feet. Only then did he walk to the edge, with a casualness I couldn't match, and peer down.

Dropping into a crouch, he kept his eyes on the wolf. "Yeah, not the route I would've taken."

Forcing my body to chill out, I moved to stand next to him, though I kept an eye on the ledge. Since my knees were still shaking, I leaned into the staff and tightened my grip. I was fairly certain it would not be wise to smack him in the head with it.

He turned to look at me, and I swore he knew what I was thinking because laughter danced in those dark eyes. "You're not all that keen on confrontation, are you, Megan?"

"Depends on the situation." My brain kept turning his question over and over, things starting to fall into place. "The wolf represents a threat."

He stood up, put a hand under my elbow, and drew me back away from the ledge. "He does." When we returned to the center of the column, he let me go.

Now that the immediate threat wasn't trying to eat my face, I was able to think things through. "You didn't like how I escaped?"

He shrugged. "It's not a matter of liking. I just found your choice for how to avoid the wolf telling."

Truly curious, I asked, "Why?"

"When faced with immediate danger, instead of eliminating it, you chose to get out of the way without use of lethal force."

"Lethal force?" Granted, I didn't know Ricochet from Adam, but he didn't strike me as someone who would take the most violent option first. Maybe if he was backed into a corner… "Seems a bit extreme in this case."

He shrugged. "When it comes down to a question of escape versus survival, you'd be surprised at what option you'd choose."

Hearing him lay it out that way, I had a sudden insight about why my decision bothered him. "Maybe you chose the wrong scenario." I tried to pick my words carefully. "Until I was taken, violence was something I understood on an intellectual level, but on a personal level?" I shook my head. "It was supposed to be used only as a last resort." I looked back to the side of the boulder, where faint snarls still drifted up. "I knew the wolf posed a threat, but his actions were based on instinct —I was the intruder, and he was doing what was natural for him." I turned back to Ricochet and gave him a small grin. "My sister works with dogs, I grew up around dogs, and to me, a wolf is just a dog in a wild fur coat." My grin faded. "If you were hoping to see how far I was willing to go, a wolf wasn't what you should've used."

Before the last word left my mouth, the scene around us had changed with breathtaking speed. It wasn't really a conscious decision but more a reflection of what I was feeling and thinking. When it was done, I was in that damn stone cell, with a storm raging outside and that hated voice demanding information I refused to give. The only way I knew I wasn't really back was that this time, Ricochet was with me.

"This is what you should've used."

If I was hoping to rattle the man in front of me, I was doomed for disappointment. He studied our surroundings, and the only sign he heard the same damn voice I did was the darkening of his eyes as the lines around his mouth deepened. "That voice…" Instead of finishing his thought, he flexed his jaw, and the voice stopped as if a switch had been thrown. Only then did I realize I had backed up to a wall, my shoulders hunched as I clutched the staff to my chest.

"It's not him, Megan." Ricochet sounded curiously gentle.

I managed a nod. This wasn't real. I forced my shoulders back and straightened.

Fortunately, Ricochet switched tracks. "This is where Wolf couldn't reach?"

Determined not be a cowering mess, I answered, "Yes."

His gaze went beyond me to the sketches fluttering on the wall as the winds from the storm snuck in through the high window to dance around us. "You hid here when they tried to interrogate you."

Since it wasn't a question, I didn't answer.

He walked to the walls and studied the images. It hit me that maybe bringing Ricochet here wasn't such a good idea, especially considering what those pictures contained—not just the nightmarish scrawls and the indistinct lines of an imaginary protector of a broken mind but also older visuals buried under the others, containing aspects of familiar faces, one in particular. But it was too late for embarrassment.

He was rifling through the images, and the moment he recognized Bishop's face, Ricochet's shoulders stiffened, not much but enough. My breath caught, and for an anxious moment, I thought I caught a familiar flutter of a shadow. Since I had a visitor, I figured it was best to ignore it. No sense in giving Ricochet more reasons to question my sanity.

I'd managed to bury the broken pieces under a false sense of calm by the time Ricochet turned to me, although I wasn't sure that would last because the person who faced me wasn't Ricochet the teacher but was, instead, the ruthless PSY-IV team member. "The ones who held you… did they ever follow you here?"

"No." I cleared my throat. "No, this is the only place I felt safe, the only place they couldn't follow. It didn't do much for blocking their voices, but here, they couldn't touch me." Memories, some sharp, some indefinable, pressed close, and a shudder ran through me. "When the pain got bad, this was all I had left to hold on to." *This and the protector my desperation created.* After watching Ricochet check out the sketches, I wasn't too keen on sharing that little tidbit.

His gaze moved from me to the walls. "There's no door."

Here was something I could easily answer. "If I can't get out, they can't get in."

His attention came back to me. "For someone with no training on how to fight a telepath, you were damn smart."

The harsh lines of his face eased. I decided compassion was better than pity, but it was a close race. Uncomfortable with his praise, I looked at my feet. "I'm not sure I was all that successful at fighting back."

"Because you think they've managed to program you to hurt the teams," he said in a hard tone, the softer emotion gone again.

Grimacing, I met his gaze and nodded.

He folded his arms over his chest. "I won't lie—it's highly probable."

As much as I appreciated his directness, I couldn't stop my wince. "Can you find out?"

"Actually, you could do it yourself."

That was not the answer I was expecting. "What?"

"Sit," he ordered as he did the same, taking a cross-legged position on the floor. He waited until I was settled, my staff lying on the floor next to me, before continuing. "Before I answer, there are some things you need to understand, one of which is why this"—he waved his hand to the tower room— "worked."

Remembering Wolf's assessment, I said, "Wolf believes it's a representation of my mental protections."

"It is, and it isn't."

"Cryptic much?"

"All the time, but I'm not doing this on purpose." His wry humor made my lips twitch, but Ricochet wasn't done with his lecture. "Psychic abilities are far from easy to explain."

He didn't need to tell me that. I was feeling way the hell out of my depth.

"Wolf is a telepath, so when he goes into someone's mind, he's pitting his mental strength against another. Most people aren't expecting someone to come in and mess with their thoughts, so most people's mental protections are few and far between. The fewer the protections—"

"The easier it is for Wolf to do his thing," I said.

"Right." He paused as though picking his next words carefully. "But Wolf being Wolf, he isn't keen on using his ability offensively unless he's left with no choice." His dark eyes flashed, but otherwise, his face remained stoic. "A telepath can either tear through a mind and leave behind a vegetable, or they can maneuver with the precision of a surgeon and never be noticed until it's too late."

My stomach pitched as his words hit deep. How close had I come to truly turning mindless? My hands curled into fists as I breathed through the knee-weakening fear. "I'm assuming Wolf is the latter variety."

"He can do both," Ricochet confirmed. "He chooses to do the second."

I flexed my stiff fingers and lay them flat on my thighs. "Good to know."

But Ricochet wasn't done. "When Wolf works with a happy individual, he's expecting the scene to be a symbolic representation of that personality."

Thinking through Ricochet's explanation, I asked, "So if he goes into the mind of a happy person, he finds what? Sunny fields and frolicking puppies?"

My comment earned me a long slow blink from Ricochet. "Sure, let's go with that." Then, regaining his serious demeanor, he said, "Once Wolf can shift the person's thoughts and perceptions, that scene changes. He can influence it, but he can't control it."

Strangely, that made complete sense to me. "So me creating this tower, that was me controlling the scene, fighting the monster's influence?"

"Exactly." Then he asked, "Monster?"

I gave an embarrassed shrug, but there was no point in not sharing. "Until we have a name, it's how I think of him."

He made a low sound of agreement but returned to our conversation. "Remember how I explained that dream-walking is a form of telepathy? How a dream-walker controls the scene, not the individual dreaming?"

I nodded, bracing. Something told me this was going to lead somewhere that would leave me less than happy.

"While your kidnapper couldn't access the core of who you

are, outside of these walls, he could convince you to shape the world to his parameters."

That made a cruel sort of sense and explained why he kept using the faces of my family to torment me. I'd lost count of how many times that hated voice used a mockery of my loved ones to twist and break my mind. Eventually, I clued in to his game because the tiniest things began tripping him up—an expression, a turn of phrase, a mannerism—that didn't ring true.

I admitted, "It was his favorite game."

Ricochet dipped his chin in acknowledgement. "I'm not surprised. Once a telepath gains the upper hand, it's hard to get it back. In your case, his attacks eventually triggered your latent ability."

"Which is why this"—I indicated the tower—"exists."

He nodded. "A dream-walker, no matter how skilled, is not without offensive capabilities."

"Offensive capabilities?"

"What happens in the dreamscape translates to the waking world. You get injured in the dreamscape, your body will believe the injury is real in the waking world and react accordingly. And it wouldn't just be you—it would also impact whoever is sharing that world with you."

It took a moment for his implication to sink in, and when it did, I felt my jaw drop. "Wait, you're telling me if someone gets hurt or killed while in whatever dreamworld I created, they're, like, really hurt or dead?"

There was a grim light in those dark eyes. "Yes. One of the best defenses a dream-walker has against a telepath is the ability to take control of the dreamscape from the telepath and turn it against them. Which is exactly why we needed to see how strong you were."

So the success or failure of Bishop's plan would rest on my ability to turn the tables on the one who hunted me. I rubbed my hands over my thighs as I tried to come to terms with this latest piece of information. "Maybe you should be the one to do that part."

"Don't underestimate yourself, Megan," he chastised me. "You managed to hold him off without even knowing what you were doing. Not for an hour, not for a day, but for months. The amount of will that requires is staggering."

Knowing I'd managed to put some protections in place eased some of my concerns but not all of them, because this tower didn't always exist, and it couldn't keep that damn voice out of my mind. Even now, my memory was seeded with dark pits of nothing, and not knowing what lay in them was almost more frightening than the idea of facing the monster who'd created them.

"But there's no guarantee I did lock him out. This tower wasn't always here." I might not remember much, but I knew that the protection had come into being after the first few days or weeks. Only when the pain became nearly unbearable had I found myself lying on the cold stone.

"How long does it take a telepath to break a mind?" I asked.

"Depends on the mind."

Part of me was grateful he wasn't pulling his punches, but part of me wanted him to shut up. "How do I find out if he planted something in my head?"

"We'll have to go looking for it."

That did not sound good, not at all.

My panic must have shown because he covered the hand fisted on my knee. "Megan." He waited until I met his gaze. "No matter what you think, he didn't break you. If he had, you never would have walked into the colonel's office and admitted your fear. Whatever trigger he buried, I guarantee it's not as solid as he thinks."

There was no way to hide the emotions tumbling through me, so I didn't try. "You can't know for sure."

"Yes, I can." He let me go, got to his feet, and went to the sketches on the wall. He searched through them until he found the one he wanted. Tearing it free, he came back and crouched in front of me, the sketch extended. "Who is this?"

I took the sketch from him and stared into the shadowy image of my imaginary protector. Color rushed to my cheeks. "My therapist claims he's nothing more than a coping mechanism. Someone I created so I wouldn't lose hope." *Too bad it didn't really work.*

Ricochet kept watching me. "What do you think?"

Jerking my gaze from the sketch to Ricochet, I frowned. "What do you mean, what do I think?"

"Do you think he's a figment of your imagination?"

"What else could he be?"

There was something working behind his eyes, a knowledge I couldn't grasp. "Let's find out."

Thoroughly confused, I blurted, "What do you mean?"

"Bring him here, Megan. Show me your coping mechanism."

Chapter Twenty

My rush of embarrassment turned to snippy temper. "You make it sound like I should just snap my fingers"—I snapped them—"and voilà, instant hallucination."

Unmoved, Ricochet didn't budge. "Is that how you normally do it?"

"I don't know how I normally do it." There was no hiding my frustration. Ricochet was asking me to do something I didn't have the first clue about how to make happen.

Ricochet sighed. "All right, let's try this. Do you remember the first time he showed?"

There was no way he would let me out of this, so instead of fighting a losing battle, I closed my eyes. As much as I loathed remembering, he was asking me to do it for a reason, so I opened the door I'd slammed shut all those weeks ago. Perched on a threshold, I felt the shiver of trepidation wash over me. Like a teen coming in after curfew, I snuck past the treacherous memories filled with that hated voice, making sure not to gain its attention. Skirting the yawning pits of blankness, I finally found what I was looking for.

"I woke in the tower." My words felt disconnected from

me, which made it easier to keep going. "I can't remember what happened, but it was bad. I was bleeding."

"Bleeding?" His question sounded far away.

"From my nose, my ears, I think." I brushed at the phantom sensation. "I don't know how long I lay there, but I felt so tired." *And so damn hopeless.* As if naming the emotion gave it power, the desperation rushed back in, sweeping me into that inescapable pit. "I just wanted it to be over."

"Wanted what to be over?"

"All of it. It hurt to keep fighting, and I wasn't sure I'd hold out next time." *Because there was always a next time.* "And I was worried…"

"About?"

What bothered me? The answer was there, floating at the periphery, but every time I reached for it, it drifted away. "I don't know." A dull throbbing started in my temples. Wincing, I rubbed them.

"Don't worry about it, Megan."

I reluctantly turned away, letting the answer escape.

"What happened next?"

I tried to bring the bits and pieces together. "There was a voice." I'd been startled by it because no one should have been there. "I opened my eyes, and he was there."

"Describe him."

"I can't."

"You can. Tell me the first things that come to mind." Ricochet's demand drifted in like a feather, and I blinked my eyes open. He was crouched in front of me, patience personified.

"Warm." It was the first thing that hit me, a sense of warmth when everything around me had become a frozen wasteland. "Strong." The innate sense of my protector's strength gave me something to cling to when mine was all but gone. "Relentless." He'd never stopped with the whispered encouragement, not even when I raged at him to shut up because I knew no one was coming for me.

"What the hell?"

The question snapped Ricochet's head around as he rose to his feet. Unable to see around him and not believing that the particular voice was really here, I scrambled up and stood at his side. Together, we stared at a puzzled-looking Bishop standing at the edge of the room.

"How'd you get here?" My borderline-rude question came out as a squeak.

Bishop looked between Ricochet and me. "I hope you aren't asking me, because I don't have a clue what just happened."

"Don't look at me, brother." Ricochet tilted his head in my direction. "It's all on her."

"What's on me?" Even as I asked the question, mortification left my cheeks hot and my fists clenched. I didn't want Bishop here, where my craziness was blatantly apparent.

Wearing a half grin, Ricochet sketched a bow in my direction then swept his hand out toward Bishop. "Megan, may I present your coping mechanism."

Oh, no, no, no. This couldn't be happening. Unfortunately, there was no denying that it most certainly was happening. Bishop was studying me with a disconcerting calculation, and Ricochet was all but grinning like a damn loon. Not ready to deal with Bishop, I turned and hissed at Ricochet. "You knew."

His grin faded, his normal seriousness sweeping back in. "No. I had a hunch, but I didn't know."

"Didn't know what?" Bishop walked over until we were standing in a loose triangle.

Choking on a mix of temper and frustration, I kept my mouth shut.

Ricochet did not. He turned to his friend and laid it all out, every damn embarrassing bit. "This is what Wolf couldn't breach. It's a mental construct Megan created to keep her interrogator at bay when her ability was triggered."

Bishop looked around, and unable to watch his reaction, I looked down, furiously wishing there was nothing but blank stone to stare at. A sucked-in breath from Bishop drew my attention. Ricochet was watching me with consideration, and Bishop was staring at the walls in astonishment... walls that were no longer plastered with sketches.

"Where did they go?" Bishop asked.

Stunned out of my ill humor, I turned in a slow circle. *Holy hell*. They were all gone, every one of those revealing sketches.

Ricochet kept going with his sharing time. "She mentioned she had a coping mechanism that managed to interact with her. Considering that this is her protective construct, the only entities that could enter would be ones she allowed. The images on the sketches are bits and pieces of her experience." He turned to Bishop. "I recognized your face in her sketches. You weren't the only one—there was one of the colonel as well as others I didn't recognize but who were probably family. Thing was, those were buried deep under the other sketches, which makes me think she was hiding them."

It was almost scary how accurate his evaluation was, and it left me off balance but unapologetic. "I didn't want *him* to find them."

Ricochet turned back to me. "The one holding you?"

I managed a nod. "He kept using faces of people I knew to trick me into telling him what he wanted."

He cocked his head. "Since he had you for so long, I take it that technique didn't work as expected."

Shaking my head, I stepped away from the two men but had forgotten about the staff, which rolled underfoot, sending me stumbling. I caught my balance with a hand against the wall. "I quickly learned to pick up on the little things that always gave away his game. Things got worse after that."

"I'm not surprised." Ricochet kept watching me but directed his words to Bishop. "There was something familiar about the shadowy figure in the later sketches. It made me curious, so I asked her to recreate her so-called hallucination, and now we're here."

"And how, exactly, did we get here?" It was hard to tell what Bishop was thinking. There were no clues in his voice or in his stony stance.

Ricochet shrugged. "Your guess is as good as mine."

Undeterred by Ricochet's evasive answer, Bishop demanded, "Want to share your guess?"

"Honestly, I don't have a damn clue." Ricochet rubbed the back of his neck. "If you two knew each other before, I could see her reaching for you, but…."

He trailed off, and my stomach sank. Unable to meet their eyes, I kept my head down because it wasn't that I *knew* Bishop, but he had factored into a great many of my stupid daydreams. If I had any doubts about labeling my previous infatuation as an obsession, this situation wiped them all away.

My discomfort must have been obvious because Ricochet was frowning at me, and Bishop's intimidation factor dropped as he walked toward me. With nowhere to go, I was stuck waiting for him to reach me. When he got close, he bent down, picked up the staff, and handed to me.

I muttered, "Thanks." Desperate to change the subject, I cleared my throat. "Can we focus on something else?" I needed to say something, anything, that would get me out of this embarrassing-as-hell situation. "Something more productive maybe?"

Bishop's shoulder brushed mine as he leaned back against the wall, looking at Ricochet. "What does this mean for our plan?"

"You mean using Megan as bait?" Ricochet didn't even

glance my way as Bishop dipped his chin in acknowledge. "It's actually a good thing."

"How do you figure?"

I wondered the same thing. I couldn't see how any of this would help when I faced the monster hunting me.

Ricochet turned to me. "You understand that Bishop's plan relies on you being able to hold the dreamscape and keep your stalker busy?"

"Yeah, but if there's a trigger buried somewhere, I'm not sure that's a good idea." The idea of luring the madman into my mind only for me to lose my shit scared me to death.

"Which is why we're going to identify that trigger before we do anything else."

Ricochet made it sound so easy that I wanted to lash out at him. Instead, I tried to keep my tone level. "Say we manage to find it—then what? Can you make it not work? Destroy it or something?"

"I'm not sure that's our best course of action."

His answer hit me with a breath-stealing punch. "Excuse me?" I wheezed in disbelief.

Bishop explained, "If we disable the trigger, it may warn him we're onto him. We need him to feel like he has control."

"He does," I snapped. "That's the whole damn problem. If there is a trigger, he could trip the ticking time bomb in my head at any time." God, did these two have a death wish? They acted like it was no big thing, but they weren't the ones who'd be eaten alive with guilt if anything happened to them. And if I ended up hurting Bishop... the thought terrified me beyond imagining.

Bishop grabbed my arms, holding me in place. "We won't let him get you."

It's not me I'm worried about. I bit the words back. Once upon a time, I might have believed him, but spending six months in hell—most of which I couldn't remember, and the rest, I sure wished I couldn't—made it hard to have faith in what Bishop had said.

"You can't promise me that." The retort came out harsh, but fear was riding my ass like a damn horse jockey.

A dark light flared in Bishop's eyes, but before he could say anything, Ricochet cut through the tension with a practical calm. "Let's find out if it even exists first. Once we have confirmation, we can figure out what it will cause and how we can use it."

I tried to push my fear and panic back. Hard as it was, I needed to trust the experience these two men held. It wasn't as if navigating danger was my day-to-day job as it was theirs. "Fine," I said tightly.

Bishop turned to face Ricochet. He didn't let me go completely but tangled his fingers with mine. *Does he think I'm going to run?* I snorted at the thought. Where in the hell could I go? Irritated as I was, I still didn't let him go as we waited for Ricochet's next move.

"Let's get this done," Bishop said.

"Megan?" Ricochet asked.

I blinked. "What?"

"Want to do the honors?" He waved at the blank wall.

"Me? Isn't this your dreamscape?"

"Not since you brought us here. Now it's yours."

Well, shit. Taking a deep breath, I glared at the blank wall. If the only way out of this disaster was braving what lay beyond my tower of solace, then it was time to leave. My irritation faded into stunned surprise when a wooden door replaced stone and silently swung open. "Cool." I took a step forward only to have Ricochet pull up short and slip by me before disappearing through the door. I reared back and shot a look at Bishop.

His fingers were smoothing down the sides of his goatee, probably to hide a damn smile. "He's taking point."

"Uh-huh." I loaded that one word with a ton of sarcasm.

He put his hand in the small of my back and gently pushed me through the door. "After you."

With my back to him, I felt safe rolling my eyes. "Let me guess—you're playing rear guard?"

That earned me a cough that sounded close to a chuckle. "It's what I do best."

My exasperated snort was cut short when I caught sight of what waited outside the tower. Whatever I expected my mind to look like, it wasn't this. We stepped past the door and found ourselves in a scene that would have fit right into a medieval landscape. A thick forest lay to our left, rolling fields stretched ahead, and when I turned to look back, the stone tower seemed miles away. It wasn't all picturesque. In fact, to the right lay a roiling bank of shadows that left my skin crawling.

Ricochet and Bishop studied our surroundings, but I couldn't take my horrified gaze off those damn creepy shadows as I grabbed Bishop's hand. "What is that?"

"That," Ricochet said grimly, "is where we need to go."

Before I could stop myself, I stepped back, dropping Bishop's hand. "No freakin' way, Ricochet."

Bishop caught me before I could retreat any farther, wrapping an arm around my waist and pulling me to his side. "This is your mind, babe, your world."

"I won't lie to you, Megan," Ricochet said. "It won't be easy, and chances are damn good that those memories you locked away are going to be part of that."

Unable to tear my gaze away from that terrifying mass, I swallowed hard. It hurt to talk. "Including who he is."

"His name or his face, yeah." Ricochet's voice softened. "Something tells me that no matter how good Rabbit is, if we can't help narrow his search now, we're going to be too slow and too late."

He had a point, and it wasn't just Bishop's team at risk—

Dev and Keelie were in danger as well because the monster wouldn't stop until my world was gone. I leaned into Bishop, taking strength from him.

He dropped his head over mine, and said quietly, "You survived it once. You can again."

I felt a core of belief in the man holding me. I cursed my inability to disappoint him. Forcing my legs to hold my weight, I straightened my spine and let go of Bishop. "All right, let's get this over with."

We headed toward the looming haze, and with each step, the sickening dread increased until it felt like I was slogging through thick mud. Dropping my gaze to the ground, I concentrated on putting one foot in front of the other, relying on Bishop and Ricochet to lead the way. We were closing in on the leading edge when Bishop took my hand and Ricochet did the same on the other side. I lifted my head and stared at that intimidating haze, feeling my heart pound in my chest.

Licking dry lips, I managed a shaky, "Here we go."

Chapter Twenty-One

BISHOP

It took everything I had not to wrap Megan in my arms and drag her back to the safety of that damn tower. Her face was ghostly pale, and her hand trembled in mine. I gritted my teeth and held tight, reminding myself that this was necessary not just for my team but for her as well. If Ricochet was right, and this thing was a manifestation of her broken memories, the keys to surviving this situation lay somewhere ahead.

The fog twisted around us like coiling snakes, leaving the same chill factor behind. Next to me, the harsh rasps of Megan's breathing indicated she was on the verge of hyper-ventilating. "Breathe, Megan. You're okay." I kept my tone steady and solid. She didn't need my uneasiness to add to the burden she was carrying. "Come on, babe. In, out. In, out."

Her first couple were shaky, but she continued to take one breath at a time. I shared a grim look with Ricochet over her bent head. If she was having this much trouble, how would she handle the increased toll that lay ahead? Maybe we needed to consider an alternate plan on drawing the bastard out.

Next to me, Megan's breathing slowed and eased, and her hand tightened on mine. When I looked down, she held my gaze with a determination I was coming to expect from her. "I'll be okay."

Not about to argue with her, I nodded.

She faced forward, and her jaw tightened. "Right, let's do this."

As if her words were a trigger, a soft hiss sounded, setting every hair on my body on end. Then a brilliant flash of light, much like a lightening strike, hit somewhere nearby, shaking the ground. I stumbled to a stop as white spots danced in my vision. Blinking them clear, I stared at the scene before me and felt my composure slip. Reminding myself that we were in Megan's mind didn't help. This skimmed too close to my nightmares. The only indication that it wasn't one of mine was the eerie silence. My nightmares were filled with moans of the dying and screams of weapon fire.

A devastating scene straight out of a post-apocalyptic war zone had replaced the stone tower and peaceful landscape. There were no signs of life— no agonized choir of the injured and dying or deafening explosions or the zip of too-close bullets—but the ghostly echoes haunted the air, leaving an uneasy feeling behind. Razed buildings were interspersed with untouched structures. The ground was a mix of churned, scorched earth and patches of undisturbed normalcy.

"Holy crap." Megan stared in stunned shock at the scene before us. "What is this?"

"You," Ricochet answered, his jaw tight, his face dark. "These are the memories you locked away."

With a hard flinch, she pulled her hand free and took a couple of steps forward, her head swiveling as she took it all in. "There's nothing left." Her voice sounded hollow and lost.

"It's not as bad as you think."

Since Ricochet wasn't known for his reassurance, his comment caught me by surprise. Megan and I both looked at him, me in disbelief, Megan with the beginnings of hope.

He shook his head as he came up to Megan's side and pointed ahead. "See that over there?"

Not about to get left behind, I moved to Megan's other side and saw what Ricochet was pointing out. It was a jarring scene of normalcy—a picturesque oasis amid the bleak landscape, as if a section of a large park had been cut out and clumsily pasted into a worst-case scenario. The bright colors of the insert faded at the border into the bleak surroundings. In the midst of the scene, a wood-and-metal park bench sat under the shade of old-growth trees, and a weathered notebook fluttered in an isolated breeze. A carpet of green, like something found during the first days of spring, lay underneath, while a mix of tall sunflowers, daisies, and marigolds encircled it. There were splashes of other flowers in the mix. The ground rose and fell in ragged hills and dips as if the path had been torn up at some point but now nature was reclaiming her domain.

Pretty it might be, but it was so out of place that it left me uneasy. As Megan and Ricochet moved closer to that weird spot, I kept pace, scanning for hidden threats. Ricochet stopped by one of the strange rock-infused grass bumps and dropped to his heels, his hands barely skimming the surface. "I'd say this was broken at one time, but now…"

"It's healing," Megan finished then winced. "Not completely, obviously, since it's scarred, but still…"

"It's just going to take time," Ricochet added, his attention focused on our surroundings.

"Time is something we don't have." Megan's voice had gained a sharp edge.

Without leaving his crouch, Ricochet stopped petting the bump and shot her a hard look. "If you go barging through here without taking care, any chance you had of recovering your memories will be shot to hell. You do understand that, right?"

Her eyes narrowed, and her chin lifted, clear signs of her

emerging temper, so I waded in. "This is purely a reconnaissance mission, understood? We're here to gain information or identify the trigger so we know what we're dealing with." I split my glare between them. "We are not going to turn this into more of a war zone than it already is."

Unsurprisingly, Megan retreated first. "Fine, but later—"

"No," Ricochet said, cutting her off. "You are not coming back until you know what you're doing."

She folded her arms, her blue eyes narrowing. "It's my mind, Ricochet."

Since time was a wasting, and as Megan had said, we didn't have it to waste, I put my foot down. "And you won't be doing anything alone until he clears you."

She opened her mouth and shut it again. "Whatever." Her capitulation came out as less than gracious, but I accepted it. The rebellious lines on her face faded to a small frown as she sighed and brushed her fingers over one of the heavy sunflower heads. "I remember this." Her fingers dropped away, and she rubbed them on her jeans. "But…"

When she trailed off, that sense of *knowing* hit me. I needed her to keep talking because something important was here. "But what?" I did my best to keep my urgency buried.

"I got a message from Keelie that she wanted to meet me before I flew out." Megan turned back to the bench, her frown deepening as she moved closer. She picked up the notebook and held it to her stomach, staring off into the distance, her tone distracted. "I was worried."

I followed along, wanting to be at her side just in case. Out of the corner of my eye Ricochet stilled with a suddenness that was all too familiar. It was the same alert he used on the battlefield when an unseen threat was on approach. Despite his unspoken warning, I kept my voice even and soft, not wanting to spook Megan. "What were you worried about?"

"Keelie. If she really needed something, she wouldn't text —she'd call."

Behind her, Ricochet straightened, but more concerned with Megan, I didn't glance over. Instead, I focused on Megan because there was a curious tension in the air that left me on edge.

Caught up in whatever she was seeing, Megan kept talking. "I got to the park, and she wasn't there. I had to get back and finish packing, so I went to call her." One hand rose as if it held a phone and got halfway to her ear before it stilled. She sucked in a hard breath, the notebook falling from her hands.

I balled my hands into fists as I fought the urge to touch her, not wanting to interrupt while she was reliving her memory. "Megan?"

"She fell." Concern and worry colored her face as she stared at something only she could see.

"Who fell?"

"The blonde. She and her boyfriend were horsing around, and she fell." Megan went to move as if to go help the fallen woman, but I stepped in front of her, my hands going to her hips to hold her in place. Megan's hands went to my chest to push me out of the way. She blinked, her eyes going from vague to focused. "Move, Bishop."

"Wait." The scene around us changed, and suddenly, I was standing in front of Megan on a sunny day in a park near the base. I could still see Ricochet and the marred scenario but now it was overlaid with Megan's memory. People and dogs went in and out of focus as they moved around us, disappearing altogether when they hit the edge of scarred memories. I let Megan go, and the busy park disappeared. I grabbed her hand, and it was back. Lacing our fingers together, I moved to her side as a blurry figure with dark hair rushed over to a young blond woman sitting on the ground and held her ankle. A brown-haired man crouched next to her.

Megan took a step and jerked to a stop, her attention on the blurry dark-haired figure with the couple. Her head tilted. "That's me."

"I kind of figured."

She shot me a look but tugged me forward. As we drew closer, I studied the faces of the woman and her companion. Their features would clear for the briefest of moments then blur again. The strange phenomenon had no discernible pattern, which made it difficult to get a clear identification, but something about the blonde and her boyfriend made me think I'd seen them before.

Megan was talking. "I went over to help. She'd managed to twist her ankle, so her boyfriend and I were going to get her over to the bench." The blurry figure went to one side, the male to the other, and together, they got the woman to her feet, her arms going around their waists. Megan and I watched the trio stagger to the bench. Next to me, Megan was rubbing a spot on her waist, just above her left hip. The memory scene faded into blurs, the three figures merging into one indistinct blob. "Did we call emergency?" Her question wasn't directed at me. "I can't remember." She looked up at me. "Why can't I remember?"

I stilled her hand at her hip, the pieces falling into place. "Because this is where you were taken." I brushed my thumb over the spot she'd been rubbing. "I'm betting they managed to inject you with something just strong enough to keep you disoriented but mobile. Less likely to attract attention helping a woozy friend out of the park than slinging an unconscious body over your shoulder."

Despite the strangeness of our current circumstances, Megan proved she had no trouble connecting the dots. "That text wasn't from Keelie."

Definitely not, but maybe Rabbit can track it back to its origina-tor. Before I could answer, a low warning whistle from Ricochet cut through the air. We turned to find him staring out over the dismal scene at a bank of fast-moving fog.

"That doesn't look good." I grabbed Megan's hand and got to Ricochet's side. "What is that?"

"Not sure," Ricochet said, his pose of coiled readiness betraying his apprehension. "But something tells me we need to be careful and fast."

"Not sure the two are mutually inclusive," Megan muttered.

I shot her a tight-lipped grin. "Trust me, it can be done."

Her hand tightened on mine, but she offered a game smile. "Okay, then."

Looking over her head, I asked Ricochet, "How do you want to do this?"

Instead of answering me, he looked at Megan. "When you look at that, what does your gut tell you?"

Following his indication, she studied the weird fog. A hard shudder shook her, but her chin lifted, revealing the hint of fear in her eyes. "To run like hell."

Her blunt response left my lips twitching. I hadn't expected humor here, of all places.

Undeterred, Ricochet pressed, "After that?"

"We need to get to the other side."

"Then lead the way."

Those slight shoulders straightened, and Megan began moving again.

⸻ •◦●◉●◦• ⸻

It was hard to determine the passage of time as Megan scrambled around and over the scarred landscape. She managed to keep us free of the leading edge of the fog, which had changed to a patchy mist, but everything else was fair game. At first I kept a keen eye on her, but after the fourth time

I nailed my knee on some half-buried object, I shifted my attention to the perils lining our path.

Conversation was scarce. Megan was focused on following a trail only she could see, I was worried about staying clear of the mist and keeping her in sight without tripping, and Ricochet kept to his standard practice of not speaking. The deeper we got inside this warped landscape, the more the oddities all but screamed that we were nowhere near anything normal. Some buildings were chewed down by fire and pitted with artillery impacts. Others stood tall and were razed by graffiti. Rusted car skeletons with flowers and weeds growing wherever they could sat right next to vehicles that wouldn't be out of place on the roads of the real world. And if that wasn't weird enough, vegetation fought with sand dunes to claim the vestiges of civilization. There was no logic to any of it. The only common theme was the presence of scarred pathways— some of them overgrown bumps and others barren ditches— left by Megan's mental wounds.

By the time we made our way through a maze of fragmented streets—they reminded me of England—lined with abandoned shop fronts with a hint of the fantastical, the ominous fog bank was holding its vigil on the horizon, neither advancing nor retreating but just hovering there. The odd behavior didn't end there. Tendrils of white trailed us at a distance. Strangely, the fog seemed as reluctant to touch us as we were to touch it. Even stranger were the low-lying wisps behind Megan, keeping the barest of distance. When she skirted a burnt-out car and jerked to avoid a sharp edge, the mist mimicked her move like a well-trained dog. I looked down to see if that behavior held true for the stuff following me. Apprehension flared when I found no signs of the mist. In fact, it was only visible around Megan.

Ricochet was about to move past me, but I held him back by grabbing his upper arm. "Hold on," I said under my breath.

He stilled at my side and raised a brow in silent question.

"Look." I lifted my chin in Megan's direction. "Why is it only following her?"

"I don't know." Ricochet kept his voice equally low as he watched the odd behavior. "But something tells me we need to find out."

Hearing the uneasiness in Ricochet's tone didn't help. Maybe it would be best to call Megan back and get the hell out of here. Before I could do that, she stopped in front of a store with an unreadable sign hanging haphazardly above it. Cracks spiderwebbed through the dark display window, slashing through every available inch. With one strong wind, that glass would fall like rain. The foreboding facade did nothing to discourage Megan, who reached for the door, twisted the knob, and shoved. The warped wood scraped against the floor, triggering a plume of dust.

As she disappeared inside, I lurched forward with a sharp, "Megan!"

Only her coughing answered.

I sped up, Ricochet at my side, and we hit the entrance seconds behind her. Relieved to find she hadn't gotten far, I paused just inside what appeared to be a bookstore. A familiar one, in fact. Back in the real world in downtown San Diego, the store hosted readings and impromptu indie music performances. Unvarnished wooden beams held the mostly intact ceiling above the narrow bookcases that took up every inch of the linoleum floor. Walls that had been black and covered in local art the last time I visited were now a murky brown-gray, and what artwork remained hung askew, some of it torn, others coated with dust. Walking under the metal chandelier, a shiver of unease snaked down my spine. This was so surreal. I crossed the dirt-encrusted floors to the stuffed shelves, where dust lay in a thin gritty layer.

"Holy shit," I muttered.

"You can say that again," Ricochet responded in a low voice. Ahead of us, Megan moved slowly through the narrow openings. "Go with her. I'll stay here and keep an eye out."

Leaving him to it, I moved up behind Megan, who was dragging her fingers along the books' spines, leaving a clear trail in the dust. Her pet mist hovered close to the floor and circled her legs. Although she seemed caught in her thoughts, I asked, "What are we doing here?"

She shot me a look over her shoulder, her expression a little lost. "I don't know, but Ricochet said to follow my gut."

I raised a brow as I looked around. "To a bookstore?"

Her smile was tiny and her shrug a little jerky, but she said, "It's my favorite one." She moved farther down the aisle, leaving me to follow. We were halfway down the row when she stopped and looked to her right.

Coming up behind her, I saw an old typewriter covered in the same dust as everything else, sitting on a table. It held a yellowed piece of paper with gibberish typed on it. It looked like a test page, proof that the antique actually worked. I wasn't so sure it would now, though.

Megan reached out, her hand trembling as it brushed just above the keys, close enough to disturb the dust layer but not close enough to touch the keys. She curled her hand into a fist and took a step back, bumping into me.

I put my hands on her shoulders, steadying her. "What is it?"

She shook her head, but when she looked at me, worry pooled in the depths of her blue eyes, turning them dark. "Do you hear that?"

My stomach clenched at the hint of fear in her question. The last time she'd sounded like that had been when I pulled her out of that damn warehouse. I tightened my hold on her shoulders. "Hear what?"

She tried to move around me, her gaze searching. "That."

Alarm raced through me because no one was here but the three of us. The small space made it difficult to hide anything, but I caught Ricochet's attention and signaled him to clear the rest of the aisles just to be sure. He slipped away, and I turned back to Megan. "No one's here, Megan."

She shook her head and rubbed her temples. "Are you sure?"

Arguing with her was pointless and would send her agitation skyrocketing. With no other option left but to watch her six, I did just that. "Ricochet is clearing the rest of the shop."

She stepped to the side, and I let her go because it was obvious she wanted her space. Only as she gained that space did I realize the unusual mist was no longer keeping its distance from her. In fact, it was now wrapped around her ankles like a living vine. That could not be good. I was about to call Ricochet over when he came around the far end of the aisle and headed toward us. He caught my eye and shook his head to let me know the shop was clear. I motioned toward the weird fog at Megan's feet. Ricochet studied the mist, but before he could do anything more, Megan sucked in a sharp breath. Her eyes widened and her face paled as she stumbled back until she was leaning against the shelves between us. Her hands went to her ears, covering them. Whatever she was hearing had to be getting worse. I went to reach for her, but Ricochet raised a hand, freezing me in place. Following his gaze, I noted that the mist was up to Megan's knees. Rico's eyes narrowed, his face going dark as he dropped into a crouch. He didn't try to touch the fog, but he studied it.

Leaving him to work, I concentrated on Megan. Moving in front of her, I caught her wrists and gently but insistently tugged them down. Holding her panicked gaze, I kept my voice calm. "You're okay, babe."

Her gaze clung to mine. "He's here." The words came out as a harsh whisper.

I didn't need to ask who. Only one person managed to carve that much fear into her face. "He's not. I promise."

Her grip on my hands tightened until it was almost painful, but I kept my flinch hidden. It hurt to watch her fight back the fear, but she managed.

Ricochet rose to his feet. "Did you touch anything?"

Occupied with her private battle, Megan shook her head.

"The books on the first set of shelves when she came in," I corrected.

"Right," Megan muttered, then she pointed to the typewriter. "And that."

Ricochet went to look at the books and then spent some time eyeing the dust-covered machine. He directed his next question to me. "When did the mist's behavior change?"

It didn't take much to follow his logic. "After the typewriter."

Next to me, Megan shivered and looked down, her eyes widening as she stared at the strange mist. Wrapping my arm around her, I pulled her close as Ricochet did a second take on the typewriter. She looked at me and whispered, "It's him, Bishop."

"I believe you," I said, and despite not hearing a damn thing, I did believe her. "But I swear to you, he's not here."

"Bishop's right," Ricochet said as he turned away from the typewriter.

"Okay." She cleared her throat and said a little more loudly, "Then how do I get rid of this voice in my head?" She stuck out a leg and shook it, but the mist didn't budge. "And this."

Ricochet folded his arms as a frown creased his forehead. "The voice... can you tell what it's saying?"

She gave a tiny shake of her head. "No, it's too soft."

Ricochet seemed unsurprised, but he gave me a grim look. "We need to bail."

Megan looked between the two of us. "I thought we needed to find the trigger?"

Ricochet grimaced. "I'm pretty sure we did."

I tightened my grip on her hand as she stiffened at my side, trying to pull away. "What do you mean?"

Ricochet motioned to the mist wrapped around her calves.

She followed where he indicated, and her face paled. "Seriously?" She scooted closer to me.

"Consider that his way into your mind." Ricochet's tone was hard, his face even more so. He jerked a thumb at the typewriter. "Add in touching that, and you've got a unique detection system. You've basically picked up the phone and called him."

I didn't think she could get any paler, but she proved me wrong. "Which means he's coming," she said.

Ricochet nodded. "Yeah, and I don't think we want to be here when he arrives."

Chapter Twenty-Two

Not needing to be told twice, I held tight to Bishop's hand as we made a hasty exit from the store. As soon as we left, the whisper in my mind gained strength and clarity, making my stomach cramp. Fragmented images of the horror-show variety joined the sibilant voice, churning a litany of paranoia until it became a nonstop loop with a voice-over from hell. Fear-induced nausea churned, and I choked it back.

"It's not real. It's not real," I chanted under my breath as I stumbled along in Bishop's wake. It wasn't freaking helping because the farther we went, the more twisted the mental barrage became until it was the only reality that existed.

"Megan!"

Bishop's voice was muffled by the hellish taunts, and his face was hidden behind the images filling my mind. "Bishop?"

I spun in a circle, trying to find him, but saw only nightmares. The fog from earlier was back, playing peek-a-boo with the scenery. It parted briefly, offering me a heart-stopping glimpse of two motionless bodies crumpled in the surreal landscape. Recognition hit. Bishop and Ricochet. Agony ripped through me, leaving my chest aching.

Pulse pounding, I stumbled forward, only to stop short when Dev stepped through the creeping fog, his hand pressed against his ravaged chest. Blood seeped through his fingers, and his pain-lined face lifted, betrayal and agonized fury blazing in his eyes. "Your fault," he hissed.

"Dev!" A mix of horrified guilt and grief propelled me forward as a choked cry escaped me. I reached for him, but my frantic hands passed right through him. His glare didn't fade even as he crumpled to his knees in front of me. I followed him down.

"I did warn you," that hated voice taunted from behind me.

Still on my knees, I jerked around and came face-to-face with writhing shadows and the same vague form that had chased me for weeks. "Fuck you!" Blinded with useless fury, I lunged to my feet, hands curled into claws. God knew what I thought I'd be able to do, but the urge to hurt and maim drove me.

I was caught in a haze of violent intent, and nothing penetrated it until an immovable object interrupted my forward momentum, knocking me back a step. Only the cruel hands locked around my arms kept me upright, the fingers pinching my nerves and sending a bright burst of flaring pain.

"Megan! Dammit, it's me. Look at me!"

Bishop's snarl cut through the taunts and whispers, and for a moment, the haze cleared. Bishop's face took its place, his expression marred by fury and concern. I quit fighting and instead clutched at him, staring hard, afraid that if I blinked, he'd return to lying dead behind me. "You're here."

Relief flickered in his dark eyes. "Right here, babe. I'm right fucking here."

It wasn't until Ricochet came up behind him, his normally impassive face revealing a matching worry in the small white lines around his mouth, that I believed. Seeing both of them upright and breathing not only allowed Bishop's reassurance to sink in but also dragged my brain back to rational thought. "Okay, okay. They're okay."

Hearing myself speak helped but didn't stop the stupid voices or the images that flickered, like mocking flames, in the corners of my eyes. Scared that those nightmares would suck me back under, I focused on Ricochet and Bishop with single-minded intensity.

"We're okay." Ricochet watched me carefully, but he directed his next comment to Bishop. "He's using her fear to strengthen his hold, which means our exit is compromised."

I knew that what he said should worry me. Panic nibbled at my heels, but I refused to chase it down, more concerned with holding it at bay. Having the living, breathing proof of Bishop standing in front of me helped keep what was real and what wasn't untangled. It left little room for pride, and fear stripped everything away except the unvarnished truth. "I'm barely holding on, Ricochet. Isn't there another way out of here?"

Oh, please, God, let there be some way out. I didn't know how long I could hold out before my composure and mind broke under the unrelenting pressure. If that happened here in a world of my mental making, it wasn't just me who would pay the price. Endangering the two men willing to risk themselves to stay with me wasn't an option.

My hands tightened on Bishop's arms. "You and Ricochet need to get out of here."

He didn't respond, but something in his expression warned me that he wasn't going to agree.

Fear and desperation rode me, and I tried to push him away, but he didn't budge. "You need to go now!" *It shouldn't be that hard, for fuck's sake. Ricochet is a damn dream-walker.*

"We aren't leaving you behind," snapped Bishop.

As my hold on sanity slipped, frustration made me speak harshly. "If Ricochet can get you out, get out!" I tried to jerk out of his hold and failed miserably. "Dammit, Bishop, let me go!"

Ricochet spoke over Bishop's growl. "Megan." When I stilled, he said, "I need you to trust me. Can you do that?"

Holding that grimly determined gaze, I gathered the shredded remains of my composure like a tattered jacket. "If it means you two get clear, then, yeah." I'd trust the devil himself if it meant keeping them safe.

"Then I need you to calm down and picture your tower. Can you do that for me?"

Swallowing hard, I nodded.

"Good. You do your part, and I promise I'll get us clear." He managed a small grin. "Don't forget the door, okay?"

Right, because he needs a way out. The clawing at my mind left me doubting my ability to follow any exit Ricochet could create, at least while I was holding the dreamscape for him, but at least the tower was relatively safe. I'd do whatever I needed to get them away from this mess. As for me, if I couldn't make it out, I could hunker down and wait it out. Maybe they'd make it back for me. Maybe.

I closed my eyes and did my best to steady my breathing as I worked through my mental chaos. It felt like forever before I pictured the stone tower, complete with a door. Since Ricochet didn't rush me, it could have been minutes, maybe less—not that it mattered. "I've got it."

The men didn't answer. Instead, the ground rolled underfoot, throwing me forward. As I lost my balance, I kept my eyes shut, desperately holding on to the image of the tower, and braced for impact. Instead of a bruising fall, I landed against something hard and warm. Blinking my eyes open at the startling sensation, I found myself sprawled across Bishop's lap, staring into his face, my heart pounding and my mouth dry. The marina photo on the wall behind him told me we were back where *he* couldn't reach.

Awkwardly, I pushed away, trying to sit up, but Bishop was determined to make sure I stayed close. I relented and sat stiffly in his lap as I ran a shaky hand through my hair, which had somehow escaped its band, and dragged the strands out of my face. Ricochet sprawled in the easy chair, his legs stretched in front of him, his fingers flexing on the armrest.

It was time for answers. "Where…? How…?" I couldn't figure out how to start.

"I had to take control of the dreamscape," Ricochet said. "To do that, I needed you to trust me."

I frowned. "I trust you."

"No, you don't." His firm response wasn't unkind. "On some level, you were determined to sacrifice yourself for us because you thought that was the only way out. To get your trust, even momentarily, I had to make you believe I'd be willing to leave you behind while we escaped."

Why did that make me feel like apologizing? It wasn't like I would have done anything differently. Not if it meant keeping Bishop—and by extension, Ricochet—safe. So if he was waiting for an apology, he had a long wait ahead of him.

Undeterred by my mutinous silence, he kept going, his voice a low whip of reprimand. "As a dream-walker, it's crucial for you to maintain control of your emotions. Emotions influence the dreamscape. Your fear paralyzes you, and you can't afford that if you intend to turn the tables on the bastard who took you."

His verbal hand slap sparked a mix of remorse and resentment. I muttered, "And here I thought fear was supposed to give you an edge." It wasn't as if I wanted to be afraid, but at the time, it had all seemed too terrifyingly real.

Bishop answered my surly comment with logic. "It can, but you have to accept it first. Once you acknowledge that there's nothing you can do to change what scares you, you realize your only option is to go through it."

I dropped my gaze as heat flooded my cheeks. Logically, what he said made perfect sense, but putting it into practice was a whole other kettle of fish.

Unfortunately, Ricochet wasn't done with his lecture. "If we're going to use you as bait, you have trust us."

Before I could respond, Bishop added solemnly, "Rico's right. To make this work, you have to know down to your soul that we not only have your back, but we know what we're doing as well."

The gravity of the conversation left little room for embarrassment or skirting the issues. Reaching beyond my knee-jerk defensive response, I acknowledged that they were right. Well, almost right. There was more to it than what they had witnessed. "I don't think it's you"—I shot a look at Ricochet to include him— "or you that I don't trust."

Ricochet's expression softened. "You don't trust yourself."

"And *he* uses that," I said in a low voice. It was a truth I hadn't forgotten per se, but I'd chosen to ignore it. "To break my hold over the dreamscape."

"He does," Ricochet confirmed.

Why it helped to hear that from him, I wasn't sure, but it did. "When we were in there, one of the things he showed me was the two of you dead."

"And you thought it was your fault?"

I nodded. Bishop's hands covered mine, and I couldn't resist twining my fingers with his, taking comfort in his touch.

"It doesn't matter how many reassurances we give you," Ricochet said. "You need to find a way to believe that we won't let you hurt yourself or us. Even more importantly, you need to find a way to believe in yourself."

I opened my mouth to argue, but what he said sank in with unsettling clarity. I kept treating this team like they were civilians, when they were the furthest thing from that. As professionals, their relationship with danger was intimate, and they survived threats I couldn't comprehend. Before my kidnapping, I'd hovered on the outskirts of their lives, or at least what they appeared to be to the outside world. Yet at the end of the day, I went home, safe in my ignorance of what really existed out there, as if their world was a book I could close and put aside. Bishop and his team didn't get that luxury. In fact, they thrived in this adrenaline-laced environment. The problem for me was my kidnapping blew that safe distance to smithereens. Now I was struggling to find my footing in a world I didn't understand next to people who knew it better than anyone else. So why couldn't I believe Bishop when he swore he wouldn't let me hurt him or them?

As if the question had flipped a profound switch, the answer blindsided me with its simplicity: because it scared me to depend on someone else. And much like when the hated voice taunted me, I was letting fear control my actions. Bishop was right—not only did I need to have faith in the team and their skills, but I also needed to find that same faith in myself.

Meeting Bishop's patient gaze, I gave a reluctant nod. "I'll figure it out." I wasn't sure how, but I'd figure it out.

⋯•◉◈◉•⋯

Unlike my time with Wolf, my most recent mental excursion had eaten up the rest of the morning and part of the afternoon. Unfortunately, just like before, it also generated the beginnings of a headache, which left my appetite nonexistent. The same could not be said for the two males discussing food options at the small kitchen table. After the third audible stomach rumble came from their direction, I decided to take a break, and I rummaged through the kitchen, piecing together a simple lunch of soup and sandwiches. Culinary wonder I wasn't, but it gave me something to do instead of being stuck on an endless wheel of worry. Bishop and Ricochet were so engrossed that they barely looked up when I set their lunches next to them. At least they managed to mumble a quick "Thanks" before going back to their discussion.

I was carrying my bowl of soup to the couch—the sandwich was a no-go, thanks to my stomach, which refused to settle—when someone's phone signaled an incoming text.

Bishop looked up from the notebook he was scribbling in, grabbed the burner phone sitting off to the side, and checked the screen. "It's Rabbit. He wants us to give him a call in fifteen."

I settled into the couch. "That's good news, right?"

Bishop and Ricochet shared a look before Bishop decided to field my question. "It could be."

"Or it could be that the colonel's demanding our asses," Ricochet muttered.

Yeah, or that. I concentrated on my lunch, and Bishop and Ricochet did the same at the tiny table. With each minute that ticked by, the air picked up tension. It made the fifteen-minute wait seem like an excruciating eternity. None of us lingered over lunch. When we were finished, Bishop and Ricochet gathered up the dishes and tackled the cleanup. There wasn't much room in the kitchen, so I had nothing to do but wait, which was a lot harder than it sounded.

Ricochet was drying the last bowl when Bishop hung up his dish towel and went to the phone lying on the table. He dialed then put the call on Speaker as it rang through.

At ring number three, Rabbit picked up. "Bishop?"

"You've got me, Ricochet, and Megan," Bishop confirmed.

"Good. Means I don't have to repeat myself." There was no sign of Rabbit's accent, and I knew that meant he had something serious to say, and not in a good way.

"Before you get started," Bishop cut in, watching me, "I have a question for you."

"Shoot."

"Any chance you can access Megan's phone records from the day she was taken?"

I blinked. *My phone records? Why does he…?* Memories cut that thought short. The call that had drawn me to the park, the one that was supposed to be from Keelie—Bishop was hoping to find out who'd made it. Silently, I wished him and Rabbit luck.

"Probably," Rabbit blithely answered. "They might be part of the file started when she went MIA." There were sounds of things being shuffled around, and Rabbit's voice was muffled for a minute before coming back clear. "Give me a couple of hours. Let me see what I can do when we're done here."

"Can do," Bishop confirmed.

Ricochet finished KP duty and took his seat at the table. With the kitchen area now empty, I made my move. My goal was the coffeepot. There was no way I would be able to sit still while Rabbit shared. Granted, the extra caffeine would cost me, but that was later.

Bishop sat back. "Okay, dazzle us, geek-meister."

Rabbit settled down to business. "Jinx and I managed to narrow our choices down to Jason Moreno and Garrett Hawes."

Ricochet leaned forward, frowning at the phone. "Major General Hawes?"

"The one and only."

Bishop let out a low whistle. "Who's Moreno?"

I cleared my throat, and both men turned to look at me. "He's with MCIA."

"Give the lady a prize," Rabbit said. "Major Jason Moreno is a chief intelligence officer within the Marine Corps Intelligence Agency."

Bishop's gaze narrowed on me. "How do you know Moreno?"

"He's met with the colonel quite a few times." I winced

because what I was about to share felt a little too close to talking out of school, even though I had no doubt these men were solidly behind the colonel. "Just before I left"—it was becoming easier not to trip over that phrase—"he was rather vocal in expressing his frustration when a funding decision didn't go his way."

"Based upon what I found," Rabbit clarified, "he was pissed because the funds he wanted for some heavily redacted project were reallocated to our teams."

Bishop's attention didn't waver, leaving me feeling like a fly under a microscope. "Mad enough to target Delacourt?"

"Maybe," Rabbit said. "He's got enough pull to undermine the colonel."

I was shaking my head before Rabbit finished. "I can't see it."

"Why?" Ricochet asked.

Why? Telling them his voice didn't fit or that it just didn't feel right wouldn't get me very far. I tried to apply logic to an illogical impression. "It's too easy. If he was so upset about the funding that he was willing to destroy the teams, he wouldn't have confronted the colonel, not with a witness nearby, because the moment something happened, he'd be at the top of this list." *Kind of like right now.* Reading their skepticism, I added, "Not to mention he's a chief intelligence officer."

"Gotta agree with her, boys." Rabbit's drawl was back in effect. "Don' make much sense to be so sloppy when you have more nefarious means at your fingertips. Those MCIA boys like their mind games."

Bishop grimaced. "Okay, I'll give you both that, but that leaves us with Major General Hawes."

"Which is a shit show waiting to happen," Ricochet supplied unhelpfully. "His connections are high and deep."

He wasn't wrong. I recognized the name even if I couldn't

bring up his face. It was a name generally linked with news out of DC.

Bishop rubbed his face before dropping his head into his hands and bracing his elbows on the table. "Fucking great."

The quiet beep of the coffee machine snagged my attention, and I made my cup of joe as we all waited for Bishop to decide if the risk of pursuing a high-level officer was worth it. Coffee poured, I turned to watch Bishop struggle with his decision.

"How deep did you dig, Rabbit?" His voice was tight.

"Couple of layers. Didn't want to try any deeper in case I sent up a warning flare."

Bishop turned to Ricochet. "What's your take?"

Ricochet shrugged. "I'm inclined to agree with Megan. Moreno is too obvious."

Bishop sucked in a deep breath and gave the green light. "Rabbit, start excavating Hawes, but for fuck's sake, be careful. Our asses are blowing in the wind here."

"Copy that." A faint knock drifted down the line, followed by Jinx's feminine murmur. Then Rabbit was back. "Megan, darlin', Jinx just confirmed our heads-up reached Dev, and he's currently on alert."

A tide of relief swept through me, and the cup wobbled in my hand. I set it down before I could drop it and leaned heavily against the cabinets as I battled the hot press of tears. "Thank you." Even choked, the words sounded so inadequate, but they were all I had to offer.

"You're very welcome," Rabbit said gently, then he cleared his throat. "One other piece of news to share."

"Does it involve not getting our asses burned?" Bishop asked in a disgruntled tone.

"Snuck a look at the police report on Megan's visitor from the other night. Fingerprints from the scene got a match." Rabbit rattled off some names. "I called in Kayden and Cyn to help run down names and addresses."

"Send me a couple," Ricochet said. "I'd rather be out poking under rocks than sitting around, twiddling my thumbs."

"Names and addies on their way." The clatter of keys accompanied Rabbit's voice. "And that, ladies and gents, is the extent of my wonderfulness."

"As always," Bishop said, "damn fine job, Rabbit."

"Aw, you know how to make a country boy blush, big guy."

"Bishop…" I hated to add to the responsibilities piling on his broad shoulders, but there was one more thing we needed to do before it was too late. He looked at me, and I laid it out. "You need to bring the colonel in." If the threat was that close, she needed to be prepared for the fallout.

His jaw flexed, but he dipped his chin in acknowledgement. "Rabbit, have Jinx bring the colonel up to speed."

There was a pause, then Rabbit asked with a hint of hesitancy, "All of it?"

Bishop pinched the bridge of his nose. "Yeah, all of it."

"'S all right. Hunker down, then, and consider it done."

"Thanks."

"Don't thank me yet." A dial tone replaced Rabbit's voice.

For a moment, we all sat there, each of us lost in our own thoughts until Ricochet's phone buzzed, probably with the names Rabbit had promised. Ricochet pulled it out, and I realized that my best guide in this crazy new reality might be getting ready to hit the road. It was time to take the next step in figuring my shit out.

"Ricochet?" When he looked up, I said, "Before you head out, maybe we could work on some basic dream-walking skills? Like how to keep *him* out without locking myself and others in? If you have time?"

Bishop shot me a look. Ricochet tapped the corner of his phone absentmindedly against the table and didn't answer right away as he studied me. His silence made me nervous but not enough to back down. I didn't want to end up in a situation where my ignorance got me or them killed.

Finally, he set the phone facedown on the table. "I've got time."

"You sure?" Bishop asked.

"Yeah." Ricochet stood up. "I recognize one of the addresses Rabbit sent me. It's a bar, no one worth talking to will be in for a couple more hours anyway." He pushed the coffee table off to the side, clearing the area in front of the couch. Motioning me to the floor, he took a position opposite of me. As we settled in, he ran a critical eye over me. "You sure you're up for this?"

Was I? Probably not, but then, if we waited for me to be sure, we'd be here forever. I shrugged. "I figure it's like riding a bike. When you fall off, best to get right back up." I gave him an unsteady grin. "Less time for the fear to grow that way."

Humor lightened his eyes. "All right. Then let's get to work on some defensive techniques."

For the next three hours, Ricochet proved to be an exacting, unrelenting teacher. When he finally called it quits, not only had I managed to not only keep him out of my thoughts, but on our last run-through, I'd even wrested control of the dreamscape away from him as well. It wasn't for very long, just long enough to slip the trap he'd laid. Then he took me through the bait-and-switch plan. The first time sucked, but determined to see it through, I made him go through it twice more before he called it quits.

Blinking my eyes open, I discovered that I was lying flat on my back while the dull throb in my temples had upgraded to a herd of elephants. When the afternoon light hit my blurry eyes, I groaned and threw an arm over them in a futile attempt to ease the pain. "Is it supposed to hurt like this?"

"Yep. Think of it like training a muscle. I'll have Bishop

grab you a couple of aspirin and some water. It should calm down soon."

I listened to Ricochet walk away, and then came the rumble of male voices followed by the sound of a medicine cabinet opening and closing. I drifted for a minute or two before something cool and wet touched my arm. I finally lifted my arm away from my eyes to find Ricochet crouched at my side with a water bottle in hand. "Drink this."

Gingerly, I pushed up until I was sitting with my back to the couch and took a few sips. Cradling the water bottle, I did my best not to think about anything. It was working. Then Bishop sat next to me, wrapped an arm around my shoulders, and pulled me in. "Here." He offered me two heaven-sent white tablets.

I took the aspirin then followed his lead as he had me lay my head in his lap. He pulled my hair free of the ponytail and began running his fingers through it. He kept his strokes soft and steady. It felt so good that I didn't bother stifling a low moan of pleasure. With the help of his soothing hands and the aspirin, the pain eased off and started to fade.

The guys talked, but I didn't pay attention, letting their rumbles wash over me as I soaked up Bishop's touch. I heard the colonel's name a couple of times and realized they were trying to figure out a proactive approach to her guaranteed irate reaction when she found out what they'd been keeping from her.

Most of my pain was gone when Ricochet said, "Well, I'm heading out. If I'm lucky, by the time I come back in, Delacourt will have vented her worst."

I opened my eyes, happy to find that the light didn't hurt, and watched Ricochet hightail it out of the house. It was strangely reassuring to know that these tough warriors were a tad intimidated at the thought of facing off against the colonel. Silence crept in as Bishop and I sat there in the quiet. Without the headache demanding my attention, I could not only feel the tension in Bishop, but I could also see it in the fine lines on his face. I caught his hand and pulled it to my chest, holding it over my heart. "You okay?"

He looked down at me and sighed. "Yeah, just trying to figure out if there's a way through this that doesn't end in a total mess."

I let him go and pushed up until I was facing him and the couch. Unable to resist, I used a finger to smooth over one of the deeper lines disappearing into his scruff. "If you manage to find one, promise you'll share?"

He caught my hand, brought it to his mouth, and pressed a soft kiss to my palm. His dark eyes roamed over my face, some of the harsh lines easing. "If we get thrown into a cell, you want to be my cellmate?"

Unable to resist his teasing, I put my free hand on his chest and leaned in close so I could rub my nose against his. Pulling back, I was happy to see his lips twitch. "Sure, but I call the top bunk."

"Babe, you can take top anytime you want."

From inches away, I couldn't miss the flare of want lighting the depths of his eyes or the need sucking out all the air between us. Taking him up on his invitation, I closed the scant distance between us and met his mouth with mine.

Chapter Twenty-Three

BISHOP

The minute she kissed me, I was lost. I opened under the first tentative swipe of her tongue. As if my permission was all she was waiting for, her hesitancy disappeared, her mouth moving over mine with a stunning boldness that left me craving more. Her taste—that unique honeyed spice tinged with the lingering hint of coffee—hit me like a fireball. Lust grabbed me by the balls, while want—and a softer tangle of emotions I refused to examine too closely—made me grip her hips with both hands as she climbed into my lap. When she settled over my aching cock, my groan was lost in our kiss. My fingers flexed against her curves as I tried my damnedest not to steal her control. As she teased and tempted, my willpower frayed. The hunger sucked me in, and my hands slid from her hips to wraparound the beautiful flame in my arms. Sinking one hand into her hair and clamping her delectable ass with the other, I dragged her close until the feel and taste of her were everything.

Eventually, the need for air became paramount, and our kiss ended. She kneaded my shoulders as she angled her head in silent request. Cupping her head with my hand, I nibbled along her neck as she sucked in air, her long lashes fanning her cheeks as her kiss-swollen lips took on a secret feminine curve. I pressed one last kiss to the base of her throat and rested my forehead against hers, waiting until those long lashes lifted and I was drowning in a midnight sea. "You are a dangerous, tempting woman."

Her slow smile was filled with mystery and promise. "Thought you liked danger." It came out on a husky tease.

Stroking her spine, I dropped a chaste kiss on the tip of her nose. "Maybe not as much as I like you." *Like.* Such a lame word to describe what she did to me, but neither of us was in the right place to finish what our kiss had started. I knew it, and she must have, too, because she sighed, her hands untangling from my hair to drift downward until she could wrap her arms around my waist and lay her head against my chest. Unable to resist holding her, I tightened my arms and rested my cheek on her bent head. For a moment, we sat there, quiet in each other's arms.

She was the first to get us back on track, lifting her head and leaning back so she could see me. "Isn't there something we can do besides wait on the others? If we're stuck hanging around here, I'm going to start climbing the walls."

As much as I wanted to offer to be her jungle gym, I reluctantly let her go, shifting mental tracks from want to necessity. "Rabbit's digging into Hawes, the others are tracking down leads on the idiot who broke into your place, and once Jinx fills in the colonel, I'm pretty sure our twiddling-thumbs time will be over."

Her gaze dropped, and she bit her lower lip, a sure sign that she wanted to say something but wasn't sure how it would be received.

Nudging her chin up until her eyes met mine, I said, "Spit it out."

"What if we go back to the warehouse?"

Taken off guard by that, I repeated, "You want to go back to where you were held?"

"Yes." There was no hesitation in her answer, and her gaze was rock steady. This was obviously important to her.

"Okay. Why?"

Her hands plucked at my shirt, the only sign of nerves. "If I went back, I might trigger some more memories."

I flattened one palm over her hands, stopping her nervous movement. "You sure you'll be okay with that? You haven't exactly taken it easy today." *Hell, even after the nerve-wracking ride with Rico, she dove right back in, determined to gain control over her ability.* Her tenacity made me wonder why she worried about breaking. She had no give in her. No matter how many times she got shoved down, she got right back up.

"I'll be fine," she said.

Yeah, she would be, but that wasn't my worry. "I don't know, Megan. You haven't been back since—"

She covered my mouth with her hand. "I'm not asking just to ask, Bishop."

Tugging her hand down, I searched her face. "Then why? Why now?"

Her gaze dropped as she tugged her hand free and scooted off of me until she was sitting back on the floor at my side. "I can't explain it, but I get the feeling I need to go back."

If anyone understood that kind of feeling, I did. "Okay." Whether it was a mistake or not, she needed this, but she wasn't waltzing in there without backup. "We don't go in alone. If we can't have Ricochet at your back, I'll call in Wolf." He was our next best option, and he'd be able to warn me if she got into trouble.

Relief filled her face. "Thank you."

Puzzled, I frowned. "For what?"

She shrugged and wouldn't meet my eyes. "For not babying me."

I leaned over until I could capture her gaze. "Hey. It's not about babying you."

"Isn't it?"

"Nope. Consider it me helping you figure out how to believe in yourself."

That made her look at me. "What do you mean?"

"This is all about facing your fears head-on and taking back your control." Her gaze slipped away, and I touched her chin, waiting until she brought her attention back to me. "There's nothing about that to be ashamed or embarrassed of, Megan. It's a hell of a move to make and takes balls. I'm happy to stand at your side while you do this. Wolf would say the same if you asked him. Besides, we'd be honored to stand by you to make sure nothing and no one gets to you." It was stupid to make such a promise, but I wasn't offering for the hell of it. She needed to know, in her bones, that she wasn't on her own in this mess and that I and the rest of the team would have her back no matter what happened. I was no therapist, but I'd dealt with enough shit on my own to know that going back with her to where her nightmares had begun would be a crucial first step to her reclaiming her faith in her ability to see this through.

She sucked in a big breath. "Okay, then. Let's do this before I chicken out."

⸻ •●◖●•• ⸻

Before we left the condo, I gave Megan my Glock, reminding her that it was for backup only. She handled the weapon with an easy familiarity as she informed me her brother had insisted that his sisters be comfortable around weapons.

Since we were trying to keep a low profile, Wolf met us a couple of blocks away from the warehouse. We made our way through the nearly deserted neighborhood. The businesses had dried up years before, leaving this section down by the bay a virtual ghost town. Not willing to clue anyone in to our presence, we did our best to remain unseen. During the rescue attempt, our team ended up taking out a handful of gunmen with rap sheets that read like a who's who of criminal intent. Most were linked to a foreign mercenary outfit specializing in questionable assignments. The ones still breathing had shut down tight and were awaiting extradition to various European countries. Whoever had hired them had deep pockets and enough power to keep them silent. Considering who our main suspect was, that was no longer a surprise.

Not many signs of the rescue still lingered—a few fire scars, pieces of police tape caught in a pile of old wooden pallets, and the drunken door hanging by a hinge and marred by black streaks from the explosives used to breach it. The rest looked as shitty as it had before. I took lead, with Megan behind me and Wolf bringing up the rear. Even though the place felt empty, I maintained a cautious approach, leading with my .45. Signaling Wolf to hold back with Megan, I stepped inside and cleared the main floor.

I didn't bother with the second floor since there were no stairs to access what little remained of it, not to mention that most of it could be seen from below, thanks to the missing floorboards. When I was sure the place was empty, I gave a low one-two whistle for Wolf's all-clear. They came in and waited just inside the door for me to join them. Wolf's gaze quartered the interior, while Megan stood with unnatural stiffness at his side.

I put my gun away and took Megan's hand. Her cold fingers interlaced with mine as we crossed the open space cluttered with rusted machinery, rotting pallets, and scattered containers before heading toward the back corner, our movements disturbing the thin layer of dust that had settled over the past weeks. The walls of the main structure were rife with jagged holes and topped by empty window frames that let in the afternoon sunlight. It didn't reach the thick solid walls taking up the back quarter of the space. As we drew closer, Megan's fingers tightened to the point of causing pain, but I didn't let go.

I stopped when she did. "Megan?"

She looked right at the pitted metal door standing partially open. Her face was sheet white. Maybe this wasn't such a good idea. Over her head, I caught Wolf's eye, and he looked grim but gave me a reassuring nod. He might not be all that keen on invading others' thoughts, but he knew why I'd called him in. He understood wanting to ensure that we didn't do more harm than good. Whatever he was sensing from Megan, it wasn't enough to have him calling it quits. Yet.

Holding tight to that, I stepped between her and the door, blocking her fixed stare. "Megan."

She looked at me. "I'm okay." It came out shaky, but she drew in air and repeated, "I'm good." This time it was stronger, surer.

Taking her at her word, I moved aside and pushed the door open. She locked her spine and walked into the darkness, Wolf and I on her heels. We stopped just inside the door, giving her space—emotional and physical. Not that there was much physical space to give in what was basically a makeshift cell. The iron ring she'd been chained to was still intact. Her movements were stiff as she moved forward then jerked to a stop, her attention centered on that damn ring. Her hands opened and closed at her sides.

Wolf was watching her, a frown furrowing his forehead. The sandpaper scrape of his voice broke the heavy quiet. "Megan, talk to us."

She flinched and half turned our way. I could see her pale face, and I could tell she was holding it together even if her voice was a little shaky. "I'm okay." Her gaze drifted over the floor, and she skirted the ring to move to the back wall. She dropped to a crouch, her fingers brushing over the cement. "I made these."

Leaving my position by the door, I went to her side. White gouges marred the cement, a stark testament to what she'd endured. It hurt to see how many there were. "You were trying to track the days."

"For a while, yeah." She pulled her hand back and balled it into a fist that she pressed against her stomach. "I lost track and finally gave up." She didn't look at me but took in the cell from her crouched position. She silently studied the room before standing up with a grimace. "I've got nothing. No flashes, nothing."

"Not quite true," Wolf countered from the door. "There's something there, just out of reach."

"That would be me being frustrated at getting nothing," she snapped.

"Beyond that," he pushed.

She glared at him. Before she could let her temper shut us down, I reminded her, "We're here to help, Megan, remember?"

She blew out a hard breath and rubbed her hands up and down her thighs. "Right. Okay." She closed her eyes, and the seconds ticked by before she haltingly said, "Fear, but not sharp, almost like it's been worn down, or I've been feeling it too long so it's just my new normal. I'm always listening."

"For?" Wolf asked.

"Him." With her eyes still closed, she cocked her head. "His footsteps are heavier than the one who brings my food," she said in a distant, flat tone.

That meant there had been someone else here at some point in time. I made a mental note of that fact.

"How long does it take to starve to death? A month? Two?" She asked the morbid question in a disturbingly logical tone, but she didn't wait for an answer. "If I stop eating now, it wouldn't take much. I think I'd prefer dying that way than whatever he's got planned because he's going to kill me. He doesn't have a choice."

I went to reach for her, but Wolf raised a hand, cutting my movement short. He shook his head at me before turning back to Megan. "What do you mean, he doesn't have a choice?"

"Someone met him here. They argued."

When she didn't say anything more, Wolf pushed carefully. "About?"

"Me, I think." She turned to Wolf, her expression a combination of worried and puzzled. "It's kind of twisted up with other crap, but there was something about cleaning up his mess when he couldn't deliver." Her head tilted as she looked at the door, clearly seeing something we couldn't. "*He* came back in, absolutely furious." When she turned back to Wolf, she wore a smile that was more of a bitter, bleak twist of the lips. "I don't remember much more after that. But I can't shake the feeling that I know him from somewhere. I just can't..." She sucked in a sharp breath and bent forward, clutching her head.

I didn't give a flying fuck what Wolf said—I caught her up and held her close. "I've got you, Megan. You're okay." I held her tight, feeling her shake.

Finally she patted my arm. "I'm okay, Bishop."

When she pulled back, I caught the crimson smear under her nose—just a drop or two but enough to alarm me. "Shit." I wiped it away with my thumb before swiping it on my jeans.

"What?" Her hand rose, but I caught it before it reached her face.

"Nosebleed. You need to take it easy." Catching her puzzled look, I elaborated, "Nosebleeds are a common sign of psychic overload. Between your sessions with Ricochet and this, you've pushed too hard."

Her eyes flashed, and her jaw firmed. "But we didn't get much."

God save me from stubborn females. "It's enough for now. We'll add it to whatever Rabbit digs up. Pushing yourself now will do more harm than good."

"Fine."

There was nothing graceful about her concession, but I'd take it. I nudged her toward the door. "Come on."

Wolf led the way back into the cavernous warehouse. "Bishop, did Rabbit ever figure out who owned this place?"

Following Megan across the floor, I said, "According to the records he found, the city owns it. They're in the midst of finalizing a deal with some developer."

"So a dead end, then."

"Yeah."

In front of me, Megan stumbled, catching herself against a stack of old pallets and knocking the top few off to shatter against the floor. The noise startled the roosting pigeons, who took flight in a rush of wings. But it was the flash of *knowing* in the midst of the confusion that had me diving for Megan while yelling, "Wolf! Down!"

The dull thud of an impacting bullet hit the pallets right where Megan's head had been, quickly followed by a second, then a third. Taking Megan to the ground, I twisted, putting my body between the ground and her. The rough cement scraped against my hip and shoulder. I continued the roll, ignoring the painful press of my gun against my spine, as I took us behind the dubious cover of a pile of containers and pallets. It wasn't much, but it was all we had. A quick look confirmed that Wolf had found a spot behind a thick, pitted column near the door. It sucked, but was better than nothing.

"Wolf?" I said in a low voice. Sitting up, I took care to stay low then helped Megan do the same.

"I'm good," Wolf said. "You?"

I swept my hands over a stunned Megan. "We're good. Where's he at?"

"From the angle, I'm guessing he's using the roof to access the second floor."

As if to prove his point, another bullet nailed the column near Wolf's head. He ducked back out of sight.

I pulled my gun out and rested one hand on Megan's head, keeping her low as I checked the angle. It wasn't good, especially as the shooter had the superior position. Not that it seemed to do him much good, considering the fact that we were all still breathing. It was safe to assume that whoever was on the other end of that gun wasn't a marksman.

Catching Wolf's attention, I switched to hand signals so as not to clue in our neighborhood shooter. Wolf did me one better when his voice floated into my mind. *He's working his way around clockwise. Probably trying for a better position.*

The bonus of working with a telepath was a built-in stealth communication system. Trusting that Wolf's angle was better than mine, I asked, *Can you intercept?*

Yeah, but you get to play distraction.

Copy that, I answered.

On two. One. Two.

I aimed around the containers, firing off of a rapid series of shots. Unless I was seriously lucky, they wouldn't hit, but they did their job in allowing Wolf to slip away into the shadows and hunt.

Return fire forced me to dart back behind the containers. Either the shooter's luck or his aim was improving because a bullet struck a nearby pallet, sending slivers of wood into my shoulder. It stung like a bitch, but at least it wasn't fatal.

It would take Wolf a minute, maybe a few second more, to get into position. To buy him that time, I needed to keep our shooter busy. I turned to Megan and cupped her face. Her wide eyes met mine, and I mouthed, "Stay here."

She gave me a tiny nod, and I gave Wolf a heads-up. *On the move.*

Using the snapshot I had of the warehouse's layout, I rushed out from our protective pile and zigzagged my way toward the cell, gun up, finger steady on the trigger. Bullets chased my heels as bits and pieces of cement pelted my calves. I felt the burn as one bullet got lucky and creased my side before I could dive behind another cluster of machinery.

A short one-two pop sounded behind me, then another gun joined the fray. Megan and Wolf were both firing, but the distinctive bark of Wolf's HK triggered a muffled curse. Then footsteps pounded, shaking the floorboards overhead and sending dust raining down.

Wolf's voice echoed in my mind. *He's on the run. Heading toward you.*

I lifted my gun and sighted along the trailing dust, aiming just ahead, and pulled the trigger. A pained yelp preceded the dull thud as weight slammed into the worn wood. A sharp crack sounded, and I covered my mouth and nose with an arm as the ceiling broke and a body tumbled through the choking cloud of dust and wood to smash into the floor.

Before the debris could settle, I was moving forward, gun aimed at the sprawled body. I could hear Megan coughing, but my attention was on the unmoving figure on the ground. I closed in, noting that our shooter had landed on his front.

"You got him covered?" Wolf asked from above.

"Yeah."

With my gun steady, I avoided the dark stain seeping from underneath one of his legs. Considering the angle, I was pretty sure it was broken. At least he wouldn't be running away anytime soon. I tried to locate his weapon, but with the way he'd fallen and the crap that had come down with him, I was coming up empty.

I'd started to circle him when I caught the slightest movement at my feet as he shifted. Before it fully registered, I had my gun sighted on his chest. "Don't do it." It was the only warning I'd give.

Unfortunately, he didn't heed it. He rolled, bringing his gun up. My finger tightened on the trigger, and my shot took him in the chest. His gun barked, but his aim was for shit, probably because he was concussed from the fall. I kicked the weapon out of his hand.

Lowering my gun, I dropped to my heels next to the mortally wounded man. "Who sent you?" I asked, even though I knew he wouldn't answer.

Sure enough, he gave me a bloody grin as the air rattled in his chest. "Fu… fuck you," he wheezed before choking on his own blood. By the time the man stopped breathing, Wolf was standing behind me.

I stayed where I was, my arms braced on my knees, my gun back in its holster at my back. "You get anything from him?"

"Not much, but he was pissed and knew the pay was too good to be true."

When greed topped skill, it generally meant a quick-and-dirty hire, not a professional hit. Together, we searched the body and, other than some gang tattoos, came up empty. No surprise.

"Bishop?" Megan asked in a shaky voice. I pivoted to find her standing over by the pallets, her face pale, two hands on the Glock aimed at the floor.

"We're good." I stood up, moving in front of the body and blocking her view.

Her tight shoulders eased, and she holstered the Glock as she made her way over. She pointedly ignored the dead man and touched my shoulder with trembling fingers. "You're bleeding."

I caught her hand and gave it a squeeze. "It's just a few scratches. Nothing to worry about."

She swallowed hard, her fingers curling with mine. She let go and gave me a careful push, and I stepped aside so she could see the body. "Who is he?" she asked.

"No idea." Wolf took out his phone and crouched down to take a picture of the shooter's face. A couple of snaps later, he moved on to scanning the shooter's fingerprints. "But we'll see if Rabbit can find out." He stood back up, his face grim as he stepped away to talk to Rabbit.

Now that we weren't dodging bullets, my brain was spinning up some serious questions, starting with, "How the hell did they know we were here?" I didn't realize I'd said that out loud until Megan went stiff at my side.

Realizing she'd taken my question the wrong way, I opened my mouth to explain, but before I could, Wolf came back over, his phone in his hand, as Rabbit's voice grimly said, "Which means y'all need to haul ass back because the colonel's called a meeting at seventeen hundred."

Apparently, Jinx had managed to fill Delacourt in, and judging by Rabbit's tone, it had gone as expected. "How pissed is she?"

"We're about DEFCON 3, *mes amis*, so be prepared."

I checked my watch. We were closing in on four, which gave us just over an hour to clean up this mess and get back to the office. "Not much time," I muttered to Wolf.

He ran his free hand over the back of his neck. "You two head in. I'll stick around and wait for Rabbit's cleaning crew to show."

"They should be there in fifteen," Rabbit confirmed from his end.

"What about a ride?" Megan asked. "We all came in together. If Bishop and I head in for this meeting, how's Wolf going to get there?"

"Ricochet," I said. "The address he was checking out. Is it nearby?"

Rabbit, correctly assuming my question was for him, said, "Yep. I'll have him swing over and pick Wolf up."

"Copy that." I looked back at the body. "Please tell me your cleaning crew doesn't belong to the local authorities." If it did, the amount of red tape Wolf would have to navigate would trump the colonel's meeting time.

"Doncha be bad-mouthin' my skills, Bishop. Like I'd sic those boys on you. We're keepin' our dirty business in-house, so no worries. Soon as they show, Wolf's free to fly with Ricochet."

Wolf's lips twitched. "Thanks for that."

"Anytime, my man, anytime."

Chapter Twenty-Four

I wasn't sure how Bishop managed it, but we made it to the office with two minutes to spare. Although I was fairly certain I could count a few more white hairs on my head after surviving Bishop's Mad Max dash through traffic, sitting off to the side in the conference room, watching him get stitched up, might be adding a few more. At this rate, a date with a bottle of hair color seemed imminent.

"Dammit, Doc."

"Stop whining, Bishop," said the man cleaning the last of the dirt and grit from the raw skin of Bishop's shoulder. "Better to get this cleaned out now than take a shot in the ass later." He jerked his chin toward the white bandage covering a bullet graze just above Bishop's waist. "Though I still recommend the damn shot."

"Your bedside manner sucks." Bare chested, Bishop sat stoically under Doc's ministrations, barely flinching as the doctor continued to patch him up.

Doc, the team medic, wasn't the typical white-coat-and-a-stethoscope type, with his close-cropped beard and long sun-streaked hair pulled back into a messy ponytail that barely tamed the curls. A faded concert T-shirt and even more faded jeans covered a body more likely to sling an ax and wear flannel.

"Embrace the suck, Bishop," suggested Kayden Shaw, the intimidating dark-haired man leaning against the wall on the other side of the table. The rather impressive arms he crossed over his chest flashed a peek of intricate ink circling his bicep.

Once upon a time, I daydreamed of meeting the entire PSY-IV team. This was not how I envisioned it happening. Not even close. Instead of being the quietly efficient and valued administrative assistant, I was squirming in my seat from the speculative looks drifting my way. I did my best to stay invisible, but with six of the nine team members and a large conference table, the normally spacious conference room felt crowded.

At one end of the table, Jinx and Rabbit huddled around a pair of laptops. Determined to keep my attention on the people I knew, I caught Jinx checking her watch again. When she frowned, my low-level hum of anxiety went up a notch. We'd been at the table for fifteen minutes with no word from the colonel. Tardiness was not her habit.

"Where is she?" asked the unforgettable woman sitting in front of Kayden. She had dark hair, spooky green eyes, and a scar that trailed down her jaw before disappearing under her T-shirt. Cynthia Arden—who everyone called Cyn—scared the crap out of me, and I couldn't even say why.

"Maybe she got hung up," Jinx offered.

Cyn made a quiet hum, neither agreeing nor disagreeing with Jinx's observation. Then she shocked the hell out of me by saying, "What do you think, Megan? Is this normal for the colonel?"

Startled, I answered honestly. "Not unless something's changed drastically in the last six months."

Cyn shot a look at Kayden, who muttered, "Right," then

straightened from his lean and moved to Rabbit and Jinx. "See if you can find out where she's at, Rabbit."

Rabbit gave a short nod. "I'll activate a trace on her phone, but it may take a bit."

Doc pushed back from Bishop, stripping off the thin medical gloves and tossed them towards a nearby bin. "There, good as new."

Bishop stood up, rolled his shoulder, and winced.

Doc's hands stilled on his med kit. "What? Too tight?"

Bishop rubbed the white gauze pad and shook his head. "Nah, we're good." He pulled his T-shirt back on before scooting his chair closer to me. "Catch us up on what you found about the major general."

"Yeah, exactly how did we end up pointing a finger at Hawes?" Doc finished neatly repacking his supplies.

"Process of elimination." Jinx looked up from her laptop, her face grave.

"That's not the best basis for starting a witch hunt." A heavy layer of concern colored Doc's voice.

"We've worked with less," Cyn said, her tone and expression not revealing whether she thought that was a good or bad thing.

"And it's ended up costing us," Doc shot back, undaunted by the glare Cyn aimed his way. Brave man that he was, he stared her down.

Jinx interrupted what was sounding like the beginning of an old argument. "Time-out, you two. We have enough going on. Let's not turn this into a soap opera."

Cyn gave a huff but dropped her gaze.

Doc shook his head and sighed. "Fine. What do we need to know about the major general?"

"I heard he lost his wife and kid twenty years ago." Kayden left Rabbit and dropped into a chair next to Cyn.

"Yeah, Lady Luck hasn't done Hawes any favors," Rabbit

said then caught Kayden's eye. "Trace is working." He turned back to the group. "At first glance, our major general reads like a tragic hero."

"With a stellar military record," Jinx added.

"Until you rub some of that shine off," Rabbit cut in. "Then those tarnished spots start popping up."

Jinx shot him a look and went back to sharing. "According to filed incident reports, he'd just completed a highly classified assignment when he got word that his wife was killed in a bungled burglary while his toddler son was upstairs in bed." She turned her laptop around and pushed it toward Doc.

The medic pulled it close. Cyn got up and came around to watch over his shoulder as he clicked through the information. "They made a hell of a mess."

Cyn grimaced. "Holy hell. Based on the level of violence, the thief did not take the interruption well."

Doc clicked. "Yeah, and based on the coroner's report, she didn't stand a chance." He shifted his attention to Jinx. "The son slept through this?"

Even I, who didn't know Doc from Adam, could hear the disbelief in his voice.

Jinx nodded. "The poor kid was in and out of therapy for years. Not that it helped, considering he OD'd three years ago."

"What a waste. God, how many drugs did they have him on? Fuckers." He frowned as his eyes moved over the scrolling information. "He was, what? Twenty-two or twenty-three?"

"Twenty-two," Jinx said. "Hawes started a charity in both his wife and son's names after that."

Doc sat back, pushing the laptop toward Jinx. "Sad as his story is, there's not much there that makes me think evil mastermind."

"Me either, until we scratched the shine away," Rabbit said. "You see, when Hawes's wife died, she left a sizable amount of family money to her only son. At twenty-five, her baby boy stood to inherit a life-changing amount of money. Until then, daddy-o controlled the purse strings. Guess who inherited when the son met his tragic ending."

"Hawes." Cyn's tone was hard.

Rabbit touched his nose. "Got it in one, *chere.*" Rabbit's lazy humor disappeared, replaced by a tone of cold practicality. "With wife and son no longer in the picture, the major general came into a shit ton of money. Money he manages behind the mask of that charity he created. But see, here's the thing. That money? It's grown substantially—as in, a hell of a lot more than can be explained by charitable donations and investments. As a matter of fact, I went to backtrack a few of the more questionable amounts, and I'm still trying to unravel the knots."

"And that's not his only sin." Jinx took back her laptop, typing as she talked. "He didn't stay the mourning widower long, because within a month of putting his feet back on US soil, he had a lover tucked away in a condo a few miles from his home."

"He's gone through quite the arm-candy selection," Rabbit added, proving that this back-and-forth he and Jinx had going was a familiar one. "And we're not talking about corporate Carols either. Think more along the lines of femme fatales of DC's elite."

Jinx grimaced and set her laptop back on the table, where Bishop snagged it. "Most of whom are kept quite discreet," she said, "but if you keep digging—"

"And we did," Rabbit said.

Jinx didn't bat an eye at Rabbit's interruption. "There are a couple of incidents suspiciously light on details."

"Incidents?" Kayden asked. "What kind?"

"The domestic-abuse kind," Rabbit said, no trace of humor in sight. "In fact, during two such incidents, Hawes made a large one-time withdrawal right when the whispers started to gain serious strength."

I scooted closer to Bishop until I could see the screen and the information he was scrolling through. I gave a soundless whistle as I read the names of the two women they were discussing—Ilene Ferguson and Margot Atler. The team had reason to be worried. These women weren't the type to keep their mouths shut if someone hurt them.

"Payoffs." Bishop continued to scroll through the files.

"That's what we're thinking," Jinx agreed. "Problem is, we tried to dig up the current whereabouts of the two women in question, and we keep hitting dead ends. It's like they disappeared into thin air."

"Maybe they moved," Doc suggested.

"Or maybe they're dead," Cyn said.

Bishop scrolled to the next screen, and everything in me stilled. I grabbed his wrist, forcing him to stop. "Who is that?" It came out harsher than I'd intended and cut the surrounding conversation off.

"Danielle Ferguson, Ilene's younger sister."

My world spun in a sickening lurch as I stared at the smiling face. "Oh my God, she's real." That face had haunted me the most because she'd died with my hands wrapped around her throat.

I didn't realize I'd gotten to my feet or that I'd backed away from the laptop until Bishop's face filled my vision. He was standing in front of me, his hands tight on my arms, holding me up. "Megan, talk to me."

"I... she... I was..." I blinked rapidly, fighting against the hot press of tears.

"Breathe, babe." The order was soft but firm.

I held on to it and him, sucked in a breath, and kept my shit together. "She's the one I told you and the colonel about, from my nightmare. The one I—" I gave an abrupt headshake. "*He* strangled."

"You're sure?"

I nodded a little frantically and braced my hands on his chest. "If they can't find her, it's because she's dead, and *he* killed her."

"Someone want to explain what's going on?" Kayden had moved closer to us.

Bishop let me bury my face against his chest as he brought the team up to speed on my role in the whole mess. Huddled in his arms, I was glad he was the one explaining. I wasn't sure I was up to it. He didn't leave anything out—not my worry about being a mole or my newly discovered ability. He finished with the latest run-in with the shooter.

There was no judgment in his retelling, just a simple statement of facts. It gave me the strength to stop hiding and face the team by his side. I couldn't help watching their faces, but they were skilled at giving nothing away.

"How did the shooter know you would be there?" Doc asked.

"Maybe he was told to hang around in case someone showed up?" Jinx's explanation might have sounded convincing if she hadn't ended it as a question.

Cyn snorted. "That'd be a hell of a long shot." She tapped her fingers on the table. "Whose idea was it to go back to the warehouse?"

I cleared my throat. "Mine. I wanted to see if going back would trigger any other memories."

"Did it work?"

"Yeah," Bishop answered. "She remembered her kidnapper arguing with another individual about her still being alive."

"Hmm," Cyn said, looking thoughtful. "Anyone know if Hawes ever tested for psychic abilities?"

"Nothing's in his file," Rabbit said.

"That doesn't mean much," Jinx added.

"What does your gut say, Bishop?" Doc asked.

The arm around my waist tightened. "My gut isn't proof."

"No, but it hasn't led us wrong yet," Kayden said.

Bishop sighed. "I think Hawes is behind Megan's kidnapping, and I think Cyn's right to think he's psychic. I'm betting he made sure to keep his ability hidden. Chances are good if we let Rabbit and Jinx dig deeper, we'll eventually not only uncover the bodies, but we'll find a tie to Falcon too."

A string of soft curses broke out, and Bishop grimaced. "We can take all of this to the colonel, but proving it will be a problem."

"Especially since it means he's probably got more than just money to keep that shit quiet." Cyn got up and paced along the side of the room.

"He'd need a powerful someone to watch his six," Kayden agreed.

"More like a couple of someones," Rabbit corrected.

"As much as I hate to remind you all," Doc said, "we can't do a thing with this unless we have actual proof."

"Give us a couple more days, and we can get you a gift with a damn bow," Rabbit said in a tone of unshakable certainty.

The door to the conference room swung open, bringing the conversation to an abrupt halt as Wolf and Ricochet walked in followed by a lanky wild-haired man who did a quick scan of the room before his expression settled into grim lines. "Risia called."

Next to me, Bishop stiffened while the room went wired.

Wild Man looked at Kayden. "Where's Delacourt?"

"She's late," someone answered.

"That's not good," Wild Man muttered.

Bishop let me go and rubbed a hand over the back of his neck. "What's going on, Tag?"

Wild Man, aka Tag, didn't waste time. "I don't know. Risia called as I was heading back here. She said she caught a flash of seeing, but nothing concrete. Just enough to let her know the colonel's in trouble. She said if I got here and Delacourt wasn't here, I was to tell you all that whatever you were talking about, you're on the right track, but you'll have to move fast or lose the colonel."

That seemed to kick the team members out of their stunned state and back into high gear. Questions and orders flew around the room until a sharp whistle cut through the rising volume. Everyone turned to Cyn, who dropped her hands from her mouth. Strangely, she shot me a sympathetic look, and some instinct flared. I knew what she was going to say, and as much as it would hurt to hear it, I couldn't fault her.

"I think Megan should go back to the condo." When a couple of protests were made, she said, "As a precaution. Whatever connection she shares with Hawes, it's enough to clue him in on what's happening."

Next to me, Bishop stiffened and took an aggressive step forward, but I grabbed his hand, pulling him to a stop. "No, she's right." Little pieces that had worried me were beginning to slip into place, thanks to Cyn's blunt assessment. When Bishop looked back at me, I managed a reassuring smile even though everything in me wanted to rage and rail. It wasn't fair —I was part of this mess. But I wasn't stupid. Despite my need to take Hawes down, to hurt him the way he hurt me, my presence with the people performing that task would be a critical liability. "It was my idea to go to the warehouse, remember? Then I got that headache, the one you said meant I was using my abilities too much. What if it had nothing to do with my abilities? What if Hawes was influencing my decisions?"

"You don't know that," Bishop said, sounding exasperated.

"No, I don't, but if there's the slightest chance that it's a possibility?" I let the question hang between us. "If Hawes is who we suspect, it's better if I'm not here while you plan."

"You wouldn't betray us," Bishop snapped.

"Not intentionally." I watched him struggle with the truth. "One session with Ricochet doesn't mean I can keep Hawes out of my head. You guys need to be able to go in with full confidence that he has no idea you're coming for him. You can't waste time worrying that he'll use this connection he forged and turn me into some mindless weapon."

"You wouldn't let him."

As much as I appreciated his confidence, I wasn't so sure. "Maybe, maybe not. He almost had me last time. I won't risk your team or the colonel just to soothe my ego." I searched his face, refusing to let my hurt show because it had no place here. "You know I'm right." Knowledge seeped in, eroding his stubbornness. Ignoring our curious audience, I braced my hands on his chest then rose on tiptoe to press a soft kiss to his chin. His hands settled on my waist, holding me close. Brushing my cheek alongside his jaw, I whispered, "I won't risk you. Don't ask me to."

The hands at my waist tightened as he dropped his head and pressed his lips where my neck and shoulder met. When he lifted his head, I saw his grim acceptance and knew I had won. I cupped his jaw. "Thank you."

I stepped back, and without his warmth, I felt a chill break over my skin. Everyone was watching us, and my cheeks heated, but I refused to be embarrassed at revealing how much Bishop meant to me. "Be safe." I wanted to say a hundred other things, but that was the most important one.

His jaw flexed, but he gave me a nod. "Ricochet."

As if he'd expected to hear his name, Ricochet was suddenly at my side. "I've got her."

The two men exchanged a look, a silent conversation, before Bishop said, "Thank you."

With nothing more to add, I turned and followed Ricochet out the door.

Chapter Twenty-Five

BISHOP

W atching Megan walk out the door sucked, but logic insisted it was for the best. It was Kayden who got us back on track. Within a couple of hours, we had a handful of certainties. One—the trace on the colonel's phone was a no-go. Even when Rabbit tried turning it on remotely, all we got was crickets, making it highly probable the phone was nothing more than shattered electronics. Two—Rabbit found one outgoing call on the colonel's phone just after Jinx filled her in. Surprise, surprise, the call was to base command's HQ, where one Major General Hawes claimed an office. Three—the last known location of the colonel was base command's parking lot, where Tag and Cyn found her locked and empty car. Cyn tried retracing Delacourt's steps, using her ability to read past events, but unfortunately didn't get much. There was too much foot traffic, she said. As a post-cog, she relied on the emotional echoes to sneak a peek into the past of a place or object, and the more personal the space or object, the clearer she could read. In this case, the base command's parking lot gave her nothing but a headache. Like any military installation, security was a bitch, so accessing the video feed on the lot meant Rabbit exercising his hacking skills. Working his magic, he found the colonel's arrival fairly quickly. Unfortunately, all we got was her getting out of her car and crossing the lot. Right before she went inside, someone off camera caught her attention, and she moved out of frame to where there were no electronic eyes.

With no other avenues to explore, we changed gears. Jinx combed through the electronic calendars, financials, and real estate holdings of the major general and, by process of elimination, got us a fairly solid schedule with an address. We also added Delacourt's home address to our to-do list, even though the chance she was home was slim to none.

We split into two teams—Kayden, Cyn, Tag, and Jinx taking the colonel's home, leaving Wolf, Doc, Rabbit, and me to scout out Hawes's expansive estate. With plans in place, weapons strapped, and comms check complete, we headed out into the early evening and the snarling mess of Thursday-night traffic in one of the bland SUVs kept in the office lot. With nothing to concentrate on but driving, my mind decided to replay the scene with Megan. Cyn's concerns were legit, but that didn't erase the smudge of guilt for kicking Megan out that lingered like a bad taste on my tongue.

"For fuck's sake, Bishop." In the passenger seat, Wolf rubbed his temples. "You want to tone it down a little?"

Wincing, I threw up the mental shields Wolf had made sure each of us had honed into nearly impenetrable walls. "Shit, sorry." Wallowing in my thoughts was not a wise move around a telepath—a point to remember, considering our suspicions about Hawes.

He waved my apology off. "It happens." He sighed and focused on the passing scenery.

Something was working in his mind. I just wasn't sure what, so I kept quiet. He'd share if he thought he needed to.

Sure enough, a few minutes later, he said, "She wasn't blaming you, you know."

I shot a look to the rearview mirror to find Doc staring out the window and Rabbit with his head back and eyes closed, both attempting to give us privacy. Getting into this now, in front of them, was not on my agenda, but they were my team. If I planned to lift up my skirt, at least they wouldn't post it all over social media.

My hands tightened on the wheel. "Yeah, I know."

"Then what's with the guilt?"

I poked at the feeling in an effort to answer, wincing when I hit a sore spot. "Admitting she could be used against us..." I shook my head. "Hearing her say it is one thing, but hearing the same thing from Cyn..." I rolled my shoulders, trying adjust the shitty feeling. "It felt like we were kicking a damn puppy."

Wolf snorted. "Fuck that. She's more like a damn pitbull."

That made my lips twitch. "I know that. You know that. But..."

"But?" he prompted when I fell silent.

Relationships were not my thing, so I had no idea if I was breaking a cardinal rule and sharing where I shouldn't, but dammit, this was Wolf and Doc and Rabbit. If I couldn't talk to them, I was screwed. Besides, they'd zip lips with the best of them. "She hates being thought of as weak."

"Who the hell called her that?" Rabbit asked.

I snorted. "No one, but it doesn't seem to matter. She can't let go of her fear that she'll hurt the team."

"Not the team. You," Doc corrected. "She's trying to protect you."

And wasn't that a kick in the balls? I wasn't used to someone trying to protect me, especially since I considered the protector role to be my job. "Yeah, she's so fixed on saving my ass that she's not watching hers." Having that kind of blind spot worried me because Megan was the type to risk it all for those she considered hers. She never said it, but in every touch, every look, those damn sketches—*hell*, even the act of pulling me into her dreamworld—all of that said what she never had aloud: that she considered me hers. And that was a damn good thing because I, too, was just a tad possessive of what I considered mine.

Rabbit lifted his head and sat up. "Good thing she has you, then, ain't it?"

No truer words were ever said. "Yeah it is," I said. *But it also makes my job that much more difficult.*

"Warned you, brother." Wolf went on to prove that no matter how strong my mental shields were, things got through. "I told you getting emotionally involved would blur your lines."

I risked shooting him a look. "Didn't stop you with Meli."

Wolf flashed me a grin before he muttered, "It's like that, then?"

"Yeah, it's just like that." Unfortunately, I'd do a hell of a lot more than just blur the lines for Megan if it meant keeping her alive and breathing. That truth sank into my battered heart, throwing my world off kilter. At the last minute, I remembered to keep my mental walls high and tight, but it was too little, too late.

Wolf shook his head. "Damn, man, you've got it bad."

Rabbit leaned forward, arms braced on the front seats, his shit-eating grin taking up my rearview mirror. "'S all good, 'cause while he's coverin' Megan's cute little ass, we'll cover his."

"Keep your damn eyes off her ass," I warned Rabbit.

Doc shoved Rabbit back into his seat. "Dare you to say that in front of Jinx."

Rabbit widened his eyes in mock innocence. "I ain't foolish enough to tug on death's whiskers."

With that, sharing time was over. *Thank God.*

Twenty-five minutes later, we pulled into a ritzy neighborhood filled with tree-lined gates guarding overly large houses that sat back from the road in tiny pretend fiefdoms. We did a drive-by of Hawes's address as we cruised through the elite neighborhood, and I pretended to be just another everyday gawker in a tinted-window SUV. I kept our speed at the limit, taking in the fifteen-foot wall wrapped around the property's boundary, the ornate gate with thick bars, and the huge-ass house sitting back behind the screen of trees. As the full extent of Hawes's estate sank in, I let out a low whistle. "Damn. That's got to be worth—what, three to four million?"

"More like five plus," Doc said. "Especially since he's got no neighbors behind him."

"Bet that's where some of that squirrelly money went." Soft clicks accompanied Rabbit's comment. "Looks like he picked a primo lot. It backs into a park."

"He's got security," Wolf said in a hard voice. "At least ten that I could sense."

At the end of the street, I took a right. "Did you catch positions?"

Wolf shook his head and turned to Rabbit. "The side neighbors looked pretty close."

"Yeah, they are, but there's a ridge along the back line we could hike over. It would bring us in from the rear of the property." Rabbit made a few more clicks and directed me out of the neighborhood and into the parking lot of a ritzy golf resort.

We pulled into the back and parked in the employee lot,

where the SUV fit in with the other reasonably priced cars. With night settling in, it wasn't hard to blend in with the shadows and make our way back over the ridge. We snaked down the ridge, our goal Hawes's back fence. While we hiked, Rabbit checked in with the others. Unsurprisingly, Delacourt's place was locked up tight with no sign of the colonel or anyone else.

Hitting our target, we separated and picked our spots for overwatch. Rabbit sent the other team our coordinates, and we settled in to await their arrival. Spread out along the back line of Hawes's property, we had an uninterrupted view of his three-story McMansion and the glittery pool caught in the spill of landscaping lights. There was enough illumination to negate our need for the night-vision viewer I'd pulled out of my pocket. The scene was straight out of *Lifestyles of the Rich and Famous*, minus the famous part. Why in the hell would one man need that much space? The whole place was dripping in pretension and left me wondering how no one found it odd for the major to afford a house like this.

I didn't realize I'd said the last part out loud until I heard Wolf's voice in my ear. "Don't forget the wife came from money."

"And he's fucking creative with his finances," Rabbit chimed in.

"Got movement," warned Doc. "Counting two, both armed."

"I've got one walking the yard." I kept my voice low, knowing how well sound carried.

"Two on this side," Wolf said.

"Got interior patrols moving in pattern," Rabbit added. "Hard to tell. Could be two, maybe three."

And that isn't counting whoever patrols the front. "Hell of a security force for a single man," I said. "Wolf, can you scan for Delacourt?"

"I can try. Distance is a bitch, and if Hawes is the telepath we think he is, he'll have precautions in place."

"Give it a shot."

We fell silent, waiting while Wolf did what he did best. One minute ticked by, then another before I heard Wolf's soft curse. "Son of a bitch is definitely psychic."

"You trip something?"

"No. Went in soft and slow. Found a few triggers and let them be, but he's shielding like a bitch."

"Any sign of Delacourt?"

"Not yet, but he's got a lower level out of sight."

Fuck. That was not good. "Rabbit, can you get—"

"Blueprints. On it." A piece of shadow broke from the others and slipped away.

We continued to watch as the minutes ticked by. Recon required patience, which was no easy thing when you knew shit was going down and you were stuck watching for hours at a time. This time, we didn't have hours to waste. Twenty minutes in, a soft warning click in my ear signaled the arrival of the rest of the team. We left Doc on watch and retreated behind the ridge, far enough away not to draw attention. Rabbit was hunched over his phone as everyone circled around. He'd managed to find a blueprint of the house, and sure enough, there was a basement level. We kept the comms open so Doc could listen in. Discussion was short and to the point.

With such a large estate, it was imperative that we search the entire house for Delacourt, which meant splitting into teams. The sticking point came when we had to figure out how to keep Hawes unaware of our infiltration. Then Cyn turned to me. "Why not go with the initial plan you came up with? The one where Megan keeps Hawes busy?"

My initial reaction was to snap *Fuck, no,* but then I shoved my emotions aside to make room for practicality. I turned the plan over and over, a sense of knowing growing with each revolution. Asking Megan to step back into that dreamworld was risky as hell. I remembered Rico's warnings. Inside that psychic sphere, it wouldn't take much for a telepath to turn the tables on a dream-walker, with disastrous results. But going in without a distraction was an even bigger risk—not just to our team but for the colonel as well. In the end, despite leaving my guts in a tangle of icy knots, the decision was simple. We needed that distraction.

I turned to Wolf. "Can you reach Ricochet? Get his take."

He nodded, tilted his head, and half closed his eyes. Everyone waited while Wolf stretched his ability out and *spoke* to Ricochet. Although there wasn't much light outside the small penlights we were using, I caught his slight flinch. He gave the merest hint of a smile, blinked a couple of times, and rubbed his chin. "They're a go, but I got to say, based upon what she threatened Rico with if he didn't say yes, you might want to make it a point not to piss her off."

That didn't exactly ease my worry. "If Ricochet isn't sure—"

"No matter what she threatened," Wolf said, "if he wasn't okay with it, he wouldn't have given the green light." His eerie sea-green eyes held mine, and his voice was steady in my mind when he added, just for me, *Give her this. She needs to be a part of this.*

Swallowing hard, I nodded.

Wolf turned back to the group. "They need about thirty minutes to pull him in, then we can move in. We'll need to rely on our comms because I've got to keep a mental path open with Rico." A round of nods came back. "All right, then, in case you missed it, Hawes is definitely a telepath, so keep those mental walls locked tight. Don't give him a crack to slither through, copy?"

I heard a soft chorus of "Copy." Then we went back over

the plan, piece by meticulous piece. The peculiar calm that preceded any mission settled over my shoulders, smoothing away the ragged edges of worry and leaving nothing but the immediate in its place. The expressions around me fell into familiar lines as we did our last-minute checks. Then it was time.

"We've got fifteen minutes to get into position," Wolf warned, twisting his wrist up to set his watch. We all mimicked him, fingers poised. "Starting now."

Chapter Twenty-Six

*G*o, dog, go.

I hit the last *o* on the dust-laden typewriter and listened to the faint snap of the key drift away into the forgotten books behind me. Brushing my dusty finger against my jeans, I turned away and walked through the bookstore, stroking dusty spines as I passed the shelves. A sense of being stalked followed me to the open doorway. Back outside in the post-apocalyptic nightmare, I looked around, tense and worried. Although nothing stared back, I shivered.

"Buck up, buttercup." My muttered comment sounded overly loud in the war-torn dreamscape. I was back in the same dreamscape that Ricochet and Bishop had followed me through earlier, but this time, I was flying solo. Well, for the most part. Ricochet was around somewhere, but this was my dream, and he was playing ghost because we didn't want to spook Hawes. Instead, I was all but staked out like the sacrificial virgin for the fire-breathing dragon.

A shadow passed overhead, and I jerked my head up, searching the gray skies as my heart pounded in sudden fear. Rico's advice about being careful with what I'd created reverberated through me. *Dammit! Why the hell did I have to pick that image?* The last thing I needed was to add a freaking dragon to the mix. A silent inky form drifted on the winds, joining a handful of others as they circled something in the distance. Faint caws sounded, and I braced a hand against the warped doorframe, dropping my head as I relearned to breathe. Crows or ravens? It was hard to tell from this distance, but I could totally handle those over a dragon.

Forcing my feet to move, I headed away from the remains of the bookstore, picking my way through the desolate city streets as I trudged toward my tower. It was Ricochet's idea to start at one of the scenes Hawes had used to torment me, not at the tower, my place of protection. We didn't have time to play the necessary mind games needed to trick him inside. It would be easier, Ricochet said, to fool Hawes into thinking I was simply asleep and dreaming than to lay a trap. Since there was no freaky, intimidating stalker fog nearby, I deduced that Hawes hadn't clued in yet.

Figures. I'd picked this scene because it was the most recent, but I had another one in mind, a darker one that left my stomach cramped and my hands shaky. My courage wasn't strong enough to dive straight into it, so I was taking the longer path to the waiting nightmare—Danielle's murder.

There were many scenes Hawes liked to taunt me with, but that one… yeah, that one got to me the most. His enjoyment, the thrill and pleasure coursing through him—and through me because I couldn't escape his demented hold—was like a drug that drew him back time after time. The fact that it made me ill and left me screaming into the void as I teetered on sanity's edge just added to his sadistic feast.

An upraised root caught my foot, sending me sprawling forward, my palms and knees hitting hard. Rock, wood, and dirt pitted my palms and stung my knees. The change in scenery barely registered as the suffocating dread pressed like a demon's hand against my spine, leaving a bone-deep chill in its wake. Something slithered in the thick greenery nearby. The flutter of wings came from overhead, but only shadows drifted through the leaves. I started to shake, and a whimper escaped me as my fear grew teeth and sank them deep into my racing pulse.

He was out there. I could feel him hunting me. When he caught me... my brain stalled under the swamping terror, leaving me blind.

I scrambled to my feet and stumbled forward, hand outstretched, sobs hitching in my chest. Branches tore at my skin and clothes, the whiplike stings adding another layer to the mindless panic driving me forward. I slammed into a tree, bounced off hard, and landed on my ass. The impact was so jarring that my fear receded just for a second—long enough for me to recognize what was happening: Hawes was playing with me, using my fear against me. Again.

Son of a bitch!

Under the sickening fear, rage woke, gaining strength as I scrambled back to my feet. My fists curled at my sides as I studied the shadowed forest from hell around me. My breath sawed through my chest in loud, harsh exhalations.

From deep in the darkness came a hair-raising laugh, followed by a mocking taunt that seemed to come from every-where at once. "Are you scared yet, Megan?"

Spinning around, I stared into the shifting shadows, trying to find him. "What do you want?" I hated the tremor in my voice, but I was holding on by my fingernails.

"You know what I want. I want *them,* and you're going to give them to me."

I was shaking my head. "No, I'm not."

"So sure of that?" The question rode an icy breath of air over my shoulder and came from behind me.

Pure instinct wrenched me forward, away from the threat

at my neck, but when I spun around, no one was there. Retreating, I put my spine to a thick tree and dug my nails into the bark. Lifting my chin, I forced a credible sneer into my voice. "You had me for six months and couldn't get what you wanted. No way in hell you're going to get it now."

Just then, a familiar feminine voice screamed my name, wiping away everything but instinct and sending me crashing through the forest.

"Keelie!" There was no way to stop my mad dash, not with my baby sister's cries cresting on the air. Images of Danielle overlapped with Keelie, pushing me faster until I broke through the forest and into a clearing. At the horror before me, I rocked to a stop. "NO!"

A figure towered over my sister's white terror-filled face. Keelie's fingers tore at the hands that were wrapped with cruel intent around her neck as her screams choked into horrific gasps. I rushed forward, carried by fear, determination, terror, and fury. Years of martial arts training were left in the dust as the need to hurt and protect took over. I grabbed a nearby branch and, screaming in useless fury, swung at the figure's head. But he was gone. With no time to check my swing, the branch slammed into Keelie's skull with a dull thud. For a breathless moment she swayed, then she crumbled into a heap.

The branch fell from my nerveless fingers as I dropped to my knees, a keening wail of grief and horror escaping my mouth. "No, Keelie! No, no, I'm sorry. I'm sorry." I cradled the lifeless body of my sister, holding her close, rocking in mindless agonizing guilt. *Oh my God, I killed her.* "I didn't mean too. I'm sorry."

Malicious laughter rang at my ear. "You'll tell me, or I'll make sure you kill everyone you love."

As I held Keelie's dead weight in my arms, the overwhelming guilt and horror of my actions closed in, leaving me screaming into the night. With a harsh caw, a dark shadow dropped from the branches above. Instinct made me turn away, but the stinging burn of razor-sharp talons raked along my skin, opening long, bloody scratches along my cheek. The unexpected attack acted like a mental slap.

This isn't real. This is a dreamscape. My dreamscape.

Keelie wasn't here—this wasn't her. Desperately, I grasped the fragile rope of sanity and hung the fuck on. Carefully, even though I knew it wasn't her, I laid my sister down. Closing my eyes, I rose and began reshaping the dreamscape, using my anger as fuel. When I opened my eyes, Keelie was gone, and I was no longer in the forest. Instead, I stood in the meadow, my stone tower rising tall and strong in the distance.

I raised my hand and aimed my middle finger at the looming storm. "Fuck you, Hawes."

Above, the sky darkened as the approaching storm moved in, fast and mean. Winds tore around me, whipping my hair back from my face in stinging retaliation and forcing me to lean into them in an effort not to drop under the pressure.

I screamed into the wind. "Grow a pair, and face me!"

"Megan."

Spinning around in the sudden quiet, I came face-to-face with Bishop. For a moment, relief left my knees weak. Then alarm spread through me. This couldn't be Bishop. He shouldn't be here. *Oh God.* Had I managed to bring him into the dreamscape again, like last time? Panic welled, nailing my gut like a fist. If Bishop was here, it meant... did that mean... and the team...? My thoughts kept slipping as my fear and worry spun faster and faster.

Hard hands grabbed my arms and shook me. "Megan, what the fuck is going on?"

"I don't know... I think..." I tried to look around, to find some way to tell if this was real or another mind game, but there was nothing to anchor me.

Bishop drew me up until I was on tiptoes, and his furious

face was all I could see. Accusation left harsh disgust and cut unforgiving lines, turning his expression brutal in its fury. "What the hell did you do, Megan? Where's the team? Why did you bring me here?"

Oh God! I fucked up! I fucked it all up!

Chapter Twenty-Seven

BISHOP

With a mental clocking ticking down the time, we split into two teams. Utilizing a nonlethal approach, we made short work of taking the exterior targets out of play. I was tightening the last set of zip ties on the unconscious male with more muscles than brains when Kayden's message, "Front clear, heading in," came over the line. He, Rabbit, Doc, and Cyn were taking the front entrance, their goal to split once inside and clear the basement level.

"In, starting search." That was Tag's check-in. He and Jinx had scaled the garage's lower roof, gaining access to the top floor through the windows. Safely inside, they would be working to clear the third floor as they moved down to the second.

Wolf tapped my shoulder and signaled that the back was clear. Our target was the smaller side entrance tucked behind a huge bush that reached almost to the second floor. Wolf popped the lock, and we slipped inside what was probably considered a mudroom even though it was larger than any mudroom I'd seen. Light from the room beyond crept under the closed door. Wolf and I stilled at the interior door. "In, holding for status."

A muffled grunt and scuffling came from inside. I waited a heartbeat, then two, then Kayden said in my ear, "Clear, move."

Wolf led the way, and we stayed tight as we cleared our way through a massive living room and kitchen, both of which were well lit. The lack of concealment made my spine itch, but on the other hand, open floor plans like this made for straightforward threat assessments. I'd be able to see people coming from a mile away. Of course, they'd be able to see me, too, so it might come down to whoever was faster. After the lazy-ass display out front, I was betting heavily on our team.

"Heading down," Kayden said.

Wolf and I split at the halls. He went left, and I took right. After I closed the door on the second room, the faint sound of a toilet flushing drifted from farther down the hall. With no cover, my only choice was a blitz attack. Since we were trying to keep bloodshed to a minimum, I holstered my HK.

The bathroom door opened, and I lunged in, slamming my fist into the guy's temple, sending him stumbling back into the narrow confines. I followed. He hit the counter with a resounding thump and swung out with an awkward punch. Taking advantage of his sloppy defense, I caught his swinging arm on my forearm, trapping it against my body, forcing him to face the sink. I sank my fist twice into his kidney. While he was trying to breathe, I shifted my stance and twisted his trapped arm into a painful shoulder lock. I followed that with a stunning smack against the back of his skull, which forced his forehead to meet the counter with a resounding thump. Granite was a wonderful thing.

Dropping the dazed guard, I pulled out another zip tie and crouched over him. Once he was trussed and gagged with a wadded-up washcloth and duct tape, I cleaned out his weapons cache. I removed his communication piece and dropped the electronics in the toilet before flushing then gathered his weapons—two handguns—and walked out, closing the door behind me. After tossing the handguns into a cluttered closet in one of the last rooms, I went to join Wolf.

"Top floor, clear," Tag whispered over the comms. "Heading down west side to second."

"First floor, clear," Wolf said as we headed toward the lit staircase.

My foot had just hit the second step when Kayden's tension-filled voice filled the line. "Possible confirmation on main objective."

A strained expectancy hung over the line as we all waited for more information.

Kayden said curtly, "Got two guards on door, south-west corner. Hold."

Frozen in place, I shot Wolf a silent question—was it the colonel? His eyes were unfocused as he tilted his head. A heartbeat passed, and he shook his head. So, either it wasn't the colonel, or he still couldn't get a reading. With nothing to go on, we held our position.

A burst of sound—the rasp of movement, muffled grunts, and a pained yip—filled my ear, then Kayden was back. "Guards down, but we've got a problem. Colonel's strapped to a chair, partially conscious. She's wired to blow."

"How long?" Wolf asked.

"Four mics, forty and counting," Rabbit answered sharply.

Fuck. Four minutes and forty seconds was not a lot of time to get the colonel clear and find Hawes. If the fucker was even here. As much as I wanted to trust the voice whispering that he was, there was always a chance it was wrong. There was another way, though.

"Can't Rabbit do his magic?"

"Negative," came Rabbit's voice. "This is one sensitive

bitch. One wrong electronic pulse, and none of us will need to worry about evac."

Rabbit's evaluation not only solidified my instinct but added a shit ton of urgency to our mission, all of which equated to hauling ass. "Copy that." I looked at Wolf. He lifted his chin, looking as determined as I felt. It was time to move. Sucking a bracing breath, I said, "Count us down."

"Copy." Then Kayden did just that. "Four, thirty-nine."

"Bishop." Something in Wolf's voice and expression brought me to a standstill. I held his gaze. "Got a heads-up from Rico. Hawes knows we're here."

For a single moment, his words didn't register, but when they did, my blood froze. "Megan?"

Wolf's face was grim. "Rico's advice is to take him alive."

Someone on one of the other teams sucked in a sharp breath, and someone else muttered, "Fuck," but they all waited. For me. Hearing those words and their underlying meaning—that if we killed Hawes, we could kill Megan—sent a soul-numbing fear spiraling through me. All the things I hadn't been able to tell her spun through my mind, shredding my heart. Yet even as I bled out deep inside, a ruthless voice laid out all the pros and cons of this fucking mission as the soldier in me took over.

"Copy that," I rasped. Those two words tasted like bitter ash.

With no way but forward, we traded stealth for speed and rushed up the stairs. As Kayden ticked down the clock, we hit the wide second floor, weapons leading the way. A figure rushed from the end of the hall, and Wolf's gun barked. The figure dropped. I flung open a door to a secondary living room. Empty. Motioning Wolf forward, I covered as he opened the next door.

A flicker of movement made me turn back to the stairs. A guard appeared. Aiming to disable, not kill, my finger squeezed, and my gun coughed. He dropped. Clearing the distance, I found the man clutching his shoulder, his face white and shocked. I kicked his fallen weapon back down the stairs and zip tied his hands.

"Three, fifty." Kayden's words accompanied my dash back to Wolf.

"Pinned on back stairs," Jinx said over the line, accompanied by the sound of gunfire.

With no backup coming and time running out, Wolf and I were left with no choice but to move forward. Tagging Wolf's shoulder, I approached the double doors with him. We were almost in place when we heard muffled voices coming from inside. We paused, holding our positions. Wolf signaled his intent, and I nodded, waiting until he got in position on the far side of the door before I took a spot on my side.

In my ear, I could hear the murmur of Kayden's countdown and the occasional sound of gunshots coming from Tag and Jinx's position. Blocking it all out, I kept my spine against the wall, straightened out my arm, and tapped the butt of my gun against the door then pulled it back fast as I called, "Major General? A word?"

Bullets tore through the door, flinging stinging slivers of wood in their wake. I half turned, dropped into a crouch, and protected my face, waiting for a pause. When it came, it was shorter than expected—a breath only—then another flurry of bullets tore through. The reverberating coughs were deeper, indicating a different weapon. *Great*. We had two shooters and no telling how many weapons.

The lead rain stopped, leaving long splinters in the doors. No light leaked out, indicating that the people inside were huddled in the dark. Wolf was crouched in a similar position to mine. Using silent hand signals as Kayden's calm countdown continued—"Three, thirty-five"—we planned.

Breaching the damn room before Hawes decided to rabbit

was crucial. Going in blind was a fucking death wish, especially since we'd be backlit, but fueled by an icy fury and a merciless practicality, I was willing to risk it, not just for Megan's safety but the team's as well. This fucker needed to go down fast and hard.

Wolf and I hit the doors, breaking through the remains, staying low, weapons up and tracking despite the shadows. Gunfire flashed in the dimness. My training took over, and I returned fire, hearing Wolf do the same. Light from the hall was not quite close enough to illuminate the room. Time lost meaning as we ducked behind darker objects and aimed at the flashes of gunfire. After someone gave a pained grunt, the gunfire lessened. *One down.* A dark shadow broke away, moving against the windows. *Stupid.* I aimed, fired. The shadow dropped. For a long moment, the only sound to penetrate the ringing silence was my harsh breathing. Crouched behind what I thought might be a huge-ass chair, I waited, listening and stretching my senses out for a telltale movement.

I counted my heartbeats, time dragging, but I kept perfectly still. Whoever moved first tended to die in situations like this. Moving just my eyes, I caught sight of Wolf lying flat on the floor, half-covered by a low-slung table. He caught my gaze and shifted his eyes upward toward the far corner on my side of the room, just to the side of the huge-ass window. I turned that way and watched the shadows, satisfaction burning bright when they moved. Taking care to keep my movements slow, I brought my gun up and aimed low. The shadow lunged, and I squeezed down on the trigger. The shadowy figure jerked back and then twisted in a futile attempt to abort the fall. The trigger completed its pull, freeing the bullet. My heart stopped, and time seemed to slow as the bullet hit. The figure dropped, and time sped forward.

Kayden kept count in my ear. "Fifty-eight, fifty-seven…"

Rabbit's chanted in time, "Almost there, almost there…"

Shoving to my feet, I rushed toward the fallen figure.

Wolf flicked on a light, illuminating a shot-up office.

I got to the body and turned it over. Hawes's eyes opened, staring at me as his mouth gaped, trying to suck in air. My bullet had gone in just under his arm and ripped through his chest, but I didn't see an exit wound. Blood bubbled out of his mouth. I knew, *fucking knew*, what that meant.

"No! God dammit no!" I slammed my hands on the hole, a useless move. "Get me something, Wolf!"

He shoved a couch cushion at me. I held it down over the wound, but Hawes flopped around, his mouth opening and closing like a fish. Everything in me stilled as his gaze met mine, dark with a vicious sort of satisfaction. His bloodied lips curved, revealing bloodstained teeth. His mouth moved, but no sound emerged. A chilling certainty built in me as his eyes rolled back and his body went limp and death claimed his due.

My mind stumbled, and horrified realization tore through my soul. Megan. I'd just killed Megan. "NO!" Hoarse with rage, my voice roared through the room. As if my agony was the trigger, the house shook, and the deafening sound of a bomb shattered the night.

Chapter Twenty-Eight

Crawling through the heavy layers of consciousness, bits and pieces of memories sparked like fireflies before falling away. Other sensations trickled in, finally breaching the last suffocating layer, forcing me to wake. My mind was curiously empty but clear. Unwilling to leave the strange peaceful reprieve, I kept my eyes closed and breathed. Winter-laced soap and the faint hint of male hit first, filling every breath I took with a familiar scent. Turning my head, I buried my nose against the heated spot covered in soft cotton. Something warm and strong curled around me. Not quite awake, I rubbed my face against the comforting brush of material and slowly opened my eyes.

Rich chocolate stared back, framed by thick lashes, their depths filled with something indefinable that sank beneath my skin, warming me from the inside out until my lips curved. I reached up and traced the high cheekbones, feeling his burnished skin, then stroked his coarse beard. He turned into my hand, pressing a kiss against my palm.

"Bishop." A chaotic mix of emotions rose, making my voice husky.

"Hey, babe." He rubbed his jaw against my hands then shifted his body along mine, forcing me to my back until I was lying beneath him, well and truly captured. Not that I minded. His wild curls fell around his face, adding an irresistible charm that melted my already compromised heart.

He lowered his head and took my lips with a fragile intensity that was quickly replaced by the dual demands of hunger and need. Clothes disappeared in our rush to touch, which slowed as his hands moved over my bare skin, leaving a devastating trail of fire in their wake. His tongue stroked and tangled with mine, leading me through a seductive dance I was more than willing to follow.

His weight settled between my thighs as he indulged. I tangled my hands in his hair, the soft strands like cool silk against my heated skin. His tongue left a line of damp skin as he traced his way down my neck, and erotic chills followed. At the base of my throat, he drew my skin into the heated dampness of his mouth before continuing over the slope of my breast. He cupped the other one, his fingers playing over the aching crest, deepening the restless hunger burning through me.

Hunger, need—it all coiled together, leaving me restless and searching. As he played, so did I, licking where I could, stroking what I could reach, filling my senses with nothing but the strength and heat of Bishop. He was there with me, alive and breathing. Every taste, every touch anchored me, reminding me that this was very real, not some tormenting mind game, and that he was safe and solid in my bed with me. The fear and worry that had been clamped so tightly around my heart slowly eased, replaced by soft gasps and husky moans as desire spread into a wildfire, burning everything it touched.

Bishop was relentless, sending me higher and higher until there was nothing left to hold on to but him. Safe in his arms, I held on tight, letting the feeling sweep me over the peak and send me into a free fall of breath-stealing beauty. All the protective barriers raised in the aftermath of a nightmare and the desperate whispers of a broken mind fell away, leaving me nothing but a single truth that escaped on a soft cry. "I love you."

* * *

After a shared shower that drained most of the hot water, we were back on the bed, but this time, I was in baggy sleep pants and a tank top and he wore low-riding sweats. I curled into his side, not able to stop touching him, reassuring myself that he was really there. I did my damnedest not to think about my blurted confession. It helped that the strange peaceful distance I woke with was long gone and my head was filled with a tangle of questions.

Bishop was carefully stroking his fingers through my wet hair as I listened to his heart's solid beat under my ear. "I can hear your mind spinning."

I was tracing distracted patterns against his bare chest, avoiding the newest additions to his battle wounds from the previous night, only hours old. My pulse stuttered. "It's a mess in there. Sure you're ready for it?"

His arm tightened, pulling me closer, as he chuckled. "Hit me."

I started with the easiest one. "Is everyone okay? The colonel? The team?"

"Yeah, everyone's good. Doc told the colonel to take it easy for a couple days. Guess Hawes used an injection to keep her compliant because she was pretty out of it when they found her."

Relief swept through me. "What happened?"

The hand in my hair stilled for a moment. Then it resumed. "What do you remember?"

His question unlocked the gate holding the memories back. It swung open under the rush of images, and my muscles tensed as I remembered, fear washing aside my earlier relief. "I thought I'd pulled you into the dreamscape and screwed everything up. You were furious, and I knew…" The mouth-drying fear and sickening guilt made a comeback. I shivered and tried again. "I knew I'd betrayed you and the team."

He stopped petting and wrapped me in a tight hug. "I thought I'd killed you."

Startled by his statement and by the pain coloring his voice, I craned my neck to see his face. "What?"

"I shot Hawes. I wasn't aiming for a kill shot, but he tripped, and the bullet took him in the chest. By the time I got to him, he was critical, but…" A dark look swept over his face. "I thought he took you with him when he died, and it would've been my fault."

Unable to resist, I cupped his jaw and looked in his eyes, pulling him back from whatever nightmare he was watching. I didn't say anything. It was up to him if he wanted to share, and nothing I said would help ease what he believed. This whole situation was rife with guilt and pain on both sides.

His gaze drifted over my face. "Right before we cornered Hawes, Ricochet warned Wolf that Hawes had you trapped—that we needed to take him alive."

He stopped again, but it didn't matter. I understood what lay behind the emotional chaos hovering like a storm cloud. He'd tried to protect me, going for a nonlethal hit, and thought he'd failed. Just like I thought I had failed. If Hawes hadn't been dead already, I'd have happily dragged his ass back and killed him all over again just as payback for the pain on Bishop's face.

Bishop vibrated with fury. He said in a low, hard, tone,

"The fucker smiled at me. He couldn't say shit, since he was drowning in his own blood, but he looked so damn smug... I was sure he was taking you with him."

We held each other's gaze, the quiet between us filled with so much. I had no idea where to start, but I wasn't about to rush in with some inane comment. Instead, I went back through those heart-stopping moments after I'd thought Hawes had won. "He fooled me," I admitted softly. "He does that... did that. But it never lasted. He always screwed up when he took the faces of those I love. This time, it was nothing major, just little things." I gave him a small smile and hoped it wasn't shaky. "It took me a few seconds to realize it wasn't you screaming at me. It helped that Ricochet decided to dive-bomb us."

"Dive-bomb?" Bishop asked.

I rubbed my chin against his chest. "Yeah, he decided to hang out in the dreamscape as a raven. He figured Hawes wouldn't pay attention to the animals." Because the arrogant ass had been a telepath and not a dream-walker, he'd never clued in to the subtler imagery dream-walkers excelled in, and Ricochet was a freaking master. I had a hell of a lot to learn still. "But the distraction worked because Hawes was so busy trying to avoid Ricochet's talons that he was ignoring me. His control slipped just long enough for me to regain control of the dreamscape."

Bishop frowned. "Ricochet thought you'd lost control, which is why he wanted Hawes alive."

A blush rose to my cheeks. "Yeah, that was my fault. When I snatched the dreamscape from Hawes, I accidentally pushed Ricochet out." I still had no idea how I'd managed that.

Bishop's looked at me sharply. "Wait, so when Hawes tripped—"

"It was probably when he was dodging Ricochet."

"Well, shit."

"Yeah."

The AC kicked on, and we just lay there. All my whirling questions slowed and drifted away, leaving one question behind. Trying not to reveal just how important it was, I fought to keep my tone normal. "Now what?"

"Now we deal with the fallout," Bishop answered, totally misinterpreting my question, as he rolled me under him. It seemed to be his preferred position, and having all that sexy heat and muscle blanketing me tended to make my brain skip. When it got back on track, and before I could find a graceful way to redirect, he continued. "It won't be easy. The colonel's going to be stuck answering a ton of questions. We still have no idea who else was working Hawes or if he was really connected to Falcon, but Rabbit's determined to unearth every one of Hawes's secrets. Once he does, we'll have to figure out our next steps."

I caught his face in my hands, and he paused. I leaned up and kissed him. It didn't take much—a soft nip to his lower lip —before it turned heated and carnal. I got lost in his taste, the rising need setting my body on fire.

When he lifted his head, red rode his cheekbones, and his eyes were dark with hunger and humor. "Not the answer you wanted?"

"Not exactly." Now that I had his attention, I couldn't find the right words, and my nerves came back with rein-forcements.

His humor faded, replaced by a heart-stopping gentleness as he framed my face, holding me still. "You told me before that if it wasn't for all this shit, you'd be willing to see where you and I would go." He studied my face with a disconcerting intensity. "Did you mean what you said?"

There was no mistaking what he was referring to. There'd been no holding those three words back when we came together. Maybe it was too soon, but so much had happened in such a short time.

Start as you mean to go. My newly embraced mantra whispered through me, bolstering my faltering courage. Swallowing hard, I nodded, my voice frozen. His place in my heart had been carved out during those hellish months at Hawes's hands, and when I began picking up the pieces, Bishop had proven he was much more than my wishful imaginings of a shadowy protector. His ability to see my flaws as strengths, his faith in my determination, his humor, his willingness to share his doubts—all of that created something much more than the undeniable attraction between us. I wasn't ready to walk away from it. I prayed he felt the same.

He dropped his forehead to mine, and I curled my arms around his neck, holding on for dear life. He brushed his nose against mine in a heart-melting touch. From mere inches away, he whispered, "Trust me?"

"Yes," I said just as softly.

He smiled as something precious filled his eyes, easing the wary lines of his face, and left my heart all warm and squishy. "Good, because I love you, too, Megan."

***

Sparks fly when Rabbit and Jinx play intimate criminal partners and risk turning illusion to truth in LINKED BY DECEPTION.
Now available at your favorite bookseller!

***

PSY - IV Teams Books

Welcome to a world where facing danger requires the unique skill set of the men and women of Jami Gray's PSY-IV Teams. As sparks, and bullets fly, love, action, and adventure will target these unique couples as they race through each breath-stealing operation.

Binge the series today at your favorite bookseller!

HUNTED BY THE PAST

Cyn & Kayden

To escape a killer from their past, can a reluctant psychic trust the man who walked away?

TOUCHED BY FATE

Risia & Tag

A seer's secrets become her only bargaining chip in a high-stakes game of lies and loyalty determining her fate.

MARKED BY OBSESSION

Meli & Wolf

A woman in hiding. A telepath who sees deeper than her scars. Can they forge a bond stronger than the obsession stalking them before time runs out?

FRACTURED BY DECEIT

Megan & Bishop

After a brutal attack by a telepath, Megan turns to Bishop for help, but how does he keep her safe when she's threat?

LINKED BY DECEPTION

Jinx & Rabbit

Forced to play intimate criminal partners, will Rabbit & Jinx risk turning illusion to truth as they race to untangle a web of conspiracies and lies?

About the Author

"This story is an emotional roller coaster, from betrayal, anger, fear, love…" —InD'tale Magazine

Jami Gray is the coffee addicted, music junkie, Queen Nerd of her personal Geek Squad, Alpha Mom of the Fur Minxes, who writes to soothe the voices crammed in her head. Her series combine high-stakes urban fantasy and edgy paranormal romantic suspense into books you don't want to put down. Buckle up and get ready for a wild ride through the fascinating worlds of the Arcane, the Kyn, the PSY-IV Teams, and the Collapse.

Come visit Jami's website at **https://www.jamigray.com** and stay up to date on what kind of trouble she's getting into and when you can expect to join in.

amazon.com / author / jamigray

instagram.com / jamigrayauthor

facebook.com / JamiGrayWriter

threads.com / @jamigrayauthor

goodreads.com / JamiGray

bookbub.com / authors / jami-gray